ALEXIS
A Dan Muncie Mystery

First Edition

Published by The Nazca Plains Corporation
Las Vegas, Nevada
2011

ISBN: 978-1-61098-027-2
E-Book: 978-1-61098-028-9

Published by

The Nazca Plains Corporation ®
4640 Paradise Rd, Suite 141
Las Vegas NV 89109-8000

PUBLISHER'S NOTE
Alexis is a work of fiction created wholly by *Jerry Lien*'s imagination.
All characters are fictional and any resemblance to any persons living
or deceased is purely by accident. No portion of this book reflects any
real person or events.

Cover, Blake Stephens
Art Director, Blake Stephens

ALEXIS

A Dan Muncie Mystery

First Edition

Jerry Lien

CONTENTS

CHAPTER 1

I had never even heard of a murderous bitch named Alexis Brogan as I watched Erika dance that night. She was a fresh-faced kid, though she was supposed to be at least 21 to be working at the Naked Maja. That was the minimum age for dancers where alcohol was being served. While Morie checked the IDs of the dancers who worked for him, he wasn't all that concerned about fakes. All he asked was that they be good fakes, and that the girl look old enough to work there.

Not that I worried about it. If Morie was satisfied, that was good enough for me. All I cared about was that Erika had a great body and she knew what to do with it on stage.

I'd just returned to the bar after sticking a dollar in her g-string when Morie came up to me. "Hi, Dan," he said. His voice had a permanent rasp from his days as a boxer. When he'd realized he'd never be in the main event he'd found another career as a bouncer and bar manager, at least until he had saved enough to buy a place of his own.

"Hi, Morie." His real name was Mortimer, but nobody ever called him that, or even Morty, unless they were ready to pay for some dental work or a nose job. "Nice girl. Has she been here long?" A job had kept me out of town for just over a month, and this was my first time back at the bar since getting home. I hadn't even been to my office yet.

He shrugged. "About two weeks now. She's working out well." That meant she got along with the other dancers and made the customers happy.

"That's good," I said. I wasn't paying much attention to him. I was too busy looking at the well-shaped ass she was sticking in a customer's face before taking his dollar. If Morie was just saying hi he'd be moving on soon. If he had something to tell me he'd come out with it when he was damn well ready.

"Yeah," he said with a sigh, "but I'm worried about her."

"Oh?" Now I gave him more of my attention, though I was watching where Erika had turned around, jammed the guy's nose between her tits, and was trying to stick her nipples in his ears. "What's wrong? Do you think she's turning tricks?"

That wouldn't have been a good idea. The girls here could get away with a lot, but there were limits. I knew the man she was giving a quick kiss as he stuck a dollar into her g-string next to mine. Steve Kellerman worked Homicide, and about a third of the other customers in the bar were cops as well. They might let it slide when a g-string 'slipped' and showed more than was legally allowed, but hooking was something they would not stand for. Especially not Tom Kelly, the next man in line. He worked Vice.

"No, I'm afraid she's hanging around with the wrong people, and she might get into drugs. If she does I'll fire her ass, even though it would pain me to do it."

That was one of his quirks. A lot of the dancers were at least half soused by the end of the night, but he wouldn't allow drug users. Well, he didn't mind a little pot when they weren't at work, but he couldn't afford a girl who used hard drugs. There were at least two men from Narco there who would spot it in an instant, and most of the others wouldn't be far behind.

As she gave Tom an eyeful I looked at Morie. "So do you want me to do something about it or what?" He wasn't telling me this just to pass the time.

"I don't know what you can do," he said after a second. "Hell, I'm not all that sure you need to do anything. I could be getting worried about nothing."

I didn't say anything. I just watched as Erika finished her set and left the stage. Her ass was decidedly watchable. As she left, Sherrie came on stage. She was a leggy brunette who could get away with all kinds of things on stage. There are advantages to doing bachelor parties for cops.

As Sherrie started dancing I looked at Morie. I'd been watching Sherrie for close to two years, so I didn't need to see what she did. "So?"

Morie grimaced. "Let me think on it, okay?" he said with a touch of annoyance. He didn't like being pushed.

I shrugged my shoulders. "You brought it up."

He glared at me. I ignored it, because he'd get over it. We had been friends for too long for him to hold a grudge. Besides, I'd helped him out of plenty of tight places. I could do things all the other detectives in the bar couldn't. They worked for the city, or the county, so they had to write reports to prosecutors and such. I only wrote one for my client.

After a moment he walked off. I glanced up at the copy of the painting that gave the bar its name, Goya's "Naked Maja," and decided to stick around for a second beer, maybe even a third. He'd be back, ready to tell me what he wanted done. Besides, I didn't have anyplace better to go.

Erika came out of the dressing room to mingle with the customers. She was in a tight red dress, with a high neck, a big opening in back, no sleeves, and that came down to all of maybe half an inch below her crotch.

When pulled all the way down, that is. As it was, it exposed about the bottom inch of her g-string in front and left an erotic display of the lower curve of her cheeks in back.

She stopped at several tables before sitting with a couple of civilians. They were wearing ties, and had a professional look to them, so they were most likely more generous to the dancers and better paid than the cops. It wasn't long before she went into the back room with one of them for some table dances.

Sherrie did her set, followed by Laurie, Shandra, Tiffany, and "randy" Sandy. Kara was dancing when Morie came back, and sat on the stool next to me. "Okay," he said without preamble, "here's the deal. Her real name is Susan Trumble, and she lives in the fifty-three hundred block of Taylor. The Armbridge Apartments."

I knew of the place. So did the two narcs. That didn't mean she was into drugs (most of the residents were honest people) but there were a couple of known dealers who lived there, and a nonfatal shooting had occurred in the parking lot a couple of months before.

"I'm not sure what friends she has there," Morie continued, "but she at least knows some residents I'd just as soon she didn't." By that he most likely meant the dealers. "Could you keep an eye on her for a couple of days? Maybe find out who she's hanging out with? I'd hate to see her get in trouble."

The out of town job had left me with cash to spare, but it had kept me from lining up any other work for when I got back. I had time to spare. "Sure, Morie," I said. "No problem."

"Thanks." He got up and headed back into the office. One good thing was that there was no need to discuss fees. He didn't expect me to do this for free, but he trusted me to keep the charges reasonable.

The stool didn't stay vacant for long. Sandy sat down next to me and put a liplock on me that would have made me horny even if I had not already been that way. She was free to do that since she was the closest thing I had to a girlfriend; though we each sometimes went out with others.

After a moment she backed off to take a breath. "Ready for a lap dance?" she asked. There was no doubt that she was.

"Sure," I said. I'm going to turn down an offer like that?

We went to the back room ourselves, and she danced for me. I won't bother to describe it except to say that if she had gone any further with what she did one of the cops would have had to arrest her for public lewdness. As it was we were both breathing heavily by the time she finished. She leaned down and asked, "You going anywhere after work tonight?"

"No, but you are," I replied. "I've got some paperwork to catch up on, so I'm going now. I'll leave the door unlocked for you."

It was my night to be glared at. "You bastard," she said vehemently. "You asshole! So you're going to go off and leave me with all these assholes for the rest of the night! Don't you dare fall asleep, or I'll cut your balls off!" She grabbed her dress and stalked off. I smiled and went back to Morie's office. There I got a copy of Erika's employment application, then headed home.

I hadn't been lying to Sandy. I did have a lot of things to catch up on. Bills, for one thing. Some of them had been paid by Mike Tailor, but there were others I had to take care of myself. And there were the reports on the case I'd just wrapped up.

I had finished everything by eleven. Afterwards I watched an old movie until I heard my door open. I had my hand on my pistol until I had confirmed it was indeed Sandy.

"Well, you did stay awake," she said.

I just smiled. She was wearing a dress that came down to mid-thigh. It looked fairly modest, until I noticed that the cloth was sheer enough that I could make out her nipples. She reached behind her and the dress fell away. Now I could see her nipples quite clearly, along with everything else, for other than a pair of shoes the dress had been the only thing she was wearing. It only took her three seconds to shed the shoes.

She headed for the stereo. She took her time, picking out a couple of CDs and programming the player. Then she came over to me as the music started and did all those things she couldn't do to me back at the Naked Maja.

After that I carried her over to the bed for round two. By then it was so late that round three had to wait for the morning.

When we were cuddling after round three I asked Sandy about Erika. "Erika? Nice kid and a good dancer, but if she's 21 I'm her maiden aunt." She grinned at me wickedly. "And I ain't nobody's maiden aunt," she said, emphasizing 'maiden.'

"I can vouch for that," I agreed.

"Why the questions about Erika?" she asked. "Aren't I enough for you?" She tried to sound coy, but it didn't quite work.

"I'm not trying to take her to bed," I said. "Morie asked me to check on her."

"Oh? What's he worried about?" She rolled over onto her stomach and propped herself up on her elbows, giving me a nice view of her nipples and the tops of her tits.

"She lives at the Armbridge Apartments, and there are some drug dealers who live there, too. He doesn't want her to get into drugs. Booze he can take, but you know all that."

"Right, especially with the number of cops we have as customers. Legal stuff only. But I don't think we need to worry about that right now. I've seen girls when they're doing drugs, and Erika isn't using. She doesn't have the signs." She was getting serious now.

"How old would you guess she is?" I asked.

She rolled over on her back and put her hands behind her head. "Nineteen," she said firmly. "Or within a couple of months of her nineteenth birthday. No older. She comes from a poor family. Dad was a drunk, died when she was young. Mom wasn't too bright, and ended up hooking part time, welfare and odd jobs the rest of the time. Not a good way to grow up."

"She told you all this?"

She shrugged her shoulders as best she could, making her tits bob interestingly. "Not in so many words. Bits and pieces, but I know how to interpret what she says. I think she's been raped, too, at least once."

At least once. If Sandy was right, two or three times was a possibility. A hard life for a young woman.

We talked for a few more minutes, then my stomach growled. Sandy grinned at me and asked, "Hungry?"

"Damn straight I'm hungry, woman," I replied. "Especially after satisfying you three times!"

She just grinned and jumped out of bed, heading for the kitchen. She didn't pull any clothes on, but I did. Boxers, shorts, and a t-shirt, because I just don't feel comfortable wandering around naked.

I didn't read anything into Sandy making some breakfast while naked. She was perfectly comfortable in her skin. It wouldn't bother her to go out in public naked if the weather were good and the law allowed it. In fact, I think she'd prefer it.

As we ate, Sandy told me some more about Erika, what little she knew. It wasn't much, but then Erika hadn't been there all that long, and the dancers don't talk about themselves much. Not about their pasts, anyway.

She helped me clean up a little, then she had to leave. I watched her get dressed, and as she picked up her purse I asked, "Wait a minute, you forgot your underwear."

She turned and grinned at me. Instead of saying anything she just gave me the finger. I knew full well that she never wore underwear, not even in the middle of the winter. If it got too cold for her 'nether regions' to be hanging out unprotected she'd just wear slacks or jeans, but still no panties.

After she had left I considered what to do about Erika. The easy thing would be to follow her around for a few days, but should I do it all at once or spread it over some time? I decided to watch her for two days, and see what happened. Then I would have a better handle on things.

Breakfast or not, I realized I was yawning. I did the smart thing and went back to bed. It had been after three before Sandy and I got to sleep, and it was nine now. I still needed a couple more hours.

CHAPTER 2

Even with the nap it was only about eleven when I reached my office. "Daniel Muncie, Investigations" shared a secretary with Mike Tailor, an accountant with only a couple of small clients. Mike was a nice guy who had retired from a major accounting firm, didn't need the money, and did it mainly as an excuse to get out of the house. He and his wife had been driving each other crazy.

Our joint secretary was driving *me* crazy. It was a good thing that Maggie had kick-ass typing skills, because other than that she was an airhead. Mike and I had to check our messages carefully to make sure we had the right ones.

One rather odd advantage was that I could let her type confidential reports, secure in the knowledge that by the time she got to the end of the document she would have forgotten what she had typed at the start.

There were no messages for me, though Maggie was pleased to see me. She pretended she didn't have a crush on me and I pretended I didn't know. "Is Mike in?" I asked as I went through his messages. None for me there, either.

"No, he's out playing golf," she said, almost simpering. That fawning attitude was enough to provoke my disinterest, even if I had been attracted to her physically. The problem was that she had a round face with all the parts arranged in the least pleasing way possible. She wasn't quite ugly, but she did take the term 'plain' to new heights. I was glad she at least had stopped wearing those short miniskirts that had shown way too much of her meaty thighs.

"Thanks, Maggie," I said as I headed to my office.

Once in there I checked the office mail. There wasn't much. Mostly advertising, in fact, that were tossed straight into the trash unopened. The credit card applications went into the shredder. Next I checked my voice mail. There were two calls that required my attention, and the rest I just deleted.

Half an hour later I was caught up. I had accepted one maybe divorce case, rejected another, and filled out some paperwork for the state. I was about to make a few calls to start checking out Erika when Mike came in. "Hi, Mike. I thought you were out playing golf."

"Morning, Dan. I will be later, but that's the easiest thing to tell Maggie, even when I'm going shopping."

Like I always told her I was going out on a case, even when I wasn't. "So how are my accounts doing?" I asked. I was one of his clients, which was why he paid my bills for me.

"You're in good shape. How'd the trip go?"

I reached into my coat, pulled out a deposit receipt, and handed it to him. He took it and whistled. "I take that back. You're in good shape. So they were satisfied with your efforts, then?"

"As satisfied as possible considering that the young woman I was hired to find was already dead."

Mike shook his head. "I'm sorry to hear that."

"Don't be. From everything I learned about her she may have been pretty, but she was pure bitch. She thought her wealth made her better than anybody not wealthier than her, and she had the morals of an alley cat. About the only thing good anyone would say about her was that she was great in the sack, provided that you remembered that you were there to please her first."

Mike tried to hide a grin.

"What is it?" I asked.

"Maggie, of course." Yet his grin was too big for his usual bantering about her, and the effect I have on her.

"Yes, I know," I said tiredly. "All I have to do is say the word and she'd be under my desk, or on my desk, or anyplace else I want her." I looked at Mike, and he was red-faced holding back laughter. "Now what?" I demanded.

He leaned forward. "Did you know she wears a nipple ring?" he asked softly. He was enjoying the shit out of this.

"She has a what?" Of all the things he could have said, that would have been, well, maybe not the last thing I would have expected, but it would have been way down the list.

"One of the couriers told me," he said, grinning broadly. "In her left tit. It seems like our little Maggie hasn't let her lust for you keep her from enjoying the pleasures of the flesh with others."

"Get out of here!" I said.

"No, really!" he insisted.

"I mean it!" I continued. "Get out of here! Go back to your own office with your dirty stories. Jeez, it's hard enough having her simpering at me without knowing that!"

Mike just laughed, but he did leave. As he did I shuddered. I knew damn well that I was going to start looking at her left tit to see if I could make out that damned nipple ring. What bothered me even more was that I find nipple rings erotic, and I was afraid that if I could see it I might give in and actually take her to bed.

I tried to remember if I had ever said anything about liking nipple rings when she might have overheard, but couldn't think of any. Besides, if she had known, she would have made sure I noticed. Well, hell. I'd just have to live with it. I shook my head and got back to work.

The first few checks on Erika went well. As hoped, she had no criminal record. Well, nothing the police were concerned with, at least. They had also had no calls from her apartment in the last two years. I knew one of the office clerks at the apartment complex from a previous case, and she confirmed that Erika/Susan paid her rent on time and caused no trouble. So far everything was going fine.

When all that was done I went down to my car. By then Maggie was out to lunch, so I was spared the temptation to look for the ring. I drove out to the complex where Susan lived. I wanted a good place to park, where I'd be hard to see but could keep a good eye on her apartment. I found a spot I liked, and then drove home. I had been in my sedan, but wanted to switch to my van. It is as non-descript as possible, but a lot more comfortable than the car.

Also better equipped. I have all kinds of surveillance equipment in it, from still cameras to video cameras to sound equipment. It's not as fancy as the stuff the Feds have, but it gets the job done. Plus it has air conditioning and a small potty for the "long" jobs. I drove it back to the complex and parked.

As it turned out I didn't have to wait long. She came out dressed for the swimming pool, in a bikini she could have used as a costume on stage at the Maja. She was glared at by some of the mothers, but none of the men seemed to complain.

She wasn't there long, though. She dived straight into the pool, swam ten laps (I could count them by watching the male heads move back and forth), then got out, dried off a little, and headed back for her apartment.

It was an hour before she emerged again, this time dressed for the street. The outfit was actually fairly modest for her, with a skirt just a few inches above the knee and a snug sleeveless sweater top. She walked with that firm dancer's stride, and got into a Pontiac Sunfire a couple of years old. As she did I could see that she was wearing no bra, and knowing what I do about dancers there was a good chance she was wearing no panties, either. Not that I intended to find out for sure.

I started the van and followed her. It wasn't hard, she drove with more caution than I expected. Not that I couldn't have handled more speed. The van had a new engine, with more power than it had when built. I can get it well into the nineties if I have to, plenty of speed for city driving.

Instead I just followed her around as she ran some ordinary errands, picking up makeup, having a late lunch, and getting groceries before returning home. After that she disappeared into her apartment until she drove to work. Then I went home myself and had supper.

After eating I headed out again. I had no objection to overlapping with the possible divorce case. This time I went to a quiet neighborhood on the southeast side of town, where I parked near an upper middle class house. I had been told that this was the husband's normal "night out with the boys," only the wife wasn't sure he was spending it with "the boys."

Well, he did, sort of. At least he started out with the boys, leaving the house shortly after seven and meeting some friends at a strip club. The Paradiso was one of the more "upscale" clubs in town, with prices to match. I went on in, and watched as he sat with some friends, tipping the dancers, having a couple of beers, and getting two lap dances.

Then I went back to the van and waited. About ten thirty he came out alone, and got into his car. Instead of going home, though, he drove to a restaurant about a mile away. He sat there in his car for about ten minutes, then got out as another car parked in the lot. I doubted seriously if this person was one of "the boys," unless the 'boy' in question liked putting on a tight dress, hose, and high heels, not to mention being endowed with long blond hair and a good figure. I focused the binoculars on the woman, and was unsurprised to see a lovely face to match the lovely body.

Considering the kiss she gave him I doubted they were simply business associates.

They went inside and had dinner. I munched on some snacks. When they came outside, I followed their cars to another house. He pulled in right behind the woman, and she waited for him before going inside. As she went in he had his hand on her ass, and she just smiled at him as he said something.

I sighed and got out my cell phone. I called the wife's lawyer, Sarah Handly. She's not a bad person for a divorce lawyer, though she is a bit cut-throat in negotiations. "Sarah Handly," she said.

"Sarah, Dan. It looks like Mrs. Brogan was right. Well, half right, any way."

"Half right? What the hell's that supposed to mean?"

"It means he did meet with some friends, male friends, at a club after he left home. He departed at about ten thirty, though, and met a young woman at the Bradley's near the club. They had something to eat, then went to a house and he followed her inside. That's where they are right now."

"What are they doing?" she demanded.

"Hell, don't ask me. I can make some guesses, but if you want to know I'll have to get technical. Do you want to go that far?" By "getting technical" she knew I meant using bugs, cameras, and other hardware to confirm exactly what they were doing.

One of the reasons I worked for Sarah was that she considered the client's wishes as well as their best interests. If all Mrs. Brogan wanted was some confirmation before confronting her husband, this would be enough. If she wanted to nail him to the wall I was just getting started. But Sarah didn't pressure her clients, so whatever Mrs. Brogan decided was the way we would go.

Which led to another reason I liked about working for her. While she was fierce in working for her clients, she wouldn't do anything unethical. If she filed papers claiming the other spouse was an abuser then there was real evidence that they actually had abused her client or their children. She never filed physical or sexual abuse charges just to put pressure on the other party.

I heard Sarah sigh. "I don't know, Dan. Tell you what, find out what you can about the woman in a day, and by then I'll know for sure. Okay?"

"Okay," I said. "Bye." I wrote down the street address and made sure I had the license number of her car, then decided to head for the Maja. Divorce cases may help pay my bills, but I don't have to like them, and I don't.

I'm too old to wash my mouth out with soap, and not enough of a masochist anyway, so I decided to get the taste of the Brogan case out of my mouth with a shot of bourbon and a few slow beers. I didn't want to get drunk, just mellow out a little. The group of girls was pretty much the same as the night before, but the crowd was a little larger, since it was a day later in the week and a night closer to the weekend. Tomorrow night, Friday, would be busy, so I planned on being elsewhere.

I was halfway through my first beer when Sandy came over. She invited me in back for a table dance, and I accepted. This one was much milder than the one the night before, but still quite enjoyable. After that she returned to working the floor, getting table dances that paid.

I didn't mind her leaving. It's not like we were dating. We were just friends who slept together once in a while. If one of us got lonely we could call the other, and if they weren't doing anything we'd get together. The rest of the time she dated who she wanted to and I did the same. As for the table dances, well, that was where she earned most of her money and I had no intention of getting in the way of business.

By one o'clock I was nicely mellow when I glanced at the door. I was startled to see Edward Brogan come in. For a fraction of a second I wondered if he could have followed me to the Maja, but I had left him behind an hour and a half before. The thought came back when he came over to the table next to mine and sat down. I relaxed, though, because he just settled in and enjoyed the show, paying no attention to me at all.

I ignored him, too, at least for a while. Then I noticed the look on his face, that slightly smug expression a man gets when he has just had his ashes hauled. I decided to take a chance, and stared at him openly. After a moment he noticed me, and he glanced back. "Can I help you?" he asked. He was in too good a mood to be annoyed.

"No," I said, "it's just that if I didn't know better I'd say you've just gotten laid, but if you had, what in the hell would you be doing here?"

He laughed. "Actually I was just with a delightful young lady, doing exactly that. But she has to get up in the morning, and so I couldn't stay late. I felt like having a drink before going on home, and why not enjoy some lovelies while I'm at it?"

Made sense to me. "She any good?" I hadn't planned on asking that question, but it just popped out. Then I realized I was staying in character.

"She was fantastic," Brogan said, smiling. "She's just what I've been needing. This is my way of getting back at my wife."

Now he had me confused for real. "Getting back at your wife?"

"Oh, yes. She has a lover, at least one, so now I do, too."

"Why not just divorce the bitch?"

He shook his head. "For the time being it's better for me that I be married. It's a business thing. Some day she'll regret trying to play me for the fool."

"Well, be careful there," I said. I picked up my beer and turned my attention to the stage. Monet was putting her hands flat on the stage with her legs straight and together, then dropping down into splits. It's impressive.

After a few minutes Brogan finished his beer and left. By now I was kicking myself for what I had done. If Sarah wanted me to go technical I had just made sure he would remember me. He might not recall where he had seen me, but he would know my face.

It was too late to worry about that now. So I concentrated on Monet hanging upside down from the pole on stage, controlling her descent using nothing but her legs.

I gave myself another ten minutes to finish the beer and watch Sandy's last stage show of the night, then I left. I knew

Sandy wouldn't be joining me tonight, so when I got home I just locked up and went to bed.

CHAPTER 3

The next morning I started the day by finding out what I could about the woman Edward Brogan had been with. The basics weren't too difficult. Her name was Cari Roland, and she worked at an appliance store called Harrison's. She was 25 years old, had a decent credit record, and seemed to be doing well.

Since I had already let Edward get a look at me, even though he didn't know who I was, I went to the store where she worked. As luck, or whatever, would have it, she was on duty and I got a chance to see her do her thing.

Her dress was toned down some from the night before. Still, there was no doubt that the male of the couple she was working was fully aware of her charms. At the same time, though, his wife was being treated with considerable respect, and all her questions were being answered. At one point I managed to pass by close enough to hear Cari speak, and even from that short time I could tell she either knew what she was talking about or had mastered the art of sounding like she did. She was specific enough on some details, though, that I didn't think she was tossing much bull.

I had to leave before I attracted too much attention, but I had discovered what I wanted to know.

I could have gone back to the office, but I had taken the van so I could continue my surveillance of Erika. I drove out to the apartments where she lived, and was pleased to see her car still there.

I hadn't been there too long when she came out for another trip to the pool. This time she was in a slightly more modest bikini, but one which still left little to the imagination. She repeated her performance of the day before, ten laps and back to the apartment. This time, though, it was over two hours before she went anywhere.

About half way through my wait my cell phone rang. It was Sarah. "I talked to Alexis," she said, "and she said to drop it. She just wanted to have the affair confirmed for now. She'll decide later what to do about it."

"Okay," I said. "I'll bill you for two days, then." That was the minimum. "Plus expenses."

I got a chuckle. "Which club did he meet his friends at?" From her tone she had already guessed it was a "gentleman's club."

"The Paradiso."

"And will your expenses include the tips to the dancers?"

That was another thing I liked about Sarah. She was a realist about these things, and didn't mind. "Of course," I said. Actually I had no intention of putting that on the expenses. The drinks, yes, but not the tips.

"Liar," she said lightly. I didn't say anything, then she continued, "Hell, go ahead and add them in. Put down an extra drink or two as well. She can afford it."

"If you say so." I was a little surprised. Normally she didn't do that.

"I'll give you a call if she decides to get more evidence, Dan. And thanks."

"You're most welcome," I replied. "Bye."

I hung up and sighed a little. I have mixed feelings about things like that. On the one hand, the right divorce case can be worth thousands of dollars. I've also gotten some scenes on video tape that are hot enough that I've kept copies for myself. On the other, I'm intruding in strangers' lives in a personal way, and at times I think I've helped ensure that there was a divorce. I've seen cases where the aggrieved party could have gotten over the knowledge that their spouse was playing around, but once they heard a tape or saw the video, it was finished.

There are a couple of attorneys I won't work for because they talked their clients into doing that when it wasn't necessary. I keep working for Sarah in part because she doesn't.

But Erika, or Susan, was my concern right now. I kept watch on her apartment, and finally she came back out. This time she was dressed differently from the day before. She had on a sleeveless pink blouse and a black leather skirt. The skirt was much shorter than the one the day before. It only came maybe three or four inches below her crotch, revealing most of her thighs. She was also wearing a flashy silver necklace, big dangly earrings and pink leather sandals. I couldn't tell if she had on anything else, though I suspected she was at least braless.

This time she went to a tanning salon. She was inside for about half an hour. For a moment I wondered why she didn't just get her tan at the pool, but the answer was obvious. When she danced there were no tan lines. She had a nice, even all-over tan. There were only two ways of getting a tan like that, and laying by a public pool at an apartment complex wasn't one of them.

When she came out she went to lunch. As chance would have it she went to a Bradley's. That wasn't surprising. It's a nice chain, locally owned and run, and there are restaurants all around the city. They are a good choice when you want a regular sit-down dinner, but don't want to spend an arm and a leg. I decided to have my lunch there as well, though I went to their takeout counter. I didn't want her seeing me, and I didn't want to risk her finishing and leaving before me.

I needn't have worried about the latter. When she finally came out she had company, a young man. It was clear she had met him there, though whether by chance or preplanned I couldn't say. They both went to another car, and drove off together. I followed, and he took her to what I presumed to be his apartment. Their intent was clear when he urged her inside with his hand on her fanny underneath her skirt, and all she did was smile at him.

I sighed, and settled myself in for a long wait. I parked where I had a clear view of the apartment door, and set up my "alarm." It's a camera that can watch for motion, and either start recording or turn on an alarm. I set the alarm and relaxed with a new novel.

It was a good thing I had the book, for other than a few birds the alarm was silent for the next three hours.

Finally the door opened, and the two of them came out. They were holding hands, and went back down to his car. I followed them at a distance, but as expected they went back to the Bradley's where they had met. Then he drove off while she got back in her car and went on home. As she went in I had a thought. I called Morie, and caught him in his office. "Yeah?"

"Morie, what are Erika's nights off?"

"Officially? Sunday and Monday."

"I see. Well, nothing has been happening." Her sex life was none of his business. "So I'm going to take a break until Sunday. See you later."

As I hung up I looked at her apartment. There was a reason he had said her "official" days off were Sunday and Monday. As a practical matter, if a girl has an especially good night, it's not at all unusual for her to not show up the next night. Relatively few girls work every shift they are scheduled for.

Even though I had told Morie I was going to knock off, I waited. Don't ask me why. Maybe I just wanted to see if she would still go to work after spending three hours with a lover. As it turned out, she did. I followed her to the Maja, went home and had supper. Then I went back for a beer. Not only was Erika dancing, but she was doing just fine. In fact, if anything she was doing better.

The hell with that. I went back home and wrote up my report for Sarah. There wasn't all that much to it, yet that was part of the problem. I had this feeling I was missing something.

Well, whatever it was, it wasn't coming to me that night. I finished up the report and set it aside.

The next day was Saturday, and I put it to good use. I caught up on a lot of things I hadn't done yet, like laundry and cleaning up the apartment. I also restocked the larder better, so I could get back to doing more of my own cooking. Then I stayed home and watched a couple of science fiction movies from my collection. By then I was tired enough to go to bed.

I was awakened about two thirty when Sandy knocked on my door. "I just didn't feel like sleeping alone tonight," she said. I took her at her word, and she sighed as she cuddled up against my back and fell asleep.

She was still asleep when I got up the next morning, and stayed that way until the smell of coffee and bacon woke her up. She came into the kitchen dressed as always, and sat down at the table. I poured her some coffee. She took a sip and said, "You're going to make somebody a good wife someday."

"Only when it comes to the cooking," I said. "She can have the housework with my blessings."

"That's why I have company on a regular basis," Sandy said. "It makes me get off my ass and clean the place up."

"So how did things go last night?"

She shrugged. "It went. Typical Saturday night. Maybe a few more drunks than usual, but they weren't too grabby and they did tip well. No complaints."

"Was Erika there?"

"Yup, and raking in the money with the rest of us. She latched onto a couple of drunks, and I think one of them was under the impression she was going home with him."

She snorted and smiled.

"She may not have gone to bed with him, but he got screwed anyway. I think she made a good two hundred dollars from him alone. At least for a while there she was table dancing for him every time I turned around."

Sandy had no sympathy for men like that. I didn't have much, either. But that was beside the point.

"Well, I'll be going over to her place later," I said as I put the plates on the table. "I want to make sure that she behaves herself over the weekend. Then I can tell Morie that she's a good little girl."

Sandy looked at me and lifted an eyebrow. "Do you mean to tell me that having a naked woman in your kitchen doesn't give you any ideas? My word, I didn't realize you were in such poor shape!"

I grinned at her. She knew better than that. "I'm an old campaigner, kid. I've seen naked women before, even in my kitchen, and some were prettier than you."

"Prettier naked women in your kitchen?" she demanded. "How many?" Now she was pretending to be outraged.

"A bunch."

"How many?" she asked again.

"Okay, a small bunch."

"How many?"

"A few."

"How many?" She knew she was "winning," and I could hear it in her voice.

"Only a couple."

"How many?" She was smiling, pleased that she had "beaten me down." Not that she had ever been upset.

"Just one."

"Prettier than me?" she asked skeptically.

"Lucinda," I said.

That stopped her. "Lucinda? From the Maja?"

"That's the one." Lucinda had been a dancer there, and had moved on not long after Sandy started working.

"She was beautiful," Sandy admitted. "How was she in bed?"

"Not bad. Though I think I annoyed her. I didn't fawn all over her because of her beauty, like most men did. She wasn't used to that." Her skill had also had something of a mechanical flavor; something done because that's the way you learned to do it rather than because you like doing it that way. When it came to her own pleasures, though, she was skilled!

"Well," said Sandy, "I must admit I wasn't sad to see her go. She was always rather stuck up, and with a lot of the men you got the feeling that they took you only because she wasn't available."

"Then that was their loss, waiting for Lucinda instead of going with you." That earned me a smile.

"So tell me who else had a good night last night?" I asked.

I make it a point to never ask her how well she did, though she would tell me at times. Still, the topic of the night before kept us occupied as we ate, even though it had been a fairly routine Saturday night.

When we finished Sandy smiled at me and stood up. She came over to me, a smile. Then she leaned forward in that manner men find so difficult, and put her hands on the seat back on either side of my head. "Are you sure that my being here doesn't give you any ideas?" she asked softly. To emphasize the point she kissed me.

I returned the kiss, then reached out and tweaked her left nipple a little harder than necessary. Well, harder than necessary if I was trying to arouse her. Just right, though, for what I wanted to do.

Instantly she stopped kissing me and stood up. "Hey, what'd you do that for?" she demanded. "That hurt!" She rubbed where I had hurt her.

"And I'm hurt you think you can seduce me like that," I told her. "If you want to go to bed with me just say so."

She grinned at me wickedly. Then she came over and sat on my lap, facing me, one leg on either side. "I want to go to bed," she said huskily. Then she reached down between us. "And so do you," she added after finding what she expected.

"That's better," I said. I grabbed her under her cheeks, leaned forward and stood up. It wasn't as easy as I made it look, but she squealed and wrapped her legs around me. "You want bed, you get bed." She laughed and held on as I carried her into the bedroom that way.

An hour later I was ready to leave, and Sandy was too. At the door, though, I looked at her, then went back into the kitchen. I dug into one of the drawers, and handed her a key. "Now you won't have to wake me up."

She grinned, and took the key. "And what if you have company? You won't want me barging in."

That was no problem. "You know the light over the door?"

"Yeah?"

"If it's on I'm alone, and you can come in. If it's out, I've got company."

"Okay. I can live with that. But what if you forget, and leave the light on?"

I shrugged. "That's my problem. Hell, maybe she wouldn't mind the additional company."

"Not out of the blue like that she wouldn't." She put the key away, and we left. She took her car and headed for home while I got the van and drove to Erika's apartment.

Things were fairly quiet when I got there. After all, it was still early on a Sunday morning. I parked the van in a different place this time, and settled in.

As it happened, I didn't have to wait all that long for the first thing to happen. I had been there barely twenty minutes when the door opened, and a man came out. He stopped just outside the door and turned around. Erika was behind him and kissed him, a full lover's kiss right on the lips. He responded by caressing her, something made easier by the red lace teddy she was wearing. It was cut all the way to the waist on the sides, and was not meant for outdoor wear, but that didn't stop her.

The kiss came to an end, and he left. Erika turned to watch him go, and as she waved to him I enjoyed the view of her ass, nicely displayed by the way the teddy cut across the center of her cheeks.

After she went back in I took another look at the man who was leaving, and confirmed that he wasn't the man she had been with Friday afternoon.

Which didn't tell me much. Maybe she went to a party and he was a pickup. Or maybe this was her regular man and the one on Friday had been a pickup.

The hell with it. I noted the license number of the car the man got into and didn't worry about it. After all, Morie didn't give a shit about the dancers' sex lives as long as it didn't interfere with their work.

And as long as they weren't taking money for it.

After that it got quiet again, until just before two o'clock, when a car pulled up. Three women got out, and I recognized all three as dancers from the Maja: Monet, Laurie, and Morgana. They all went up to Erika's apartment, where she greeted them still dressed in nothing but that teddy. They went inside, each of the visitors carrying one of those oversized purses that dancers seemed to like.

Ten minutes later the door opened again, and all four came out dressed for the pool. I wasn't surprised. The three visitors shared a house, and I doubted the house had a pool. Clearly Erika had invited the others over to use hers.

With the complete approval of the men of varying ages who showed up within the next ten minutes. A sociologist could have had fun studying the actions and reactions of the men there, from openly ogling the four, to trying to show off (a waste of time), to just plain enjoying the view.

This time Erika didn't just do laps and go back. With friends there she stayed for a bit over half an hour. By then all of them had had their fill of the men. They enjoyed being the center of attention, but even that can get old, especially when money was not involved. And when the men start doing stupid things to try to show off.

One man managed to fall in the pool and splash the girls, so they got up and headed back to the apartment. Then they disappeared for almost three hours, when the four of them went out to eat, using two cars. That was followed by a movie (I couldn't tell which one), and then back to the house the girls shared.

It was late when Erika left the house and drove home. She went in and as near as I could tell she went to bed alone. I went home and did the same.

CHAPTER 4

I arrived at my office bright and early Monday morning, and found Maggie already there, simpering at me. I knew she thought I spent every minute of every weekend in bed with a variety of beautiful women, and this was her way of letting me know that I was forgiven.

Given my mood that was bad enough, but what was even worse was that she was wearing a lightweight bra and a snug blouse, and I could make out the ring in her left nipple. It had to be an inch across, which is on the large size for a nipple ring.

Fortunately, I was going straight to my office, and I believe I managed to hide my reaction. Once I was through the door, though, I let loose the shudder I had felt coming. Then I breathed a sigh of relief. The nipple ring did not make me want to reconsider doing anything with her.

With that out of the way I looked over the mail and got my phone and e-mail messages. little required any real attention, so I dumped them. Then I double checked the report I had written for Sarah, put my bill together, and took them out to Maggie.

With no other work in the day's business, I went back out to finish checking on Erika. I parked in another slot a bit after ten, and settled in for a long wait.

Or maybe not all that long. I had only been there about fifteen minutes when I noticed her car wasn't in its parking spot. It caught me by surprise. Dancers tend to be late risers, at least when working evenings, and this was far sooner than I expected her to be up and gone.

Still, with no idea where she might have gone, I just stayed put. She had to come back eventually, didn't she?

By three o'clock that afternoon I wasn't so sure. I had finished one book and was well into another, and there was still no sign of Erika. Suddenly the front passenger door opened, and Linda Dorret climbed in. "Hi, Dan," she said.

Linda was the clerk at the complex I had called the previous Thursday. She's a slender, pretty girl of 20, maybe 21, who was friendly but not my kind of woman. Mainly because she had a fiancé, and she was totally committed to him. "Are you still checking out Susan Trumble?" she asked.

"I am." There was no good reason to deny it.

"Okay. Just wanted to make sure. Anything we should we know about?"

Ah, so this wasn't entirely social. "Not that I'm aware of. Especially since you've still got those two dealers living here."

She grimaced. "They may well be dealers, but so far they haven't given us any reason to break their lease. As long as they behave themselves on our property there is not much we can do about it."

"What about the shooting?"

She shook her head. "Not good enough. Officially it went down as a robbery, where one junkie tried to steal drugs from another junkie. The source of the drugs could not be quote proven unquote, so we can't use that as a reason."

She looked at me again. "Are you sure you don't want me to send you an invitation to the wedding?"

"Heck, Linda, I'd just turn you down. You don't want me there anyway. I smoke, I drink, I leer at the ladies and use bad language. I'd be a terrible influence, and it'd bore me."

She laughed, a delightful sound. "Just what I thought. You're afraid you'd be bored. I'd be insulted, but you're probably right. Though I'm sure you'd liven things up quite a bit."

"That kind of livening you don't need. Want to liven things up? Spike the punch."

"Actually, we're going to have two punches, Dan. And one of them will be 'spiked.' Some of our members do have a drink now and then, and we do want to be open." She was a member of one of the more "fundamentalist" churches, and the reception was going to be held in the church hall.

"Have you and whatshisname anticipated the wedding yet?" There were some girls I wouldn't insult with a question like that, but Linda had a good sense of humor.

She laughed again. "No, I'm still a virgin." Another reason she wasn't "my kind of woman." "But Don will take care of that in due time."

"By which time you'll be Mrs. Market."

"That's the idea," she said cheerfully. "Well, I've got to be getting back to work. See you later."

She got out, and I wished she had stayed. I watched for a little longer, then left to go back to the office. If I was going to waste my time I could do it more comfortably there.

But I didn't forget about Erika entirely. On my way home after five I drove by her apartment again. Her car still wasn't there. I went on home troubled by that, for no good reason I could name. After all, there were dozens of perfectly innocent reasons for her to not be home.

Which didn't stop me from worrying.

The next morning I got myself up bright and early. This time when I went to the complex I did something I should have done before. I drove around the entire complex, and checked out the whole parking lot. Still no car.

Fortunately for my sanity, a job was waiting for me. It wasn't much of one, and didn't even take the entire day, but at least it gave me something to do besides sit around and brood about a maybe missing dancer. I didn't forget about her, though, and when I felt I could leave the office I went back to the complex. She was still not there.

Now I was getting seriously concerned. I had supper, then went to the Maja. The evening girls were coming in, but Erika wasn't among them. By the time I finished my second beer she was decidedly late.

Morgana was there, though. She had said "hi" earlier, and now as she passed by I waved her into the other seat at my table. "Hi, again," she said cheerfully. Her stage "personality" was that of a dark-haired vamp, with hints of witchcraft and sorcery, but personally she was a bright, friendly girl.

"Morgana, did Erika say anything about plans for Monday or today when you were with her Sunday?"

"No," she said, shaking her head, "she didn't say anything. Why?" Then she cocked her head at me. "And how'd you know we were together Sunday?"

"Morie asked me to check on her. I saw the four of you go swimming and to the movies."

"I see."

"Anyway, I went to check her out on Monday and her car was gone. It was gone today, too, and she's not here when she's scheduled to work tonight."

"Hmm, you're right." She looked quickly around the club. "She isn't here. Well, you know us dancers. It's probably nothing to worry about." She stood up and patted me on the cheek. "Gotta go. There's a customer waiting for me."

I didn't feel like trying to maintain a cheery disposition, so I finished the beer and went on home. If she was still missing the next morning I was going to do something about it. I was just thankful that Monday and Tuesday were the nights Morie usually took off. I didn't want to worry him yet.

The next morning I found that I had more than that to concern me. I got up and turned the radio on. Before long the news announcer came on and the lead story, a killing. "Local businessman Edward Brogan was killed last night while visiting a friend, Miss Cari Roland. Miss Roland told the police that he attacked her, and she defended herself." The rest was carefully written to say he was with his mistress without saying he was with his mistress, and left the impression that he had gotten violent.

I have trouble with coincidences. Yes, sometimes things happen strictly by chance, but in my experience most of the time there is nothing coincidental about it. Now here a man is killed by his mistress just after I confirm for his wife he has a mistress? I found that hard to believe.

But I had something else to take care of first. I headed out to the Armbridge Apartments, but this time I went to the office. Fortunately Linda was working at the front desk. She looked up and started to smile at me, then got serious when she saw my expression. "This isn't social, is it?" she asked.

"Not at all," I replied. "I need to have a look at one of your apartments."

"Let me guess. Susan Trumble."

"Yup. Can you let me in?"

"Not alone. On the other hand, our leases do permit us to enter apartments if there could be a problem, and I'd say this fits. Want to tag along?"

I smiled at her a little. "Thanks, yes."

She went back into another room, and opened up a locked cabinet filled with keys. She came back out with what hopefully were the keys to Erika's apartment. On the way over she asked, "Just what's the problem?"

"She had Sunday and Monday off, and was supposed to be back at work last night. She had some friends over on Sunday, but when I came here on Monday morning her car was gone. It wasn't here yesterday, either, and she wasn't at work last night."

"I see. So she could have gone somewhere, or she could be in the apartment after someone stole the car."

"Those are two possibilities," I agreed. "There are others."

"You think she could have been kidnapped?"

"I think I don't know what to think," I admitted. "All I know for sure is that nobody has seen her since Sunday."

"When she had company." Linda grinned mirthlessly. "We had some people complain about the four of them. Interesting thing, none of the complaints came from men." I didn't bother to answer, for we were at the base of the stairs up to her apartment. We went up, and Linda started by knocking at the door. She knocked three times, waiting between times. After three minutes she unlocked the door.

I felt a sense of relief when there were no unpleasant odors. Not unless you count what could have been stale perfume, maybe, but certainly no smells of decomposition.

Linda stuck her head around the door and loudly called "Hello! Anybody home?" No answer.

After another ten seconds or so she opened the door the rest of the way. She went in and I was right behind her. The apartment wasn't spic and span, but it wasn't a mess, either. It simply had a lived-in look. Linda called out again as she went and quickly checked the other rooms.

Linda came back into the living room, and shook her head. "It's empty. Nobody's here."

"Mind if I look around?" I asked.

"Don't take too long," she said. She didn't bother telling me not to touch anything. She knew I wouldn't. Even aside from not wanting to upset Erika if she came home, I wouldn't want to disturb anything that might be evidence.

"Do me a favor, will you?" I asked. "Look around and let me know if anything seems out of place."

"Out of place?"

"Like something left behind that a woman would take with her, or something missing that should be here."

"Oh, like if her purse were still here."

"Exactly, though I don't expect it to be that obvious."

And it wasn't. Not to me, anyway.

I didn't find anything that indicated that there was anything wrong. There were no signs of violence, no scrawled messages, nothing that looked out of the ordinary.

I finally went back into her bedroom, and Linda was peering into the open closet. Actually, it would be more accurate to say she was frowning at the top shelf of the closet.

"What is it?" I asked.

"She's a dancer, isn't she?"

"She is."

"And most dancers are concerned about their appearance, right? Always want to look their best?"

As do most women, but I knew what she meant. "That's right."

Linda turned around and pointed to a desk at the foot of the bed. "See that mirror?" It was a fancy lighted mirror for putting on makeup.

"Yeah, I see it."

"That's a professional mirror, too big to take on a trip. Not without good reason. But most women have a second smaller mirror for just that purpose. Susan does, too." She faced the closet again and pointed at the top shelf. "Right there."

Sitting on the shelf was a small blue lighted mirror, with the cord still wrapped around it. "I see."

"There could be explanations," Linda continued. "Maybe this is a spare, and she's got her regular traveling mirror with her."

"Maybe," I agreed, but she didn't believe it any more than I did. "Just one thing, though. I followed her around Sunday night. She came home at about one in the morning. I was here a little after ten on Monday, and the car was already gone."

Linda stared at me. I could see the wheels turning in her mind. Home about one and gone by ten? "Family emergency?"

"Maybe, though I get the impression she has pretty much cut herself off from any family. For one thing her father is dead."

Linda glanced up at the mirror, and shuddered slightly. "I can't even imagine being without a family," she said softly.

"Not everyone is as lucky as you."

"I know. In my head I do, at least." She looked up at me. "So what do we do now?"

"We do nothing. We go about our business as if we haven't been here. I've got something else to do right now."

"So I should just go back to work?"

"That's right. Now it's my problem."

"Okay, if you say so."

"I do."

She hesitated for a second, then started for the front door. As she did she couldn't resist another quick glance at the makeup mirror in the closet.

I followed her back to the office, then thanked her again before getting in my car and heading for a house I had only seen one time before. When I got there things were still busy, though it looked like they were wrapping up.

I got out of the car and watched from the sidelines for a few moments. Then I got lucky. Steve Kellerman came out of the house. I moved to where I could get his attention, and signaled for him to join me.

He hesitated for a moment, then did. "Hi, Dan," he said. "What're you doing here?" The question was a mix of personal and professional curiosity.

"Asking questions," I said. "Tell me a few things and I'll let you know if I'm here for a good reason."

"Go ahead, though you know I can't reveal much."

I ignored the warning. "I understand Brogan was shot by his mistress."

"Three rounds right in the pump. He was dead before he hit the floor. She had an Astra nine millimeter in a drawer. He punched her, then came at her threatening to do it again, she grabbed the gun and fired."

"That's her story?"

"Well, somebody punched her. She's got the beginnings of a beautiful shiner. Left eye. Now, what's it to you?"

I shook my head. "I don't know, Steve. It could be nothing, but just last week I was hired to find out if he had a mistress. I followed them here, and he went inside for a good while."

"Really?" New information for the cop gristmill.

"Really. They certainly seemed friendly enough then."

"Doesn't matter much," Steve said almost automatically while his mind processed what I had told him. "All kinds of men can become abusers."

I knew that as well as he did. "But not all kinds of men are followed by a PI on Thursday and shot dead the next Tuesday." I shook my head. "I don't like that kind of coincidence, Steve. I have this nasty suspicion I've been used."

I had his attention again. "Used by who?"

"I don't know. If his wife had shot him I'd guess her, but this way …" I shook my head. "Damned if I know. All I do know is that I've got this sneaky, nasty suspicion."

"So what do you want me to do about it?"

"Hell, your job. Look close, though, and at least consider the possibility that it could have been a murder."

He cocked an eyebrow at me. "A murder? Not just a homicide?"

"Murder," I repeated. "With malice aforethought. I have this nasty feeling that things aren't as you're supposed to believe they are. Hell, Steve, three bullets in the heart? That's either fast shooting or she stood over his body!"

"That bothers me a bit, too," he admitted. "We'll be checking the bullet paths in the body."

I nodded. That was about all I could ask for, at least at this point. "Keep me informed, will you?"

"As much as I can."

I nodded again. "See you later."

He said the same, and he headed for police headquarters while I drove to my office. I had some thinking to do.

CHAPTER 5

I was in no mood to talk to anyone when I got to my office. Even Maggie could see that, so other than a quick "Good morning" she left me alone.

I've had cases go bad on me before, but for two cases to go bad at the same time was a new low. Of course, the Brogan murder wasn't my case, except indirectly, and that was close enough.

It was having Erika turn up missing that bothered me. Here I was supposed to be keeping an eye on her, and she had disappeared on me. It seemed rather sloppy to me, letting a subject get away like that.

But worrying about what had happened wasn't going to do any good, so I set aside the self-recriminations and started looking at what I could do to find her.

The first problem, of course, was that I didn't know for sure that she hadn't left on her own. I pulled out the copy of her employment application and picked up the phone. An hour and over a dozen calls later, and I had an answer of sorts. If she had gone anywhere on her own it wasn't to see family. Her mother called her a slut, interesting coming from a woman who had done some hooking. One sister called her a whore, while another said she was sorry, but "I can't let Susan back into our lives until she has accepted Jesus Christ as her personal savior." I think she would have continued, but I managed to cut her off there. That was just as well. Whatever happened to Christian forgiveness? I considered her to be a pompous hypocrite.

Then there was the brother who gave me the feeling that he might have been one of the men who had raped her. At least he spoke of her in an overly familiar way that made me uncomfortable, and that doesn't happen often.

It was a good thing I was talking to him over the phone. I'd left the police force after an incident with a man who had raped his daughter, aged 12. He *had* resisted arrest, but I'd caught him under the chin with my baton hard enough to break his jaw.

In two places.

He'd tried to claim police brutality, but fortunately for me a news camera crew caught the confrontation on tape, confirming that he had resisted, and that I had only hit him once.

Still, I had decided that I'd be better off outside the force, where I could pick and choose which cases I investigated. So far I hadn't regretted the choice. While it wasn't a life of adventure and wild women (well, not all the time), there were advantages. And I still had my friends in the Department.

I kept those friendships with one rule I had yet to break. I never took a case where the person being investigated was a cop.

Which came in handy at times like this. I called the police Missing Persons office, and got lucky. Detective Tom Posner answered. Tom was one of the good guys who tried to find the missing person. The other detective, Claude Barnaby, was there because the department bosses figured that was where he would do the least damage. Even within the department he was better known as "Clod" Barnaby.

"Hi, Tom. I've got a bit of a problem."

"What, the mighty Daniel Muncie has a problem?" he asked, going overboard about my request. Then his voice returned to normal. "Sure, if I can. What is it?" There were two reasons I was hoping to get him. Not only was he a good guy, but while I may not take cases where the target was a cop, the reverse was not true. In fact, I gave cops a discount.

In his case I had been able to prove that his now ex-wife was messing around at the hospital where she was a nurse's aide. Worse yet, it had been with a security guard!

But it made him inclined to help me when he could. "Listen," I asked, "could you get a license plate on the 'look, don't touch' list? There's a girl who's been missing since early Monday, and I'd like some extra eyes to see if her car can be found." The list was usually for the gang unit, to keep track of certain people, but others could also use it for various reasons.

"Oh? Anyone I'd know?"

"Erika."

"What, the underage girl at the Maja? She's missing?" With his work with missing kids and runaways I wasn't surprised that he had spotted her for being underage.

"She hasn't been seen since late Sunday night."

"How do you know that?" he asked.

"I'm the one who saw her." I quickly filled him in on the Sunday night get-together. "So I watched her go into her apartment on Sunday night, and when I went back on Monday morning about ten the car was already gone. Then she didn't show up at work last night. I checked with her family, and she isn't with any of them."

"Hmm. Okay, give me the number and car description."

I gave him the information, and he said he'd get it right out. We talked for a few moments, and then he had to go back to work.

I would have, too, except that there wasn't much I could do. That was the worst of it; the lack of anything positive I could do to find out where Erika was. If I were still a cop, and working this case, then I could have done a variety of things, from checking with the credit card companies to checking phone records to searching her apartment in detail.

There wasn't much I could do, so I called Sandy. She answered the phone with a vague sound that could have been anything from 'good morning' to 'go to hell.' "Good morning, sleeping beauty," I said, making my voice more cheerful than I actually felt.

"Drop dead," she said clearly in return. But at least she didn't hang up.

"I need some help, Sandy," I said. "Erika is missing."

There were some vague sounds, as she moved around a little. I suspected she was sitting up, and I could picture her in bed, the sheets down around her hips. I didn't find the image as pleasing as I usually would. "What was that?"

"Remember I told you Morie had asked me to check Erika out?"

"Yeah?"

"She got together with some of the other dancers Sunday night. I saw her home after midnight, and she was gone when I went by her apartment Monday morning. She was supposed to work last night and missed her shift. I went through her apartment this morning, and there was no sign of violence, but Linda pointed out she had left her makeup mirror behind."

"Linda?"

I grinned to myself. I shouldn't have been surprised that she had picked up on that. "Linda, who works at the complex. I didn't break in."

"Oh." There was a short pause, and then she asked, "She left her makeup mirror behind?"

"There was a fancy one in her bedroom, and a smaller blue one in her closet. Of course, she could have had another one she did take."

"I doubt it. Those things last for years. And when one breaks you throw it away."

"So you agree she probably left against her will?"

"If she was going away for more than a day she would have taken a mirror with her, unless she knew there was one she could use where she was going. So either she thought she was leaving for a short time, there's a mirror where she is, or yeah, she didn't plan on leaving." I heard a yawn.

"Listen, can you do me a favor?"

"Whazzat?"

"Can you find out if anyone has any idea where she might have gone? I know she hasn't gone back to her family, but there are other possibilities. Maybe some friends somewhere else, or maybe someone hired her for a job."

"Hmm, possible." She yawned again. "I'll check around, but it'll take a while. I don't have many of their phone numbers, you know. We're not all that close away from the club. Why don't you go to Morie for the numbers?"

"I'm not quite ready to. Besides, I'm not sure he has the current numbers for everyone. More to the point, I think they'll be more open with you, especially about any jobs she might have gotten."

"You got a point there. Okay, I'll see you later." She hung up, and most likely went back to sleep. I was only mildly annoyed because she wouldn't talk to any of the dancers for a good while. The problem for me was that this still left me with nothing much to do.

So I dug out my report on Edward Brogan and reread it. It took me nowhere new, which was no great surprise. After all, I'd only written it a couple of days before. But it did give me an idea. I started going into more detail on Cari Roland's background. It didn't take long for some interesting holes to appear. For one thing I couldn't seem to find any evidence she had even existed prior to six years before.

It took a while, but eventually I found the birth certificate for a Cari Marie Roland, born on the proper date and in the proper town in the northern part of the state. The problem was that on this certificate her race was given as "black." Even more interesting, I also found a matching death certificate dated nine months later, from "crib death."

I sat back and thought about the Cari Roland I had seen. While it was possible she might have a black ancestor in her background, there was no way I would consider her a black. It wasn't just the blond hair, but her features as well. Her facial structure and everything else were simply too European. And her green eyes were real, not contacts.

I was caught by surprise when the phone rang. It was Steve Kellerman. "Hi, Dan. I got some news for you, and you're not going to like it."

Oh, shit. Just when I was already in a bad mood. "Okay, what is it?"

"I've already spoken with our illustrious District Attorney and he's decided to close out the Brogan shooting as a case of justifiable homicide."

"Really," I said flatly.

"Really," replied Steve. "Even though the three bullets went through his chest at three different angles." I sat up straight. "Three different vertical angles," he added.

"How different?" I demanded.

"Not that different. No more than ten degrees or so. But at the range he was supposedly shot that was enough to make three shots while he was standing unlikely. At least one of them had to be after he was already down. That one would seem to indicate murder, not self-defense."

"But he's not going to prosecute?"

"Nope. He's writing it off as self-defense by an abused woman." I could hear the disgust in Steve's voice. He was either personally convinced it was a murder, or he was suspicious it was. Or maybe he thought it was just too soon to make such a decision.

"Suppose you were to tell him that Cari Roland isn't who she says she is."

"Won't wash. Her prints came back negative."

That startled me, but in a way it fit in nicely as well. "No match?" I asked, to confirm.

"There's no record of her." His voice changed, becoming suspicious in another way. "What do you mean, she's not who she seems? What do you know?"

"Nothing, yet," I said. "I just have suspicions of my own."

"But you'll let me know if you find out anything?"

"Of course." He knew better than to ask exactly when I would tell him.

"Okay, then. I just thought you'd like to know."

"Thanks, Steve. I do appreciate it."

We said our good-byes, and hung up. Ten degrees, huh? It wasn't much, but as far as I was concerned it was enough to turn a self-defense claim into murder.

Yet there was another call I had to make. As I said, I didn't like the coincidence of the timing. I called Sarah Handly. Her secretary put me straight through. "Sarah, Dan Muncie."

"Yes, Dan."

"Has Alexis Brogan paid you yet?"

"No!" I could hear the surprise in her voice. "I just sent out the billing."

"Get paid," I said. "Get your money from her and stay away."

"Why should I do that?" She sounded mystified.

A thought occurred to me. "Are you alone?"

"I am at the moment. I was just about to call in a client."

"Okay, you heard her husband was killed?"

"Of course."

"Sam Ackright has decided to call it self-defense, but I'm going to prove it was murder."

She was quiet for a moment. "Murder? And you think Mrs. Brogan was involved?"

"I can't believe the coincidence," I told her. "Doesn't it strike you as a bit odd that his girlfriend kills him less than a week after I prove he has one?"

"I'm not sure I take your point," she said, though from her tone I could tell she did at least a bit.

"Suppose this had happened last week," I said. "How would it look if he were killed by a girlfriend nobody knew he had? This way their relationship is already established, by me. When the police went to tell her, she could admit that she knew he had another woman."

"I think I see what you're getting at."

"Then there is the way I found the girlfriend on the first night. How often does that happen? I've had cases where I couldn't confirm a lover for months."

"I definitely see what you are getting at."

"Then you'll understand how I don't like being used like that. It annoys me, and I react badly to that kind of annoyance."

"Don't get mad, get even," she said.

"Exactly. By the way, are you going to share any of this with Mrs. Brogan? Such as telling her I'm going to try to nail her?"

She hesitated. "I'm a divorce lawyer, Dan," she finally said. "Divorce is out of the question now, and I don't handle criminal cases. All that remains is for her to pay her bill."

I grinned. "There is one more detail."

"Oh? What's that?" she asked curiously.

"As it happened, after he left Cari on Thursday night Ed Brogan went to the Maja. Not only that, he sat next to me, and we got to talking a little. He admitted he had just come from being with his lover. But the interesting thing is that he said he took a lover because his wife had one."

"Really!" she said thoughtfully. "How certain are you of that?"

"That she actually has one? Sarah, I can't answer that. All I know is that he said it as a fact. He was convinced she had a lover. Maybe he had proof, maybe he didn't, but I don't think it was an idle claim."

"I see. That does change things, doesn't it? So why didn't he divorce her?"

"I asked him. Business reasons, he said, whatever those were, but he would have divorced her in due time."

"Interesting indeed. No, I don't think you need to worry. My relationship with Alexis Brogan is at an end, or will be once my fee has been paid. How long do you think it will take to prove your case?"

"Hell if I know. I've got another case I'm working on, a missing dancer. Since she may still be alive I've got to give that one priority."

"I can understand that. Besides, it will give Alexis longer to pay me."

"Take advantage of that."

"I plan on it. By the way, speaking of money, think I should have a word with the insurance company?"

"What, for his life insurance?"

"Yes. They may want to know that there are questions about his death. Shall I let them know?"

"Hell, that's up to you." I didn't want to get involved in that. Especially given the legal relationship between Sarah and Mrs. Brogan.

"Off the record, of course," she said. "I may even have them contact you."

"I'm not sure that's a good idea."

"Why not? You've done insurance work before."

Whenever I could. Then I had a thought. "Wait a minute. Are you going to suggest they hire me to investigate the killing?" I had thought she meant just to tell them there were reasons to be suspicious about the death.

"Since you're going to do it anyway, why not get paid for it?" She sounded almost amused at the thought.

I smiled. Getting paid was good, plus having a client would give me good cover. And if Sarah told them there wouldn't be a question of me going to the insurance company. "I can live with that," I said. "Thanks for the suggestion,"

"No problem," she said, all humor gone. "If she used you, she used me, too. I don't like being used any more than you do." She hung up without another word.

CHAPTER 6

After talking to Sarah I noticed the time. It was later than I had realized, so I went out for supper before going to the Maja. As I expected, Sandy was there, and she had already talked to the other girls.

She came over to the bar as soon as I had my beer. "Sorry, Dan," she said, "But nobody has any ideas where she might be."

That was what I had been afraid of. Well, there was nothing left to do but make it official. "Thanks, Sandy. I appreciate the help. In the meantime I think you have a customer waiting."

"I do, but he can wait another minute or so. What're you going to do now?"

"Tell Morie and let him make the official missing person report. I think it's been long enough."

She looked behind me. "Well, here he comes. See you later." She stood up and headed back to her customer. Morie dropped down in the same seat. He wasn't near as pretty as Sandy.

"So what's going on, Dan? This is the second shift Erika has missed." He tried to hide it, but he was concerned.

I shook my head. "I have no idea where she is, Morie. She hasn't skipped town, though, since her clothes are still in her apartment. I saw her back home Sunday night, and when I went to watch her on Monday she was gone."

"Gone?"

"Her car was gone, and she didn't come back to the apartment that day. As far as I know, I'm the last person to see her."

"So you think I should call the cops?"

"I do. Talk to Tom Posner if you can. He'll actually do something. Other than that, I'm out of options for the moment."

Morie nodded. "I'll call first thing in the morning."

"Good." I said. It was, too. Posner worked the day shift. Barnaby came in about two or so, and worked into the evening. If he called now he'd get Barnaby for sure.

Morie just nodded, and went about his business. I finished my beer, tipped Laurie, and headed out. I didn't want to stick around there, but I didn't feel like going home, either. I compromised and went to the home of the Widow Brogan.

I had to remind myself that the murder had only happened the night before. There was a string of visitors to the Brogan house, presumably friends and a few relatives. More than a few came with covered dishes, following that old tradition of feeding the bereaved. I hoped Mrs. Brogan had plenty of space in her freezer.

It wasn't until late that I got a good look at the wife of the late Edward Brogan. I was able to move the van closer, and as she started going to the door with departing visitors I was able to see what she looked like. She was older than Cari, of course. Like Ed, she looked to be about 35 or so, but a good looking 35. Good legs and a good figure all wrapped up in a well fitting black dress. I put the binoculars on her, and saw that the face matched.

As I watched I saw something else. There seemed to be another figure in the background. From some of the glimpses I got it looked to be a man, but only once did he come close enough to the door for me to make anything out. It was indeed a man, in a dark pair of pants and a dark turtleneck. Other than that I never got a good view of him.

I moved further away again, for in this neighborhood I didn't dare stay put for too long. Now I couldn't see into the doorway as well, but I could still notice when people left. And I could observe Alexis Brogan when she came to the door.

Shortly after ten what seemed to be the last couple left. Alexis was at the door, and accepted their condolences. She watched as they drove off, her arms crossed in front of her. As they started driving away I caught a faint glimpse of what looked like a hand resting on her right shoulder. Then her left hand came up and rested on that hand until the car was gone from sight.

As it disappeared her face changed. The grief went away, and she smiled, a lover's smile. She turned to face whoever was behind her, looking up and still smiling.

For a moment I wondered if she was going to kiss him right there, but they went in and the door closed. Gradually lights started going out until only three lit windows were left, in an upstairs room I presumed to be a bedroom. For a short while a small window next to the bedroom was lit, most likely a bathroom. Not long after the bathroom light went out the bedroom went dark.

While it was possible that the other person could have stayed in a room on the other side or in back, one I couldn't see from where I was, I doubted it. And the other person hadn't left, either. If I could have found anyone to take the bet, I'd have put money on his being in the same bed as the grieving widow.

Make that the supposedly grieving widow.

Suddenly I felt disgusted. I started the van and headed for home. Who did this bitch think she was? Her husband is killed one night and she has to spend the next night with her lover? That wasn't bright. If she was that careless then there were other things she had done that would give her away.

In fact, the only thing saving her nicely rounded ass right now was that Sam Ackright had made his decision before all of the evidence was in, and Ackright was not the kind of man who reopened cases willingly.

On the upside, when I was ready to nail her it shouldn't be all that difficult. As a start, I had written down the license plate numbers of the three cars still in the driveway. With any luck one of them belonged to Alexis' "guest."

I went on home and resisted the temptation to have another drink. Instead I went to bed and read for a while before going to sleep.

In the morning I woke up and realized I wasn't alone. Sometime during the night Sandy had come in, and slipped into bed without waking me. That upset me. I didn't like thinking I could sleep through something like that. Suppose it had been someone less friendly? That could have gotten me dead!

As I looked at her she woke up. She smiled and said, "Good morning."

"Good morning to you, too."

"Are you always that jumpy at night?" she asked.

"What do you mean?"

"Well, I came in and you had your gun out. Scared the hell out of me."

"I didn't shoot you, did I?" I made myself ask.

"No, but it made me glad I had already undressed."

Now I knew what had happened. My unconscious mind had taken care of the situation without really waking me up. It doesn't happen often, only when something is bothering me. And there is a trigger, like Sandy coming in. I just smiled at her. "Well, once I saw you standing there, naked like that, I knew you were unarmed."

She looked at me as if offended. She whipped down the sheet. "What about these?" she demanded.

I grinned at her. "Wrong kind of thirty-eights, kid. Let's go eat." I stood up and headed for the bathroom, then the kitchen. I had breakfast halfway done by the time she came in. She had combed her hair.

"How are you doing this morning?" she asked.

"Just peachy," I replied. "I've already got another case half solved." She looked up at me and I quickly added, "Not Erika. I presume she didn't show up later?"

"You presume correctly." She snatched a piece of draining bacon. "No Erika, no call."

I finished breakfast, served us both, then sat down. As we started eating I looked at her. "Sandy, mind if I ask you a personal question?"

"Depends," she said. She looked up at me. "Mind if I tell you to go to hell?"

"Not if I deserve it."

"So what's the question?"

"You've got a degree, don't you?"

She grinned. "Yup."

"What in?"

"Ready for a laugh?"

"Sure."

She looked me in the eye for a moment. "Elementary education."

That startled me. That would have been one of the last things I would have guessed. "Elementary education? As in teaching the little ones?"

She nodded. "I did my student teaching with a bunch of fourth graders. I was pretty good at it, too." She grinned again. "Now you're wondering why I didn't go into teaching, aren't you?"

"The thought has crossed my mind," I admitted.

She sat back for a moment, remembering. "It was the last day of my student teaching," she said. "I was standing there, watching all the little rug rats head for home, feeling a little sad that I wouldn't be seeing them any more, and their regular teacher was telling me about how good I was, and how well I had done with the kids, all the things I was supposed to be glad to hear. But you know what? The only thing I could think of was that my bra itched, and if I didn't get out of those pantyhose in the next ten minutes I'd go crazy. That's when it hit me. If I became a teacher, every damned school day I'd have to wear a bra and panties at least, and most of the time pantyhose, too. Oh, I could get away with pantyhose with the built-in panties, something like that, but if I had on a dress I'd have to wear some kind of panties."

"And you hate underwear."

"And I hate underwear. Oh, I finished getting my degree. It would have been stupid not to, I was already so close, and damn near made cum laude. But actually teach?" She shook her head emphatically. "No way. By the end of the first semester I'd have been in long dresses so I could at least go panty-less!"

I grinned. She looked at me and asked, "So what case is it that's half solved?"

"Did you hear about the man who was shot by his girlfriend Tuesday night?"

"Yeah. Something about him trying to beat her up."

"I don't think it was self-defense. I don't even think he hit her. I think it was murder."

"Why's that?"

"I was hired to follow him last week. I followed him on Thursday, and saw him meet the woman who shot him. They had a late meal together, then went to her place. I left them there, and went to the Maja. Remember?"

"Sure."

"Well, later on he went there too. The Maja, I mean. He wasn't ready to go home yet, and we talked a little. Not much, we didn't even exchange names, but he mentioned he had a girlfriend because his wife was fooling around on him."

"Tit for tat, huh?"

"Something like that. Then Tuesday night he gets murdered."

"And you don't like the timing."

"That's right. It's too much of a coincidence."

"His coming into the Maja after leaving his girlfriend was a coincidence, too."

"Yes, or maybe fate. Not that it mattered, really. I wouldn't have liked the timing of his murder anyway. The only thing it did was give me a starting point."

"A starting point?"

"When I left the Maja last night I went to his house. The widow was having lots of company. After a while they left. All but one, that is. A man. He spent the night."

Sandy stared. "In her bed?"

"I don't know for sure, but if I had to bet I'd say yes. I saw the way she smiled at him after the others were gone. She didn't look anything like a grieving widow."

"What did he look like?"

"I don't know." I let my frustration show. "I didn't see him clearly. White male, medium build, maybe half a head taller than her, wearing dark slacks and a dark turtleneck. That's all I could make out."

Sandy was thoughtful for a while. "So if you're right, that proves the husband was correct in saying that his wife was fucking around on him. But that seems to be a strange way of murdering him. Why that way?"

"Think about it, Sandy. What are the best ways of getting away with murder? You can't always count on your lawyer convincing a jury you're innocent. And you can't always count on never being arrested. But suppose that you arrange for him to be shot under conditions that allow the shooter to get away with it? Such as pretending that he was trying to beat her up?"

"I see. Still not easy to do, you know. Like what if the girlfriend likes him and doesn't want to kill him? She could tell hubby, maybe the police."

"So you get to her before she's his girlfriend."

Sandy looked at me suspiciously. "He was set up with her? Still not easy."

"No, but it could be done."

"I suppose." She checked her watch. "Well, I need to be going. I'm meeting Zenobia at the gym before long, and I've got to go home and get my leotard."

Zenobia was another of the dancers, a tall, striking black girl with tits even larger than Sandy's. She was also a good dancer, with some modern dance training in her background.

Sandy stood up and walked into the living room. She stopped at her dress, laying where she had left it in the middle of the floor, her back to me. She picked it up by bending over at the hips, giving me a good view of what I had missed by getting up to fix breakfast so soon. She dropped the dress over her head, putting it on like a large t-shirt. After that she stepped into her shoes and picked up her bag and purse. "Bye," she said, waggling her fingers at me.

I watched her go out the door, wondering why I hadn't taken advantage of what was mine for the taking. Breakfast could have waited a while longer.

Yet I knew why. It had to do with Alexis Brogan spending the night with her lover. Her husband had been dead for less than 24 hours, yet she was willing to have him stay the night. That was stupid, and I was offended, even if it was going to make my job that much easier.

CHAPTER 7

With breakfast out of the way I headed for the office. Like I said, while I had every intention of nailing Alexis Brogan for the murder of her husband, my main concern right now was Erika. Ed Brogan was dead, and was going to stay that way no matter what I did. Erika, though, could still be alive.

I had a pair of starting points I hadn't used the day before. I had the auto licenses of two men she had been with, and the address of one of them.

The first, the fellow she had met at the Bradley's, was Marcus Matthews. He was a night bartender at the Graywood Hotel, one of the best non-chain hotels in the city. He had a clean record with the police, and a good credit history. That was about all I could tell, not a good start.

The other man was much more promising. Maximilian Sharf was a salesman, with a history of working for a variety of companies of varying reputations, mostly poor. He had several arrests on his record, with the word "fraud" mentioned prominently in the list of charges, but apparently most of the charges had been dropped. There had been only one prosecution, on reduced charges, and that had only resulted in probation.

One thing that mildly surprised me was that he was older than I had previously thought. I had guessed his age to be the late twenties, but he was actually 36. That suggested he put considerable effort into keeping his appearance youthful, which in turn suggested a certain amount of vanity.

The downside with him was that he had no record of violent crimes. While it might be that she had gone off with someone willingly, it just didn't feel like that was the case. It was asking too much to expect that someone would take off late on Sunday night and be gone for several days without telling anyone where they were. Especially when it meant missing two days of work.

But what could I tell from the little I knew? There wasn't much to go on, yet I could draw some conclusions. To begin with, if there had been any violence in the apartment it was sharp, fast, and left no signs. It also didn't leave any blood behind. Not any that was visible without a close examination, that is, and I was in no position to conduct such a search.

It also happened in a relatively short span of time. I had left her at her apartment at midnight, and by ten she was gone. It seemed likely that it hadn't happened during daylight hours, so the period was further cut from about ten hours to roughly six.

Presuming that it was indeed involuntary, that is. Yet could it have been her own decision? Only if she was inconsiderate enough to not call anybody and let them know.

Then I had a thought. The problem with taking Linda into the apartment was that she didn't know what was there to begin with. What I needed was someone who had a better idea what had been there to start with. The obvious choice was one of the three women who had spent Sunday with her. There was a good chance that they had looked at her clothes.

But it was early, yet. So instead of bothering one of them, I got back in my car and drove out to the Armbridge Apartments. There I started knocking on doors and asking questions. I got nowhere for a good while. All I could get was "negative" answers, nobody had heard anything. Then I got lucky.

Bill Masters was annoyed when I knocked. He worked nights, and had just gotten to sleep, and I woke him up.

"I'm sorry, Mr. Masters," I explained, "but it's important. I'm investigating a possible kidnapping."

"You are?" he asked suspiciously. "Who?"

"Susan Trumble," I said.

"Don't know her," he replied instantly.

"She's a dancer," I continued, "and she lives in B-23."

"Still don't know her," he said, and started to close the door. Then he stopped and looked at me. "Wait a minute. You mean that good looking kid who goes to the swimming pool practically naked? That's her?"

"That's her."

"Yeah, and she drives a bright red Sunfire?"

"Yes, she does." At least I hoped she still did.

"Now I know who you're talking about. I like to park my truck over there. It's a bit big, and I've got more room to get in and out. So what do you want to know?"

"Just if you might have seen or heard anything Monday morning. We know she came back here around midnight Sunday night, and was gone by mid-morning or so."

"No, I didn't. I got home about six, and didn't hear anything out of the ordinary. Just people getting ready for work, as always. By seven thirty or so I was asleep, and slept undisturbed until about three."

I started to thank him when I noticed him frown. "One thing, though," he added. "I don't know if it helps or not, but her car was gone when I got home."

It helped! Still I kept my voice even as I asked, "Are you sure? It could have been parked somewhere else."

"I'm sure." He grinned. "When you've got a neighbor as pretty as her you pay attention. I can see the walk from her place to the swimming pool, and since she'd go between the two in just that skimpy thing she swam in I've enjoyed the view more than once."

The grin faded. "Yeah, I know where she liked to park, and that slot was empty. And it's a bright orangey red that I would have seen if parked somewhere else."

"Thank you Mr. Masters. You've been a big help."

"She's really missing?"

"She is. Nobody has seen her since she came home late Sunday night." Nobody but her kidnapper, that is.

"Well, I hope you find her. She's not my kind of woman, but she was certainly good to look at."

"That she is," I agreed. "Oh, did you happen to notice if there was anything on the ground around that parking slot?"

"Hers, you mean? No, I didn't see anything."

"Well, thanks again for your help." I waved and left.

Now I had something a little more concrete. I saw her home at midnight, and she was gone by six. Well, her car was, which meant that most likely she was, too.

I kept checking around, but nobody else could tell me anything new. Bill Masters was the only one with relevant information. The most I got from some of the others were complaints about the way Susan/Erika dressed, especially at the pool.

By the time I finished I was more than ready for lunch. I had some burgers, and then I called the girls Erika had spent Sunday with. I was lucky, and got Morgana.

"Hi, Dan," she said, cheerfully. "What can I do for you?"

"First I've got a question. By any chance did you get a good look at Erika's closet when you visited her on Sunday?"

"Did we ever! She and I are close to the same size, and I got to try on a few things."

"Would you be willing to do me a favor, then? I'd like to go through her clothing and find out what might be missing."

"She still hasn't turned up?" There was no humor now, just concern over a missing friend.

"No, and I'm not sure if she's gone somewhere on her own or been kidnapped. The thing is that if most or all of her clothing is still in the apartment then she has likely been kidnapped."

"While if enough things are gone she might have left on her own," said Morgana, finishing the thought. "Sure, I'll help. When do you need me there?"

"As soon as you can get here. I'll get access to the apartment while you're on the way."

"Okay. I'll come as soon as I throw on a dress. Bye."

I had no doubt that she meant that literally, so I headed back to the apartments. Fortunately Linda was working, and I was able to explain to her what I wanted to do.

"I can't let you have a key, Dan," she said, "but I'll go in with you. That would be okay."

"That's fine, too," I replied.

She got the key to the apartment and walked over to it with me. "So this will be one of the other dancers joining us?"

"Yes, Morgana. She was here Sunday. She and Susan went through Susan's closet, so she has a fairly good idea of what clothing Susan has."

"While you and I don't," Linda commented.

I didn't need to reply. We reached the apartment, and found Morgana waiting for us. Her black hair practically gleamed in the sunlight, and she was wearing a sundress of some sort. It wasn't too bad from the front, but there was no back worth mentioning above the waist. At least the skirt came down most of the way to her knees.

I performed the introductions, and the girls seemed to get along at first, though I did get the impression that Linda was more curious about Morgana. We went inside, and I stood back while the two of them went through the closets and drawers.

Morgana may have been cheerful and friendly on the phone, but she was all business here. Finally she finished and stood back. "Well, I can't say for certain," she said, "but if she did take any clothing with her it wasn't much. Most everything I remember seeing on Sunday is still here."

"Most everything?" I prompted.

She shrugged. "Hey, my memory isn't perfect. Let's say that everything I remember seeing is here, okay?"

"Okay. What about the mirror?"

Morgana glanced up at the mirror. "Yeah, she likely would have taken that." She looked over at me. "So you think someone took her?" I could see she was concerned about the possibility. I glanced at Linda, and she was also worried, but for two different reasons. Not only was she concerned for Susan's safety, the same as Morgana and I were, but there could be legal problems for the complex as well.

"Yes," I said, "I think there is little doubt now that she was kidnapped some time early Monday morning after coming home from visiting with you."

"But by who?" asked Linda.

"By someone she knew," I replied. "The door is undamaged, so they didn't break in. And since the door has a deadbolt there was no way they could slip in with some plastic. The only logical conclusion is that she opened the door to someone she had reason to believe she could trust."

"Someone she could trust?" asked Linda.

"Yeah, like someone in a cop's uniform," said Morgana. "Someone she thinks she should be able to trust just because of who, or what, they look to be."

There was something about the way she said it that made me look closer at her. She shrugged. "I was almost raped by a fake cop once," she said. "What was good for me is that I have a cousin who's a real cop, so I was able to tell he was a fake before anything bad happened to me."

"I see," said Linda. "So someone got her to open the door for her, and then kidnapped her. But wouldn't she have fought back?"

"Not if he was able to disable her before she could."

"But shouldn't there be some sign of that?"

"Not necessarily, Linda," said Morgana. "Look, come with me." She led the way back into the living room. "Now, suppose she's standing by the door. The bad guy gets her to open it, and she invites him in. She turns and walks away," Morgana turned her back to the door, "and bingo, she's at his mercy. He can hit her over the head, grab her around the neck, or do a variety of other things to knock her out before she can put up a fight."

Linda nodded. "I see what you mean."

"Which brings us back to the question of who she would trust enough to open the door early in the morning," I said. "I found another tenant who says that her car was gone when he got home from work at six that morning, so what ever went down it happened between midnight and six."

"Dead of night," said Morgana, nodding. "Some real slimeballs out then."

"It certainly is looking like she was kidnapped," said Linda. She sounded a little frightened.

"But by who?" asked Morgana. "And why?"

It was my turn to shrug. "No telling just yet. But when we do find out the one it will help us answer the other."

"Is there anything I should be doing?" asked Linda. "The complex, I mean. To keep it from happening again."

"You could have a guard on patrol at night. Will the owners go for that?"

"I don't know, though they might if you can prove she was kidnapped. At least they would have to consider it."

"Or you could put in gates," added Morgana. "My last complex did that, but it didn't help all that much. Too many other ways of getting in."

I had to agree with her. The only kind of "gated" complex that really did any good was one where there was a guard to let people in. Just putting in a gate doesn't do much good, since you have to allow for people who forget codes or lose keys, not to mention guests of the residents.

"Well, I'm sorry to rush, but I need to be heading on home," said Morgana. "Good luck, Dan. I'd hate for anything bad to happen to Erika. See you, Linda."

There wasn't anything else Linda or I could do, either, so we followed Morgana outside. Linda locked up, and we walked back to the office, where I had left my car. It was a quiet walk, with each of us involved in our private thoughts.

CHAPTER 8

It was time to do a more complete check on the two men I knew about. I started with Marcus Matthews, in part because I had a good contact who could tell me about him. I knew the assistant manager at the Graywood Hotel, where Matthews worked. Louis Carrington was a gentle man who had worked his way up from bellhop to assistant manager. He was so gentle, in fact, that this movement had taken forty years, from starting as a bellhop at the age of 15 to making assistant manager at 55. Nobody had ever accused him of being overly ambitious. Or ambitious at all, for that matter.

Now Louis, better known as Lou, was 67 and working because he enjoyed working. I went to the hotel, asked to see Lou, and was sent right up. Lou came out to see me, a pleasant, white haired man, only five foot seven but bulkier now than when he was a bellhop.

"What can I do for you, Dan?" he asked.

"I'm looking for a missing person," I said. "She's a young dancer, and may have been kidnapped."

"Dancer? What kind?" I knew Lou had a soft spot for artists, especially dancers. I knew he had photos of himself with a wide variety of celebrities who had passed through the hotels where he had worked, but the ones on the walls were mainly of dancers.

"She works at the Naked Maja."

"Ah. Is she any good?" The kind of dancing made no difference to him. He still cared. Some of the dancers in the photos were classical dancers, ballerinas and the like, but others were burlesque, and the more recent photos were 'exotic' dancers.

"Good at that kind of dancing. And pretty."

"You say she's missing?"

"Yes. She disappeared between midnight Sunday night and six on Monday morning."

"So what can I do to help?" Besides which he just cared about people.

"I'd like to speak to one of your employees. My missing dancer spent some time with Marcus Matthews last week, and I want to know if he can tell me anything useful."

"Do you think Marc might be involved? He's a nice kid and I'd hate to think he had done anything like that."

"I don't know for sure, but I'm inclined to think not. It was likely just a case of a beautiful young woman and a good-looking young man getting together and letting nature take its course."

"You've seen him, then?"

"Yes, I have. Morie Weisel, owner of the Naked Maja, asked me to keep an eye on Erika for a while. Last Friday she went to a Bradley's, and later came out with a young man. She got in his car, and went to what I presume was his apartment. After a few hours he took her back to the Bradley's where she picked up her car and went home."

"That would be long enough." Having worked in hotels for over half a century he had no doubts about how they spent the time. "Let me see when he'll be in."

I sat back while Lou called the bar and checked. I didn't pay any attention until Lou said, "He is? Send him up to my office, will you? Thanks."

Lou hung up and said, "He'll be up in a couple of minutes. He came in early to help with the happy hour."

"Thanks. What can you tell me about him?"

"Let's see." Lou sat back and looked at the ceiling. "Marc has been working here about two years now. A little less, maybe. He studied bartending at one of those schools, but you know we don't worry about that much. He gets along with the others in the bar, the customers like him, and he's pretty reliable. I know he's bedded at least one of the waitresses, but they still work together." He looked at me and grinned. "That can be a problem, you know. Bedding co-workers can be hazardous."

I grinned back at him. "What about marrying them?"

"That's much safer," he said, smiling back. Forty years before he had married an assistant housekeeper and they had been together ever since. One son was a career Army officer, their daughter was an OB/GYN, and the younger son was already a manager with one of the hotel chains.

I caught up on his family news until there was a knock on the door. When I turned around the young man from the week before was standing in the doorway. "Excuse me, you wanted to speak to me, Mr. Carrington?"

"What, there's company so suddenly I'm 'Mr. Carrington?' Relax, Marc. Nobody's in any trouble." He looked at me. "At least not as far as we know."

"I know of nothing," I said.

Lou stood up. "I'm going to make my rounds now, so you two can talk in private." He left, closing the door behind him.

"Have a seat, Marc," I said. As Marc Matthews sat down I considered the short bio Lou had given me. I knew he could do that for everyone in the hotel who had been there more than six weeks. Marc sat down warily. "I'm here to see what you can tell me about Susan Trumble."

That got his attention. "Susan Trumble? Who's that?"

"She may have called herself Erika."

"Oh, her! Yeah, I remember her real well." He smiled. Clearly it was a pleasant memory. "What about her?"

"She's missing."

His smile disappeared instantly. "She is?" Either he was truly surprised or he was a good actor. "What happened?"

"We're not sure right now," I said. "That's why I'm talking to you. I know you've been with her. When did you first meet her?"

"Last Friday. How did you know about that?"

"In a moment. Do you know what she does for a living?"

"She's a dancer at the Naked Maja. A good one, too, I'd bet."

"She is. Erika is her stage name. So you met her for the first time that day? At the Bradley's?"

"Yes, I did. How'd you know about that?"

"Because her boss wanted to make sure she was taking care of herself and not using drugs. I'm a private detective, and he hired me to follow her. I was watching her when the two of you met. So just how did you meet?"

Marc hesitated. "She's missing?"

"She is. We suspect she was kidnapped."

"Okay. She was supposed to meet someone, a date, I think. I was there because sometimes I get tired of eating my own cooking, and want a change of scenery from the hotel. I saw her when I went in, and watched her getting madder and madder. We were in adjoining booths, and facing each other. I finally asked her if she had been stood up, and she said yes. We talked for a few minutes and she invited me to join her."

"Then what happened?"

"We talked, and got along real well. After a while I asked her if she'd like to go to my apartment for a while. She said yes."

"Just to come to your apartment? To do what?"

"What else? I didn't say what for, but she knew what I was talking about. She agreed, and said I should drive us both there."

"Which you did. Did she say why she wanted you to drive?"

"No, she didn't. But on the way she showed me. I opened the door for her, and by the time I got around to my seat she had pulled up her skirt and was sitting on her bare ass. That's when I found out she wasn't wearing any panties. And when she spread her legs a bit it was pretty clear what she had in mind."

"So you started fondling her. What else did she do?"

He grinned at me a bit. "She didn't try to blow me, if that's what you're thinking. She knew how dangerous that would be. Besides, there wasn't enough room for her head between me and the steering wheel. She also didn't want to distract me from what I was doing with her clit. She did grope me, though."

"Sounds like an interesting drive," I said dryly.

"It was. By the time we got to my place she was soaked and I was hard. We got inside, and I barely had the door closed before she was on her knees grabbing for me. We didn't even make it to the bedroom." He stopped and looked at me. "But that's not what you want to know, is it?"

"No, it isn't, actually. By any chance did she mention the name of the person who stood her up?"

"Not really. She called him Mackie, but that sounds like a nickname to me. Other than that she talked about some of the people at work. And she got me to talk about my work." He grinned. "She said I should try to get a job at the club where she worked."

"Do you like interacting with people?"

"Yeah, I do. The best part of bartending is talking to the customers."

"Then don't change jobs. People don't go to places like the Naked Maja to talk to the bartender. Or talk too much of anybody but the dancers, for that matter. Besides, the music is so loud you can't hear a thing." I decided to get him back on the subject. "Other than her boss, did she mention any other male names? Any that might have been former boyfriends?"

"Just someone from back in high school she called George the jerk. He was a junior or senior, something like that, when she was a freshman, and he seduced her. Then he went off after some other new girl."

"That wasn't a nice thing for him to do," I agreed. "I'm not surprised she calls him a jerk."

"What, for leaving her? That's not why she called him that. She'd been raised real uptight until that happened. Once she discovered sex she says she blossomed. He fucked her and she loved it. She called him a jerk because when she got to know some other boys she came to realize what a rotten lover George was. She said that if he was going to go around seducing girls he could at least learn how to do it right."

"So she called him a jerk for being a poor lover?"

"You got it."

"Did she say where she went to high school?"

"In Marcy. Some dinky little town south of here."

Southwest, actually. "Did she mention anyone else?"

"No, those were the only ones."

"Did she mention going anywhere soon?"

"Like last weekend? No, she didn't. In fact, I was hoping to get together with her this week, and I thought she wanted to, as well. She was supposed to call me, but she didn't."

"Now you know why."

"Got that right. Do you need to talk to me any more? I should be getting back to the bar. Things will be getting busy before much longer. The early shift, you know."

The early shift I didn't know, but I let him loose. I got out one of my cards, and gave it to him. "If you think of anything else, anything at all, give me a call. Sometimes even things that seem useless can be helpful."

"I'll do that." He got up and left.

Mackie and George the Jerk, I thought. Could 'Mackie' be a variation on 'Maximilian?' Or maybe a misunderstanding of 'Maxie?' The only way to find out was to find either Maximilian or Erika and ask them, and of the two Sharf would be the easier to find.

With his license number I had an address. For the moment I had no employer for him, but it wouldn't take long to find out. Either way, I decided to start by going past his house. I was mildly surprised to find that his car was there, so I took a chance.

I pulled up in front of the rather modest house. It didn't live up to the fancy car he drove, but that wasn't uncommon. Lots of people with modest houses have upscale cars, since those are more "public" than their homes.

I had no idea what to expect from Sharf, so I decided to play this straight. As long as he wasn't the kidnapper he had nothing to fear from me. While it was possible, I didn't believe it. People who get involved in frauds seldom commit violent crimes. Many have as much larceny in their hearts as anybody who has ever pointed a gun at a teller, but they tend to consider themselves to be 'above' violence.

I only had to knock once before Sharf answered the door. "Yes?" he asked rather frostily.

"Mr. Sharf, I'm Daniel Muncie," I said, showing him my identification. He glanced at the card, then looked at me sharply. "I'm investigating the disappearance of Susan Trumble."

Unlike Matthews, he recognized the name. "Disappearance?" he asked. "She's missing?"

Either he was a good actor, which given his "profession" was entirely possible, or he was honestly caught by surprise. "You didn't know she was gone?"

"No, I didn't! I've tried to call her a couple of times, but I kept getting her answering machine. She never returned my calls."

"May I come in?" I asked.

"Sure." He opened the door and let me in.

I looked around the house. It was neat and tidy, with a comfortable feel. I had expected something a little flashier.

"She's missing?" Sharf asked.

I pointed to the phone sitting on an end table. "Go ahead and call the police. Use the non-emergency number, not 911. Ask for Missing Persons. You'll get either Tom Posner or Claude Barnaby. Ask if Susan Trumble has been reported as a missing person. They'd likely want to talk to you about her. You were one of the last people to be with her."

That startled him almost as much as her being missing. "I was? But I haven't been with her since last Sunday!"

"We know. She disappeared that night."

"How do you know that?" he demanded.

I ignored the question. For the moment I wanted him rattled like this. "Were you the one she was supposed to meet at the Bradley's on Sixth Street last Friday?"

"Yes, I was! How'd you know that?" He shook his head. "Look, I'm not answering any more questions until you tell me how you know I was supposed to meet her, and that I was with her on Sunday." He was a little belligerent now. He was rattled almost enough. Just one more item would do it.

"In fact," I said, "you left her apartment around ten thirty that morning. She was pretty in that red teddy, wasn't she?"

"Not another answer until you tell me how you know all this," he said angrily.

I smiled at him. "I was watching. Don't worry, it had nothing to do with you. I presume you know what she does for a living."

"I do," he said, the anger replaced with suspicion. "She's a dancer at the Naked Maja."

"Have you ever seen her dance?" I asked casually. "At work, I mean. I presume she did some private dances for you." I know Sandy did for me at times.

He looked uncomfortable. "No, I haven't," he admitted.

I smiled at him. "I don't blame you. If I were you all those cops would make me uncomfortable, too."

"So you know about my record."

"Of course I do. But your record is all for non-violent crimes. They don't make you out to look like a kidnapper, so let's get down to the issue at hand, Susan. You were supposed to meet her last Friday."

"You still haven't told me what you were doing where you could see us together."

"I haven't? I'm sorry. Her boss at the Maja wanted me to check her out for a while, to make sure she wasn't getting involved with drugs. That's what I was doing when I saw you leaving her place."

"I see." He wasn't completely satisfied, but he decided not to push the issue. "Yeah, that was me. I was supposed to meet her for lunch, but a business appointment ran late, and I couldn't get away to call her. I went by later, but she was already gone." He hesitated for half a second, and then asked, "You were watching her then, too, weren't you?"

"I was."

"Did she leave alone?" When I hesitated he smiled and said, "Relax. I know girls like her. She's a great lay, but any man who expects her to stick with one guy is a fool. That's why I didn't bother asking her about it when I did meet her after work on Saturday night. I knew she'd lie to me."

"Why ask me if you're so sure of the answer?"

"Then will you at least tell me if he was good looking? Hell, at least tell me he wasn't ugly!"

"He wasn't ugly," I admitted.

"Well, at least that's a relief," he said. "I'd hate to think I could be replaced by some ugly SOB. Now, what else do you want to know?"

"For one thing, did she call you Mackie?"

"Yeah. She didn't like the name Max, or Maxie, or anything like that, and Maximilian was too long. So we compromised on Mackie. I'm not fond of it, but for a great lay like her I can live with it."

We talked for about half an hour, but there wasn't much more he could tell me. Mostly he reported the same things Marc had already told me about, just in more detail. He even had more of a name for 'George the jerk.' His last name was 'Rawlings, Rollins, something like that.'

There were a few things that might prove useful, but it was too early to tell. Finally I thanked him and left.

CHAPTER 9

By the time I had finished talking to Sharf it was too late to do the one thing I wanted to do, drive to the town of Marcy and see if I could find out about this 'George the jerk.' That didn't mean I had nothing to do, though.

I went back to the office first. It was the tail end of the day, but I still needed to see if there were any messages. I could have called, but I didn't know if Maggie had left. Even if she was there I never counted on her getting the messages right. I needed to see them for myself.

I wasn't in the least surprised to find that Maggie had already left. If Mike and I were both out of the office her work day tended to end somewhere after three. I checked my messages. There was nothing on voicemail, and the e-mails could all be dumped, but I found a message slip about someone by the name of Roger T. Youngblood.

I called the number left with the name, and he was still at work. "Mr. Youngblood," I said when he answered, "I'm Daniel Muncie. I got a message that you wanted to talk to me."

"Yes, Mr. Muncie, I do. I represent a pair of insurance companies who are interested in your theory that Edward Brogan was not killed in self-defense during domestic abuse."

I had the image of an older man, possibly a bit stuffy and self-important; definitely a man of precision. "Are they, now? So what would they like to do about it?"

"They would like to hire you to prove this."

"Prove it how? Enough to give them an excuse to block payment on the accounts? Enough to stand up in civil court after she sues for the money? Enough to put people in jail?"

"Enough to stand up in civil court, certainly, Mr. Muncie, though we are both well aware that the best way of ensuring that would be to find enough evidence to put Alexis Brogan and Cari Roland in prison on murder charges. A jury would find it difficult to give her the money if she is in prison for conspiracy to commit murder."

"Quite true, Mr. Youngblood. Shall we discuss this in more detail in person?"

"I believe that would be a good idea, Mr. Muncie. It is too late for a meeting in my office. Would you care to share a drink with me?"

"I would. Where would you like to meet?"

"I understand you are a regular at the Naked Maja. May I presume that you would have no objection to discussing business there?"

"None at all," I said. How did he know I was a regular? "Are you familiar with the Maja?" His selection surprised me. I was expecting a regular bar, most likely one of the upper class ones.

"Indeed. Some lovely ladies work there. How soon would you care to meet?"

"I can be there in about ten minutes." Well, he wasn't all that stuffy!

"It will take me a few minutes to finish some paperwork here, but I will meet you not long after that. Good bye, Mr. Muncie." Without another word he hung up.

I wondered how he would know who I was, but that was his problem now. I hung up the phone and closed up the office behind me as I left. It actually took me eleven minutes to reach the Maja, but two minutes after that I had a beer in my hand and was telling Morie what I had found out so far.

It didn't take long, and when I finished Morie was thoughtful for a moment. "So you don't know where she is?"

"Unfortunately, no, though I am getting a better idea where she is not. There's only two possibilities, Morie. Either someone kidnapped her for a specific personal reason, or it was a random event. If her door had been kicked in I'd be willing to consider a random act, but if she let him in I'm inclined to think it was done by someone she knew, or at least had reason to trust."

"Reason to trust?"

"Like someone in a police uniform."

"Oh, okay. You'll keep me informed?"

"Of course."

He just nodded and I left his office. I went out front to where Laurie was starting the first dance of her set.

She was just collecting her tips when I noticed a man coming in. He was in his late thirties, a well-dressed businessman type I'd seen in there a few times before. He glanced around before paying the cover charge, but when he got his change he came straight to my table. "Mr. Muncie," he said when he reached me, "I'm Roger Youngblood." He had his hand out.

It was him, all right. There was no mistaking that voice. I shook his hand. "Dan Muncie. Candy can take your drink order."

Candy was right behind Roger, a young woman with a body as good as any of the dancers, and a face that almost lived up to the rest of her. She was saving money for plastic surgery to build up a severely receded jaw.

"Yes," said Roger, "How are you doing today, Candy?" he asked with a pleasant smile.

"I'm doing fine, Roger," she said. "Your usual?"

"Yes, please." He smiled as he sat down, his point made. He and Candy already knew each other. "Under the conditions," he said, "I think it would be more appropriate if we were Roger and Dan. Unless you like being formal?" His faint smile said he knew the answer.

"That won't be necessary, Roger," I said, smiling back.

"It's interesting we haven't encountered each other before," Roger said. "I've been in this business for some time, Dan, and know many of the private detectives in town. It's about time we worked together."

"To our mutual profit?" I asked with a smile.

"Of course." He paused as Candy brought him his drink, whiskey and water on the rocks. He pulled a wallet out and got out two bills. He put a five on the tray and stuck a ten down her ample cleavage. From her smile and the way she just stood there I guessed this was the way he always paid.

"I do so love the ladies," he said as she walked away. "That's one of the reasons I never married. I could never be faithful to only one woman." He took a sip of his drink and nodded. The drink met with his approval. "The other is that I'm not sure I could stand living with one."

That was a strange thing to confide in me. "Edward Brogan," I said. Time to get onto a safe subject.

"Yes, Edward Brogan," said Roger. "Mr. Brogan has, or rather had, a thriving business, Brogan Plastics Incorporated. The company provides plastic parts to other companies, as components for their products. Whether or not it is able to continue depends on a variety of factors, some outside of the business world. Our main concern, though, or rather our immediate concern, is his insurance. He had two main policies through two main insurers. The first, through his business, would pay Alexis Brogan one million dollars. The second, a personal policy not related to the business, is for one point five million dollars."

I whistled. So the two policies together were for two and a half million! That was a nice piece of change no matter how you look at it. Especially on top of the value of the business itself.

"Precisely," said Roger. "Excuse me." He stood and walked to the stage, where Sherrie was dancing. She put on a good show for him, and he put a buck under each side of her g-string.

When he came back he continued, "Now, neither company is particularly eager to give all that money to a murderess. On the other hand, if the shooting was exactly what it was reported to be, they will willingly pay what is owed under the terms of the policies. So give me one fact that I can take to the companies to tell them you have something more than suspicions."

"I presume you've seen photos of Cari Roland."

I got a smile.

"Of course," Roger said. "A beautiful woman like that, involved in shooting her businessman paramour? The media love showing someone like that. How could I avoid seeing her?"

"I was able to trace her back several years before hitting a gap," I said. "A large gap."

"That's hardly unusual," he said after taking a sip of his drink. He was listening to me, but he was watching the stage.

"True, except before that I wasn't able to find any trace of her until I got back to her birth certificate."

Roger mulled over that without taking his eyes off the stage. Sherrie was doing her usual flamboyant and damn near illegal finish. "Somewhat more unusual, but hardly proof of wrongdoing."

"I found what is supposedly her birth certificate. At least it has her name on it, for the date she says she was born, and the town is the same. The problem is that the real birth certificate gave her race as black."

He had been raising his glass for a sip. Now he lowered it untasted, his eyes on me instead of the stage. "Black?"

"Yes. There is also a death certificate nine months later, from crib death."

"Indeed." Now he took a sip, a small one. "What color are her eyes again?"

"Green," I said. "Without contacts."

"I hardly think a green-eyed blond could be mistaken for a black, do you?"

"It would be rather difficult," I agreed, even though I understand that most babies have gray eyes and dark hair.

"It sounds to me like at the least her identity is, shall we say, questionable?"

"I would agree with that." There was also the way that most of her 'history' had that squeaky clean feeling of a created background, but I wasn't ready to bring that up yet. "The one complication is that when they ran her prints through AFIS she came back clean. No record."

"Very interesting. Have you got anything else?"

"Alexis Brogan has a lover. I went by her house last night, and there was a wake of sorts going on. Friends, and family, the usual. By the end of the night everyone had left except for one guest, a male. He spent the night."

"I see." He took another sip, then excused himself while he tipped Morgana. When he came back he said, "I have no doubt that you will be hired. What are your normal rates?"

"Corporate? Eighty an hour plus expenses." That was double my standard rate.

"Really? I may bring you more work."

That was interesting confirmation I could charge more. "I'd appreciate that," I said.

"In addition, I'm sure that if you succeed the companies will be willing to reward you with a percentage of the policies. Easily one percent, say for a case which will stand up in civil court, more if you are able to find the evidence needed to put both women in prison. Possibly up to five percent."

I could certainly live with that! Even one percent would be $25,000, and five times that would leave me set for the year!

I saw something in his eyes. "Payable upon conviction?"

He shrugged. "Most of it, at least. Though your regular bill will be paid immediately."

"I'll be collecting, then. I have no doubt that this was a murder for hire, and I'll get the proof needed to put them in prison. Maybe even Death Row."

"You are that confident?"

I smiled at him. "Yes. More to the point, they are that overconfident. Would you consider it a good idea to have your lover stay with you on the night immediately after your spouse has been murdered?"

"It was not the wisest thing to do," he agreed. "Do you know who the lover is?"

I shook my head. "Not yet, but I will soon. I also intend to find out how deeply he's involved in this."

"That is an amusing question, isn't it? Was he merely part of the incentive for Mrs. Brogan to have her husband killed, or was he an active participant in the crime?"

"Amusing" wasn't the word I would use, but I understood his point. "We'll find out," I promised.

"I have no doubt of that," Roger said. He finished his drink. "Now, if you will excuse me, I have another call to make." He stood and left, but not until he had stopped by the stage and tipped Shandra.

I wasn't too far behind him, on the way to supper. I was in the mood for a steak, and that was not one of the things Morie's kitchen had available. After supper I went home, but my day wasn't over either. I still had three license numbers to run.

The first was for a BMW. I thought the car had looked familiar and I was right. It was the car I had followed the night I tailed Ed Brogan. Someone had been efficient in getting her dead husband's car back to her.

The one closest to the house, a Lexus, was also registered to the Brogans. It was two years old, and paid for.

I ran the plates for the third car, a Mercedes, and cursed. The damn thing was registered to a leasing company! I was going to have to identify him some other way.

I was just annoyed enough that I drove back out to the Brogan house. This time I made sure I had a camera with a good telephoto lens with me. I also parked where I had a clear view of the front door. That was made easier this time because there were only five cars at the Brogan house.

It was almost an hour before the first people left, an older couple. Alexis Brogan saw them to the door by herself. There was an exchange of hugs, and they left in a Cadillac. Alexis was in another chic black dress.

Twenty minutes later the door opened again. It was another couple, a man and woman of about forty. This man was wearing a minister's collar, with what looked like a purple shirt. His wife was nicely, if somewhat modestly, dressed, but a minister's wife or not, she was quite attractive.

Alexis came out further with this couple, and there was a man with her. While the light was far from the best, the digital camera I was using had enough to do the job. Watching them I could almost see the pantomime playing out. There were the final condolences, and the assurances that "I'll be fine." At one point the minister said something to the man, and he turned around with a sweeping gesture at the house. I had the feeling he said he was going to stick around to "help clean up."

Before long the minister and his wife were gone. Alexis and the man stood on the sidewalk until they were gone, and had turned the corner, then they went back into the house, holding hands.

While it could have simply been intended as reassurance, within five minutes the lights on the first floor were being turned off. Several windows on the second floor lit up, and I concentrated on them. Before long there were figures against the curtains, shapes going back and forth. Usually it was only one, but once there were two, and they came together. Even as shapes against the curtains it was clear that they were kissing. I got three shots, and could have gotten plenty more.

Maybe five minutes later the lights in the room went off, leaving the house in the dark. I considered that my cue to leave. When I got home I checked the plates on the two new cars. As expected, the Buick belonged to a Presbyterian minister, the Reverend Daniel Moyers, and his wife, Helen.

The Caddy was more interesting. It was registered to Richard and Patricia Brogan. Had the widow Brogan actually had the audacity, the chutzpah, to entertain the parents of the husband she had just had murdered?

I didn't let it worry me too much as I went to bed. Tomorrow would be a long day, and I needed some sleep.

CHAPTER 10

When I woke up the next morning I finally did something I should have done earlier. I checked back through the newspaper until I found when and where the Brogan funeral would be. As I half expected, it would be today, at three.

I also got online, and after a few minutes I was able to find the website for Brogan's business. A few more minutes were needed to get to a section for the company's officers. I was sourly amused to see they were already eulogizing Ed Brogan while making no mention of the circumstances of his death. He looked dignified in his photo, with its broad black border. Harder to take was the way Alexis was discussed, as his "devoted wife, shattered by the loss of her beloved husband."

I decided to have a look at the company officers. There was a man involved, and it occurred to me that it could well be someone from the company. I started with Executive Vice-President James Casey, and there he was. As soon as I saw his photo I recognized him as the man Alexis Brogan had spent two nights with after the murder of her husband.

Well, only last night for sure, though I found it seriously doubtful that she had spent Wednesday night with some other man.

I looked over Casey's bio, and one thing I noticed missing was any mention of a wife. Brogan's had mentioned Alexis, but it seemed that Casey had no spouse. On the other hand, it did mention how much Brogan had "trusted" Casey, and how he and Brogan had been " close friends."

No spouse right now, anyway. There was mention of how Casey had taken over operation of the company since the death of its founder, even though Alexis Brogan was the majority stockholder. It looked to me like a "merger" was in the works, as soon as they deemed an acceptable amount of time had passed.

With stories about how they had fallen in love while working together to lead the company, no doubt.

I left the site and logged off before I completely lost my appetite. I still had things to do before the funeral, primarily to find out what had happened to Erika.

I called Maggie, and let her know I wouldn't be in until later. Then I got in the car and headed for Marcy. It only took me an hour to get there, and another ten minutes to find the high school. There I identified myself, and asked if I could see the yearbooks for Susan's freshman and sophomore years. It didn't take long to find what I wanted.

George Rawlin had been a senior during her freshman year, a good looking kid on the football team. It was a small school, and the only other 'George' in either the junior or senior classes was a 'special ed' student, praised for being a nice person, since he didn't have any activities they could talk about.

When I took the books back I asked the secretary, "By any chance has the vice-principal for discipline been around here for long?"

"Oh, yes, for fifteen years now."

"May I speak with him, please? I believe he can help me with a case I'm working on involving one of your former students."

"I'll see if he's available."

He was, and was curious about how he could help. "Richard Nickelby," he said, introducing himself. "What can I do for you?" Nickelby was about six foot tall, heavyset and with a crew cut.

"Daniel Muncie, Mr. Nickelby. One of your former students is missing, possibly kidnapped. I'm looking for some information that might lead to finding her."

"I see. Just who might that be?"

"Susan Trumble. She graduated two years ago."

He shook his head. "She would have graduated two years ago if she had graduated. She left after the first semester of her junior year." He shook his head again. "She had a tough life. Her father was an alcoholic and died when she was still young. Then her mother went through a succession of live-in boyfriends. We didn't know what had happened to her." In a small school like that in a small town he would know such things.

"She ended up as a dancer," I said.

He raised an eyebrow. "Could I take my family to see her?"

"Only your sons, and then only if they are over 21."

"That's what I thought you were talking about. I'm sorry to hear that. She was a nice girl."

"She still is, even if she dances almost naked for a living."

"She's happy?"

I shrugged. "Happy enough, I suppose. She was liked by the other dancers, for what that's worth."

"I suppose that's something," he sighed. "Just what is it you needed to know?"

"There's a possibility that she might have been kidnapped by someone from her past. Given her age, that can't be much in her past. One of the names she mentioned to one of her boyfriends was a 'George the jerk,' and I found a George Rawlin in one of your yearbooks who seems to fit the bill."

Nickelby grimaced. "That sounds about right. George was an asshole who used his being on the football team to further his sex life. He especially liked going after the impressionable freshmen and sophomores, maybe because the older girls knew better."

"How good a player was he?"

"Not good, actually. On his good days he was a passable second string defensive lineman. Most of the time, though, he did just well enough to keep from being kicked off the team."

"You seem pretty sure of that." I could guess why.

I was right. "I am sure. In addition to being vice-principal, I'm also the head of the athletic department and head football coach. I know all the kids here, one way or another."

"So do you have any idea where George Rawlin is?"

"I do. His ways didn't change after he graduated, and he finally caught one girl at the wrong time of the month. He married her rather than have her three rather large brothers rearrange his face. Actually, he's settled down quite a bit, and has turned surprisingly responsible. Parenthood can do that sometimes. If you want to talk to him he's working at a hardware store downtown. I'll give you the address."

My reaction must have shown, for he continued, "Sorry if that bursts your bubble."

"Just goes to show you shouldn't pin too many hopes on a long shot," I said.

Nickelby grinned. "That's why I don't bet. And why I wouldn't even if I wasn't a coach."

"Are there any others who might have given her a hard time, though? Any romances gone bad, where there might be a grudge? Anybody who might turn into a stalker, or a kidnapper?"

"Hard to say," replied Nickelby. "You can never be sure with these kids. Most turn out more or less the way you expect, but some surprise you. We had one kid here, a quiet boy, but he came back from the Gulf War with a Bronze Star he got while serving with the Rangers. Another kid a few years later was much like him, enough that they could have been twins, but he's over at Waterford, where they sent him after he casually cut some stranger's throat and then sat there watching him bleed to death."

I couldn't match his experience, but I knew what he meant.

He stood up and looked at a couple of photos on the wall, his back to me. They were class photos, showing all the members of various classes. He said nothing for a few moments.

"I can't say for sure, you understand," he finally began, "but there are a couple you might want to check out." He sat back down and wrote out a short list, only three names. "I could have added two more," he said, "but one is dead and the other is in prison."

"Prison? What for?"

"Rape. Rape and attempted murder, actually, but he wasn't good at either of them."

"What's his name?"

"Harvey Malik. He had a visible crush on Susan for the whole time she was here, but she wouldn't have anything to do with him."

"What about the one at Waterford?" I asked. Waterford was the hospital where the state took care of the real crazies, the ones who qualified as being criminally insane.

Nickelby shook his head. "You can forget him. He graduated the year before Susan started here, and he's mentally long gone. The only way he'll leave that hospital is in a box."

"Thanks for the list, Mr. Nickelby. I'll let you know what happens with Susan." I stood up to leave.

"Please do."

I left the school, and as I was passing through town I saw a hardware store. On impulse I went in, and looked around. There were three people working there, an older couple and a younger man, in his early twenties. He seemed bright and cheerful as he helped a customer. The battery on my cordless drill was going bad, so I bought a new drill, and the young man was at the cash register. His name was George, and his face was an older version of the one I had seen in the yearbook. I decided I could stop worrying about him.

I drove home, and made it in time for a slightly late lunch. Then I started trying to trace the people Nickelby had mentioned. One was living out of state; another seemed to be in college, but the third I couldn't find. I was about to check on Malik when I noticed the time. If I was going to go to the Brogan funeral I needed to leave.

I made the service with a few minutes to spare, so I waited outside until everyone went into the chapel. I sat in the back, watching as Mrs. Brogan came in on the arm of James Casey. At least she didn't try to look like the sobbing heartbroken widow, but the stoic grieving widow instead.

From the varying expressions of the other people around me, some of them weren't any more convinced of her grief than I was. Just as interesting, James Casey didn't seem too popular, either, when he delivered the eulogy.

This was confirmed at the end of the service when most of the people went up to the urn that held his ashes, and to speak to his parents, but no more than about half went up to the widow to express their condolences. The same held true at the cemetery. Plenty of people showed respect for Edward Brogan, and sympathy for Robert and Patricia Brogan, but only about half of them showed any compassion for the widow.

I followed two women out of the cemetery, listening to them complain about how Alexis hadn't pulled the wool over their eyes! I took a chance. Stepping closer, I said, "Excuse me, but I'd think you'd feel more sympathy for her than this. After all, he was killed by his mistress! That has to be hard on her." I tried to look mystified and confused.

"Hmmpf," one said, a woman in her late fifties or so. "That's because you don't know what was going on." She kept her voice low, conspiratorial. "He wouldn't have had a mistress if it wasn't for her, messing around with Mr. Casey like she was." Clearly, by "her" she meant Mrs. Brogan.

Disbelief. "No, you can't be serious! What makes you think that was going on?"

It's amazing how challenging people can open them up, while agreeing and asking for more can just lead them to wonder if they've said too much. "I've seen them together. At work, no less. She used to hardly ever come in, then suddenly she starts coming in several times a week. And she would always make sure she saw Mr. Casey when she did."

"That's not all," said the other woman, a slimmer version of the first. "She'd come by, and ten minutes after she left he'd leave for lunch. You could almost set your watch by it. On those days he'd have a longer than normal lunch hour." She looked at her friend. "That's so he'd actually have some time to eat."

I tried to keep the look of disbelief. "Surely you aren't saying that they were-, that they had-, you don't mean-."

"When I was younger we called it a nooner," said the first. "Yes, that is exactly what I mean. They were having an affair."

"But wouldn't Mr. Brogan have suspected?" I asked, aghast.

"Of course he knew," said the second, not wanting to let her friend have all the fun. "That's why he had a lover of his own. If Alexis Brogan had stayed faithful to him," she managed to make the "Alexis" sound like an insult, "he would never have taken up with that Roland woman. Everybody knew that."

It sounded like a delightfully gossipy office. "But what is this to you?" asked the first suspiciously. "Why would you care what happened?"

I glanced around, and made a quick decision. "Thank you, ladies," I said, smiling. "You have just helped convince me that Alexis Brogan was involved in the murder of her husband."

The gasping was quite satisfactory, as was the shocked look from both of them. "Murder!" said the first. "Murder?" asked the second. They looked at each other, stunned.

"Yes, murder. I have reason to believe that Miss Roland was not defending herself, but that she murdered him, with Alexis Brogan's approval."

"Oh, my!" said the first.

"Well, I never did consider Mr. Brogan the kind of man to hit a woman," said the second primly. "He was much too much of a gentleman." It didn't occur to her that her willingness to accept Roland's story was in conflict with this statement.

I leaned forward, "joining" their conspiracy. I pulled out a couple of my cards, and handed them each one. "You've got to keep this quiet," I said, "but I'm investigating the case, trying to prove that he was murdered, and that his wife was in on it. Maybe Mr. Casey, too." Another set of gasps. "Now I don't want this to get around, you understand. You can only tell your closest friends, and make sure they understand that this isn't to be spread around. Okay?"

"Okay," they agreed eagerly. As soon as I saw the gleam in their eyes I knew that I had succeeded. If I had asked them to spread the news, they might well have become suspicious, and kept quiet. If I had tried to get them to keep it to themselves, they might have done so, or at least held off for a few days.

But the combination of allowing them to tell a few 'friends' and saying it was to be kept quiet ensured that the news would spread rapidly. By the end of the day tomorrow, no, tomorrow was Saturday, make that Monday, everyone in the company, with the possible exception of Alexis Brogan and James Casey, would know what I was doing.

Since they would have "friends" among the employees, not to mention toadies, I fully expected that they would know before long as well. That was fine with me. I wanted them under pressure. It would increase the chance of their making a mistake.

A fatal mistake, since conspiracy to commit murder, murder for hire, and murder for profit were all on the list of the "special circumstances" that warranted the death penalty.

But there was one more hook, an important one. "There is one thing you can do for me," I said, ostentatiously looking around. "If you hear anything or find out anything which might help prove it was a murder, could you let me know? I'm sure you wouldn't want them to get away with murder, would you?"

They didn't. I thanked them for their help, and let them leave. They immediately headed directly for a car where some other women were talking. In less than a minute the other women were looking in my direction. I revised my estimate. Most of the employees would know before the end of the day.

But there was something else that had drawn my attention while I was talking to them. Before this I had simply had the feeling that James Casey had been involved, but suddenly I realized that his involvement answered a key question.

Who had popped Cari Roland in the eye?

It is difficult to give yourself a black eye. Some people can do it, but most people just can't bring themselves to hit themselves in the face hard enough to get a "proper" shiner. Yet one was needed to support the claim that Brogan had hit her.

But suppose someone else hit her? A male would be preferred, someone who could hit her hard enough to ensure enough bruising. Alexis might be strong enough, but it would also be useful if she was busy elsewhere when the murder happened, especially if that 'elsewhere' had witnesses to what she was doing when her husband was being shot.

James Casey as an active conspirator solved the problem. Alexis could be someplace with witnesses, while James Casey could give Cari the black eye.

Still, I was left with two rather sticky problems. First, how had Cari and Edward met? What had brought them together under conditions where Alexis could be certain that Edward would start an affair with Cari?

Second, how could Alexis and James be sure that Cari would actually commit the murder, rather than telling Edward that his wife wanted him dead? How could they know she wouldn't either fall for him for real, or tell him and make a better deal with him?

Then there was a third question. How had James and Alexis come to know Cari Roland, or whatever her real name was? By now I had no doubt that Cari Roland was not her real name.

I came out of my reverie and noticed that two thirds of the conspiracy was coming toward me. I stepped into their way, and gave them the meaningless "sorry about your loss" pleasantries they would expect from someone who might have known Edward, but who they did not know. In the process I shook hands with James Casey.

The knuckles of his right hand were bruised, and slightly skinned. Tender, too. He winced when I squeezed his hand.

As I left them I felt vindicated. Casey was physically an office drone. His hands were office soft, without the calluses a man would get who does a lot of physical work. No hunting, no boxing, no carpentry or metal working. He may have been a good businessman, well qualified to be the executive vice-president, and interim president, but physically he was just an office drone. Punching a woman in the eye left its marks.

But satisfied or not, it was time for me to head back to the office. Finding Erika was still my first priority.

CHAPTER 11

At the office I picked up where I left off. Harvey Malik may have been in prison, but I wanted to know where. While rare, it wasn't unknown for a man in prison to "arrange" for something to happen to a girl he coveted.

It took a little while, but in due time I found that Malik had been sent to the Roseville Minimum Security Unit. That bothered me. It was his first felony conviction, but he had been in trouble for some time, and he had been convicted on charges of battery and sexual assault.

Then I realized what had happened. All his other crimes must have been misdemeanors, and not felonies. Even more important, this was his first conviction as an adult. When it came to his sentencing, a record of juvenile misdemeanors wouldn't matter all that much.

Still, Roseville? I could see medium security for someone with no previous felony record, but a minimum security unit for a person with a violent crime?

Next I did a search on a news service. As soon as the stories came up I took one look and said "Oh, shit!" Harvey Malik had escaped from prison a week before, on Friday afternoon.

I started pulling up the stories, and found out that he had managed to get away while on a crew working outside the prison. People assigned to such units are considered to be low flight risks, but Malik was an exception. He had behaved himself at first, earning the ability to work outside on a road cleaning crew. It was during one of those assignments that he slipped away. The guards had lost sight of him for a moment as he worked in some shrubbery at the side of the road, and they had not seen him since.

More disturbing was a later story about a missing motorist, a possible victim of escaped convict Harvey Malik. Wilamina Farrell had been reported missing after she had disappeared while driving home on a business trip. The route she was known to be using passed within four miles of where Malik had been working. So far there had been no sign of either her or her car.

One good thing was that Malik had committed his rape in Mansfield. Well, it wasn't good, but at least this way I could easily contact the prosecutor. Before much longer I found a story on the trial, and it mentioned that the prosecutor was Sherry Lake. I knew Sherry, a divorced single mother in her middle thirties who thrived on putting rapists in prison.

I called the district attorney's office, but she was gone for the day. I hadn't realized that it was getting that late, but it was already a few minutes after five, and on a Friday at that. Still, I got a clerk who promised to call her and give her my message.

To my surprise, the clerk kept her word. Barely ten minutes later my phone rang. "Dan Muncie," I said.

"Dan, Sherry Lake. I understand you want to talk to me about Harvey Malik. What is it you need to know?" I've been on her good side ever since I helped her convict a rapist.

"For a start, what was he in for?"

"He was originally charged with rape and attempted murder. The rape we could prove, but even though he had said he was going to kill her we couldn't prove attempted murder. I was happy to let him plead to assault and battery, plus the rape."

"Public defender?" I couldn't see an experienced defense attorney doing that.

"Yup, and a new one. He didn't realize just how weak our case was." Which clearly did not upset her in the least.

"But Roseville?"

"That part I wasn't too happy about, but Judge Haskell is a sucker for sad eyes. And since this was Malik's first felony he got Roseville."

"What's your evaluation of Malik?"

"He's a control freak who's going to kill someone one of these days. If he hasn't already."

"I presume you're talking about the missing businesswoman, Wilamina Farrell."

"Sure am. Fifty-three passes within about four miles of where he escaped, but I doubt she would pick him up at the side of the road. There is, however, a truck stop another two miles away, and we know Farrell stopped there to use the rest room and get some coffee. That was the last time anyone saw her."

"Really, now. So he could have taken her in the parking lot when she got back in her car." That part, that she had been seen at the truck stop, had been kept out of the news.

"That's what we're thinking. What's your interest in him?"

"Maybe another kidnapping victim. He went to school with one Susan Trumble, and she's been missing since late Sunday night."

"I see. And you think he kidnapped her?"

"He's the best bet so far."

"Well, good luck. We haven't seen any sign of him, and we've been looking."

"Thanks, Sherry."

"You'll keep us informed, won't you?"

"Of course."

"Oh, by the way, did you hear what happened to Jake Karplan?"

Karplan was the rapist I had helped put in jail. "No, I didn't. What happened?" Something unpleasant, I hoped.

"You remember his preferences, don't you?"

"Of course. How could I forget?" Any rapist was bad news, but Karplan liked doing it anally, especially unpleasant since he had a preference for girls in their mid-teens.

"He's dead. Someone returned the favor with a wood rasp."

"Ouch!" That was even more unpleasant than I wanted!

"Ouch, indeed," she said dryly. "He bled to death. There's no suspect that I know of, but one of his victims has a brother in that unit, serving time for battery and attempted murder."

"Sounds like he may have succeeded this time."

"They'll never solve it," she added. "Karplan had made lots of enemies there, so nobody will ever rat out the killer. Take care and I'll see you later."

"You take care, too. Bye." I hung up and considered the implications of what she had said about Malik. Harvey could well be a murderer by now, even leaving Erika out of the picture. But if he did have Erika, and she was still alive, did she know about Wilamina Farrell?

If Malik had taken Ms. Farrell captive, that changed a lot of things. At the least he was now a kidnapper, and given his record most likely added a few counts of rape on top of that. Then there was the possibility that Farrell was already dead, which added murder. Plus whatever crimes he had committed with Erika besides the kidnapping itself.

I looked out the window and took the Lord's name in vain a few times, as well as throwing in some other language that mothers wouldn't want their children to hear. It may have still been sunny out, but it was well after five on a Friday, not the best of times to go investigating things.

I needed to know some more about Malik. I pulled out my address book and called Alvin Hobbs. He had been a police sergeant, and when he retired he had moved back to Roseville and gotten a job with the prison.

"Hobbs." I was lucky. I had gotten Hobbs himself.

"Hey, Al, Dan Muncie."

"Hi, Dan, how you doing?"

"Not bad, but I need some information."

He laughed. "So this isn't a social call after all? How unsurprising." The laughter faded. "So who do you need to know about?"

"Harvey Malik. What can you tell me about him?"

"He's bad news, Dan," Al said, all humor gone. "He scares me. He looks at you and there's nobody home. His eyes are cold. He's dangerous, Dan. Deadly dangerous."

"So you think he's going to kill someone?"

"No, I think he has killed someone. That woman they think he kidnapped? I'd bet she's dead. I think he raped and killed her."

"If he's so dangerous why was he allowed on that road crew?"

"Because there was no good reason to keep him off of it; especially as far as the front office was concerned. He hadn't caused any trouble with the guards or with the other inmates. We couldn't get across that the reason things were quiet with the inmates was that they were scared of him."

"They were scared of him?" I found that hard to believe.

"Dan, this is a minimum security unit. We don't have the hardcases like they get at Bensonville. He'd be dead there. The people who come here are more like embezzlers and drunk drivers, with a few for things like involuntary manslaughter or negligent homicide. They see him and they see someone different, someone dangerous, so they leave him the hell alone."

"So the front office didn't see any trouble from him, and decided he could be trusted on a work crew?"

"That's about the size of it. His name came up, there was nothing in particular to keep him off the list, so he went out."

"And made his escape. I presume that the guards are being disciplined."

"Yeah, but not that severely. They were short a man, and besides, he did it smart. It was towards the end of the day, everyone was tired, and he had been working right along with the others until then. There was no indication he was even thinking about escaping until they looked around and he was gone."

"I see."

"Yeah, he's smart, but he's a wacko, too. He is fucking crazy, and it was only a matter of time before he killed someone. If he'd stayed here, eventually one of the other prisoners would have done something to annoy him enough, and he'd've kill the guy."

"Why'd you say it was only a matter of time? Because you think he killed the woman he kidnapped?"

"Exactly, Dan. I will be surprised if she isn't dead. Especially after this long."

"Okay, and thanks a lot, Al."

"One thing. What's your interest in the case?"

"I think he committed another kidnapping. An old flame from high school."

I could almost picture him shaking his head. "Well, I wish her luck. She's damn well going to need it!"

"Yeah, she is."

"One more thing, Dan," he added. "Don't be in any hurry to send him back here."

"I don't think you'll have to worry about that," I said. The escape alone would be enough to send him to at least a medium security unit. Throw in the others and it was hard time for him, even if not Death Row.

"That's true enough. Well, take care, Dan. I wouldn't want to see you get hurt."

"I'll be careful," I promised.

We said our good-byes and I hung up. As a matter of curiosity I got onto the county tax collector's web site and I looked to see if Wilamina Farrell had any property. I wasn't sure what she might have, if anything, but they came up with three addresses. One was her home, mentioned in the news stories. The other two looked to be residences, presumably rental properties. I used a reverse phone directory, and found that one was occupied. There was no number for the other one.

That didn't necessarily mean anything. It could have been an unlisted number or no phone at all. I called a friend at the phone company anyway, and she confirmed that there was no active phone there, unlisted or otherwise, and hadn't been for six months.

After thanking her I considered the situation. While it wasn't confirmed, suppose that Malik had indeed kidnapped Wilamina Farrell. And suppose, for purposes of discussion, that she had the keys to her rental property, the one that seemed to be empty. That could be a good place to hide. The more I thought about it, the better I liked the idea.

Depending on where it is, I realized. If it was in the middle of a busy neighborhood then it wouldn't be anywhere near as useful. I didn't recognize the street name, so I checked my map. It looked promising, but there was only one way to tell for sure. I had to go there and have a look for myself.

It was a small house on a narrow road on the south side of town called Trace Lane. The name fit. The road was a nominal two lanes, but if two full sized cars met they'd both have their right wheels off the road. Especially since it hadn't been repaved in quite a few years, and the shoulders were badly crumbled.

It wasn't likely to be repaved any time soon, either. There were only three houses on the half mile road, and one of them was empty and falling apart. I drove past the house I was interested in, the last one on the street, and parked where a clump of trees blocked the view from the house.

I grabbed my binoculars, got out, and looked at the house. It wasn't big, but unlike the other two it was brick. Worse yet it was in the middle of a large lot, with no cover. There was no way to sneak up on the house without being seen well before.

Next to the house on my side was a garage. The door was open and I could see a car, one matching the description of the car Wilamina Farrell had been driving. The license number was wrong, though, but only by two characters. Then I realized he had used some paint or tape to turn an "F" into an "E," and a zero into an eight. It was her car for sure.

Still, I would bet that if the police had checked the house the garage door had been closed, and the car hidden. It was likely open now because after a week of hiding there he had gotten cocky and careless.

One thing I looked for was outside lights. My fear was that there would be lights with motion sensors around the house. That would make it difficult to sneak up at night. I didn't see any in the front, but they could have been hidden. There could also be sensors that would sound an alarm in the house, but I didn't think so. This wasn't that kind of neighborhood.

I slowly worked my way around to the back of the house, still looking for a good way in. If there was one it escaped me, but at least I didn't see any sign of sensors back there, either.

When I got back to my car I had a stroke of luck. The house had a mailbox beside the road, and a mail truck came by, making a late delivery, though lord knows why at an 'unoccupied' house. Junk mail most likely, I told myself, and on the last part of his run before heading back to the post office.

I waited, and ten minutes later a man came out of the house, walking the hundred feet or so from the house to the box. I had to be careful to not let him see me, but I was able to get a good enough look to confirm that it was Harvey Malik.

I have a good deal of self-confidence, but I do know my limitations. Trying to bust in by myself would have been too dangerous, not to mention of questionable legality. I got back in my car and drove back up the road. This time I turned the corner onto Banford and stopped. I wasn't visible from the house, but I could keep an eye on who went in and out.

As soon as I was parked I called Grant Parker. This was a job for specialists, and Grant was the sergeant in charge of the police SWAT team. They were a good group, proud of the fact that in the last six years they had made it through every incident but one without firing a shot, and in that case they had no choice but to kill an escaped convict busily shooting at anything that moved.

"Dan Muncie, Grant," I said when he answered. "I've got a job for you."

"You do?" he asked, sounding amused. "What kind of job?"

"Capturing an escaped prisoner and rescuing at least one kidnap victim, maybe two."

"You have? Who?" There wasn't a trace of humor now.

"Harvey Malik, from Roseville. He escaped last Friday. There's an excellent chance he kidnapped Wilamina Farrell, and a good chance he took a dancer who went missing last weekend."

"Where is he?"

"South side. One oh seven Trace Lane."

"Hang on. I've never heard of that street."

Goes to show how small it was. "It's off of Banford," I said. Beyond that he could find it for himself.

"Okay, got it," he said after a few seconds. "Where are you?"

"On Banford, at the corner of Trace."

"We'll be there in a little while."

"Get here quietly, Grant. You've got plenty of time." Either he had plenty of time or it was already too late. Either way there was no rush.

"That's good," he said. "I hate rush jobs."

I sat and waited, and smiled when a few minutes later the police helicopter flew overhead slowly, making a single loop before flying off. Five minutes later Grant showed up in a police truck, a former ambulance, parking nose to nose with me. Seconds later a patrol car parked behind me, on the other side of Trace Lane. It only took me a few seconds to figure out he was there in case Malik made a break for it.

Grant got out and headed for the back of the truck, waving to me to come along. I got out and followed him. There were two other officers with him, Tyrone Powell and a younger officer I'd seen around but didn't know. All three were in SWAT black.

Grant didn't bother introducing me. Instead we went inside where he pointed to a TV monitor. "Okay, which house is it?" It was showing a video shot from the helicopter just moments before.

"That one," I said, pointing. "It's not going to be easy. As you can see, he's got clear fields of vision all around the house." And clear fields of fire, but I didn't need to mention that. They could see it as well as I could.

Grant was concentrating on the image, running it backwards and forwards as he looked at it. "You've had a look?"

"Yes, I was behind those trees over here." I pointed to the trees when they momentarily appeared. "I'm pretty sure he didn't see me."

"Positive ID?"

"As positive as I can be through a good set of binoculars. The car is there for sure."

"We've got a go, then."

"I looked, but I couldn't make out any motion sensors."

"That's good," commented Grant. He wasn't paying attention to me. He was thinking about how best to get in. I wasn't offended. I was thinking about the same thing.

After a few minutes of quiet he looked at me. "What's your take on this guy?" he asked. "I know he's an escaped prisoner, and that he's kidnapped a woman doing it, but that's about all I know about him."

"He's a loose cannon, Grant. If he was an ordinary criminal I'd likely have chanced knocking on his door and overpowering him. He may have been in a minimum security prison, but I talked to Al Hobbs, who's a guard there now, and Al said he's a total wacko. He hadn't killed anyone yet. but I think he's crossed that line. I have this nasty feeling he is pure nutcase now."

"Dangerous?"

"Very."

He pursed his lips and looked in the direction of the house. "Do you think she's still alive?"

"She which? If I'm right he's got two women in there with him. Gut feeling, yes on Susan Trumble, no for Wilamina Farrell, but it's only a feeling. I think Farrell was pure victim, so he killed her when he couldn't think of a good reason to keep her alive. The only reasoning I can put to Susan is that he brought her here to be with him, but if she were dead he'd cut out. Then again, she could be dead, and he's so whacked out he thinks she's still alive. Lord knows stranger things have happened."

Grant nodded, but I wasn't sure to what. "Okay," he said decisively, "we'll go based on the one still being alive. Tyrone, let's go over some options."

I stepped away from them as Grant and Tyrone started going over entry methods. He had accepted some limits by deciding to assume that Erika was still alive. If she were not involved, say if we knew she were dead, then they would likely just surround the house and wait him out. But they couldn't afford to let him use Erika as a hostage.

That meant that they would have to find a way to get in fast, and get Malik down and under control before he could do anything harmful to anyone. This was where the location of the house was a problem. In a regular neighborhood they could get within a few dozen feet of the house by using trees or other houses as cover. Or just pull up in front and run the thirty or forty feet to the front door. But there was no cover within at least a hundred feet of the house in any direction. Even the dark, now that the sun was setting, would only help so far; especially if he turned on lights.

I may have stepped away, but I could overhear enough of what Grant and Tyrone were saying that I knew they had decided that there was no way to safely get in without some kind of distraction to pull him to one side of the house while officers approached from the other side. They were discussing some possibilities, but I had one of my own.

"Grant," I said as I walked back to them, "I've got an idea for a distraction."

He looked at me curiously. "You do?"

"Sure. One thing guaranteed to get a person's attention is having a siren stop directly in front of their house, right?"

"Right," he agreed warily.

"Especially if they're an escaped criminal."

"Right," he said, a little less warily.

"So how about this. Get your people in place at the back of the house. When everyone's in position we send that officer over there," I pointed to the one on the other side of the intersection who had arrived just after him, "down about a mile or so. He comes back, at a safe speed but with his lights and siren on. Just before he gets back here I go down Trace Lane, and he follows me, lights and siren going full blast. I go down and stop in front of Malik's house, and get out of my car."

Grant and Tyrone were starting to smile. "You're giving the officer who stopped you a hard time," contributed Tyrone.

"Exactly. I get out and start yelling. The officer gets out of his car and tries to calm me down. Put another of your people in the back seat where he can't be seen, but where he can watch the front of the house. When Malik looks out the front window, he gives the word and everyone runs to the back of the house. When everyone is in position at the house you give the word, and the assault begins. Then the officer and whoever's in the back seat can join the fun."

Grant mulled it over, as did Tyrone. "What do you think, Ty?" he asked after a moment.

"Sounds good to me," said Tyrone. "But put one of us in a regular uniform to do it. I've got mine handy."

Grant nodded. "Okay, get the rest of the troops here."

The other members of the team had been alerted, and Tyrone told them to join us. They hadn't wanted to do that right away, to avoid drawing public attention. Well, not any more than the curious looks we were already getting from passing drivers.

As we waited for the others to arrive Ty came up with a modification. While he and I were arguing, he would make a "radio call," and a second car would join us.

"Do you think that might spook him?" asked Grant.

"Not too much more than the first one," I said. "After all, if I'm giving the first officer that much of a hard time, he'd have to expect the officer to ask for backup. A sergeant maybe. But a third car would be too much. Two's the limit."

Grant agreed, and when Jerry Tyburn arrived, that was the plan presented to him. Tyburn was the lieutenant in charge of various special operations, including the SWAT team, the bomb squad, and a couple of other operations. He didn't especially like me, and I thought he was a bit of a putz, but he was too professional to let that get in the way of doing what needed to be done.

When we finished explaining what was going on, he looked at me skeptically. It was a long ten count before he finally said, "I'm not wild about the idea, but since nobody else has a better one I'll go along. Just one thing, Dan."

"What's that?"

"You'd better not be the first one through the door."

"Cops through first, Lieutenant," I promised. Inside I was delighted. He might have told me I couldn't go in at all.

After that it was just the doing. Tyrone changed uniforms and took over one of their regular cars. The second car was to be manned by Henry Walthers, an officer with over twenty years experience. He had been one of the first SWAT officers, and left it only to get more regular hours to keep his marriage together. He had also been promoted to sergeant, and his sergeant's stripes would fit into the scenario quite well.

While we were making some preparations the other team members moved into position behind the house. It took a while for them to get where they wanted to be. By then Tyrone was sitting a mile away, waiting for the signal. Finally the radio announced that everyone was in position.

Walthers acknowledged the transmission, and I got into my car. I kept the window down for a moment, until I heard the sound of a siren. Then I started my engine.

It wasn't too many seconds after that when I saw the flashing lights coming down the road. When he was about a hundred yards away I put the car in gear and started down Trace. I didn't need to get too much speed, and besides, the road was in bad shape. I saw no need for real high speed for this role.

In seconds I had Tyrone right behind me, lights and siren going. He turned on just about every light he had, and started with the special noises. Not just the regular warning siren, but the high-pitched warbles and the other attention getters. A person would have to be deaf to miss them.

I drove as fast as I dared, then braked when I approached Malik's house. I stopped right in front of his mailbox, and instead of waiting in my car like a good little citizen, and as I would have if stopped for real, I got out prepared for "battle." I also breathed a sigh of relief. None of the external lights had been turned on.

Tyrone got out, and I walked up to him. "What the hell you stop me for?" I demanded loudly. He made like he was trying to calm me, but I was into a tirade. I pulled out all the nasty things that drivers had said to me over the years I was a working cop, and used many of them quite loudly. As I did Tyrone backed off and "called for backup." He didn't actually. What he said was "he's at the window."

That was the signal for two things to happen. The first was that Walthers drove down the lane with his siren off, but his lights on. He joined Tyrone, and I started yelling at both of them. I was careful, though, to do nothing that would force them to 'arrest' me. That wasn't part of the script.

Seconds later, as I spun around to walk back in the direction of my car I caught sight of armed officers in almost full gear coming out of the woods behind the house. I could also make out the figure of Malik in the front window, apparently absorbed in our little drama. At least I hoped he was, since it was all for his 'benefit.' In the meantime I ignored the officers running along both sides of the house.

Instead I was yelling about the cowardly cops needing two of them, and why don't they get more. I was also wishing that I had a police radio on me, at least a receiver, but I hadn't felt like pressing my luck with Tyburn. My signal came soon enough, when I heard the sound of doors crashing, and Tyrone and Walthers suddenly sprinted up the sidewalk. They pulled their weapons as they ran. I followed behind at a slower pace, and I left my handgun holstered. I was allowed in, but this was still a police operation.

By the time I got inside there were cops all over the place. Malik was down, but not yet cuffed. He was resisting with an almost maniacal strength, making it impossible for them to get the cuffs on him yet.

But I didn't worry about that. He was their problem. I headed for the back of the house, just in time to hear a call, "She's here, and still alive!"

Right behind that was another, "We've got one too, but this one is dead." That officer's voice was tired and angry.

I went into the bedroom where the body was, to get the bad news out of the way. I'd never met Wilamina Farrell, but she was the woman tied down spread-eagled onto the bed, stab wounds in her naked body. Clearly she had been raped, likely more than once, before he had killed her. From the looks of her she had been dead about a day.

I went into the other bedroom. Erika was indeed still alive. She had lost weight, she hadn't been able to clean up since being taken, her hair had been chopped shorter, and she was a nervous wreck. She looked like hell, but as far as I was concerned, she was simply beautiful. She was alive, and she could recover from all the rest.

She was tied to a chair, wearing only what was left of one of those long T-shirts some women sleep in. I whipped the bedspread off of the bed and wrapped it around her, then got out my pocket knife and cut her loose from the chair. "Can you walk?" I asked.

"I think so," she said softly. "Just get me out of here."

She managed to stand up, and I led her out into the hallway, my left arm around her, helping to hold her up. As we did I realized the fight was still going on.

But not for long, unfortunately. Malik saw us, and screamed like a wounded animal. I immediately decided he had to be on some kind of drug, because insanity alone didn't explain the way he was suddenly able to toss the officers holding him down off of him. He jumped to his feet and grabbed something from a nearby table, the cuff they had gotten on his left wrist swinging wildly.

Now the number of officers there was a problem. For just about everybody there, shooting was out of the question because there would have been another officer in the line of fire.

I hated to let go of Erika, but there were more immediate concerns. As I pulled my own gun I saw that the object Malik was grabbing was a machete. I had no doubt that his first target would be Erika, and then me, since I had had my arm around her. After that he'd start on the police, doing as much damage as he could.

All that didn't particularly appeal to me. But I had one advantage over the majority of the officers there. I enjoy shooting. Most cops don't fire their weapons but once or twice a year, when they qualify. While the SWAT officers fired more often, those not knocked sprawling were mostly armed with carbines, not good weapons in a a confined area. area. As soon as I realized what Malik was doing I knew I couldn't go for the usual shots. There were too many officers in the way. But he was spinning around on his right foot, stretching his left leg out to start running at Erika. Almost quarters. I shoot several times a month at a range with variable moving targets, and even with my arm around Erika I had easy access to my pistol.

As soon as I realized what Malik was doing I knew I couldn't go for the usual shots. There were too many officers in the way. Almost without thinking I lined up and, using the skill developed with many hours at the range, I fired. Malik immediately crashed to the floor, the machete falling separately and sliding in my direction.

This time they were able to subdue him in seconds, even as he screamed in pain. They didn't try to take him out of the house, though. Instead they called for the ambulance that had been standing by. He was their problem now.

"What happened?" asked Erika as I helped her back off the floor. "You didn't kill him?"

"No need to do that," I said, with a little more bravado than I actually felt.

"So what did you do to him?" she asked, still not recognizing what I had done.

I looked at her. "What do you think would happen to you," I asked, "if you were pivoting on your right foot and your ankle suddenly shattered?" Then she understood.

CHAPTER 12

With Erika rescued there were some calls I had to make. The first was to Morie, to let him know that Erika was alive, but that it would be a few days at least before she was ready to dance again. I let her talk to him, just to prove she was okay.

We had just hung up from that call when the gurney came out of the house with Malik. I looked at Erika, and she was staring at the gurney with an expression I couldn't read. "He won't hurt you again," I said.

"I know," she replied. "But he's already hurt me enough. I heard him kill her, you know. It will be a long time before I stop hearing her begging for her life."

As the ambulance drove off, with a police car right behind, she looked at me. "So where are you taking me?"

"The hospital. The police will want a full record of any injuries, and it would be a good idea for you to be there overnight for observation. Besides, some people can come in and talk to you. I think you should consider getting some therapy."

She nodded. "I think I will. I had a little once before, and it helped." That told me Sandy was right about her being raped.

I was relieved. Some people refuse to get therapy no matter how badly they need it. I reached for my keys, then thought of something. "Oh, is there anything of yours here? Anything I should get before we leave?"

"No," she said flatly. "Even if there was I wouldn't want it." She opened the blanket a little and looked down. "As soon as this thing comes off of me I don't want it any more, either."

I couldn't blame her. I started the car and pulled out. I didn't say anymore and neither did she for a good two miles. Then she asked, "What's going to happen to him?"

"Death Row, most likely. A brutal murder after rape? Not to mention auto theft, kidnapping, and false imprisonment."

Erika looked at me, startled. "False imprisonment?"

"That's what they'll call it for the way he kept you a prisoner after kidnapping you."

"So keeping you prisoner after kidnapping you is a separate crime? I didn't know that."

We were quiet from there until we got to the hospital. There I explained to the hospital personnel what needed to be done, but that didn't take long. All I had to say was "rape victim" and they knew the drill. I did pull one of the residents aside and told him what had happened to her, though.

While she was being processed I called Sherry Lake. I had her home number from the caller ID at the office, and had made a note of it. "I heard you were successful," she said.

"Fortunately, yes. Susan was rescued and Malik is in custody, but he had already killed Ms. Farrell. So do you think you'll get another chance at Malik?"

"I doubt it," she said. "One of the homicide prosecutors will be the lead, though I may get to assist."

"Sounds good either way. By the way, I haven't heard any news reports, but I had to shoot the bastard."

"You did?" By her startled answer that detail had obviously not been in the news. "There was something about a shot, but that was all. Nothing about anybody being hit." There was a short pause, and then she continued, "Obviously you didn't kill him, or you wouldn't be talking about who gets to prosecute him."

"No, I didn't. He broke loose from the officers who were trying to arrest him, and came at me with a machete. It was so crowded that they would have had trouble shooting, so I shot him in the ankle. That brought him down and they were able to restrain him."

"A machete? How'd they leave that in the area?"

"They were busy. He was going loco, and there were at least three cops on top of him when he stood up to come at me."

"That many?"

"Yup. I know he's loco, but I think he might have been on something, too." I had become convinced of that during the drive over. "Crazy is one thing, but what he was doing was a bit much."

"Have tests been ordered?"

"Don't know, but I can ask."

"That's all right. Not your concern anyway."

"Okay, but I do want to find out how he's doing."

"You know he's going to try to sue you for this," she said, sounding amused.

"So I should have killed him? Sorry, but that would involve way too much paperwork. Not that I'm worried about the shooting itself. It was fully justified."

"I'm sure it was. Well, thanks for calling. I've got to get back to my family."

Next I gave Al Hobbs a quick call. He got no pleasure about being right that Wilamina Farrell had been murdered, but he was relieved that Malik was in custody.

I hung up and started looking around for someone who could tell me about Malik. It didn't take long for me to find a nurse who pointed me to a doctor on a phone. He was talking that doctor jargon that's damn near as hard to understand as what lawyers say. I understood enough, though, to know that whoever he was talking about was in bad shape, and it had something to do with the bones. Considering that the nurse had sent me to him because he was the doctor who had been working on Malik, it was no great feat of deduction to figure out that Malik had serious problems.

I didn't have to wait long before he finished. He hung up and turned to look at me. Clearly he had noticed me, and was now ready to talk to me.

"Yes, what is it?" he demanded. Well, maybe 'ready' wasn't quite the right word.

"I'm interested in how Harvey Malik is doing," I said. "How bad was the injury?"

"Who the hell are you and why the hell would you want to know?" he asked belligerently. "You're not from the press, are you? If you are I can't talk to you."

"My name is Dan Muncie," I replied, "and I have a personal interest. I'm the one who shot him."

"Well you certainly fucked him up," the doctor said. "Why the hell did you do that to him?"

"It was either that or kill him."

My answer startled the doctor. "You mean you weren't trying to?" he asked after a second.

"Shit no. If killing him was my intent he'd be waiting for the medical examiner, not here being treated."

He looked at me narrowly. "Why the hell did you shoot him? And why haven't the police arrested you?"

I could almost hear the click of the light bulb turning on over my head. Obviously the doctor knew nothing about what had happened except that Malik had been shot. Nobody had told him anything about how he came to be that way.

"I shot him because he was coming at me with a machete," I said, "and the police haven't arrested me because I was with them. They were trying to arrest him, but he broke loose and grabbed a machete they hadn't had a chance to move yet."

"So why did you shoot him instead of the cops?" he asked suspiciously. "And why in the ankle?"

Since I knew what he meant I resisted the temptation to ask why I would want to shoot a cop. "The room was packed," I said. "None of them had a clear shot without another cop being in the line of fire. Well, I didn't either, but I saw another way. I put my round in the floor right behind his ankle. Not that hard a shot since he was standing on it."

He was still suspicious. "What the hell were all those cops doing there, then?"

"Trying to arrest him. He was already wanted on a variety of charges including escaping from prison, grand theft, and two counts of kidnapping. While they were trying to arrest him they added murder to the list."

"Murder?" That took him back.

"Yes. I fully expect he will be tried for capital murder."

"Shit!" He said it almost reverently.

"By the way," I said, "you may want to run some tests on him. He was face down on the floor with three cops on his back, and still managed to get to his feet."

"Really?"

"He did indeed. That's when he grabbed the machete and tried to attack me."

"Then you must be the bastard he was threatening to open up like a deer," he said with the ghost of a smile.

"Doctor, I'll have you know my parents had been married over two years when I was born," I said solemnly.

That earned me a grin. "Hang on a sec." He turned to the nurse at the desk and ordered some additional tests on Malik, stat. When he turned back he said, "So you want to know his condition? Bad. His condition isn't life threatening, and I don't think he's going to lose the foot, but I think there is an excellent chance that he's going to end up with a permanent limp. The bullet hit the base of the tibia and fibula, pretty well wrecking the joint. A couple of the tarsal bones are in bad shape, too, and I suspect that at least one was shattered beyond repair. My guess is that he'll end up with an ankle that won't bend, or at least won't bend much. That's up to Sampson, though."

"Sampson?"

"Doctor Sampson, the orthopedic surgeon I was talking to a minute ago. Virgil Sampson. Damn good man."

"Tell him he needn't go out of his way. The only place that ankle is going is to prison."

"You seem pretty sure of that."

"I am. It's a three-way choice between Death Row, a life sentence without parole, or Waterford."

"Waterford?" The doctor didn't know what I was talking about.

"The hospital slash prison where the state sends those found to be criminally insane. Not a pleasant place to work, I hear."

"Or be sentenced, I presume," the doctor commented. "By the way, I'm Harry Oldcamp." He stuck his hand out.

We shook. I guessed I had been forgiven for shooting Malik.

We talked for a couple of minutes longer, and then he said, "By the way, why didn't you shoot him in the chest? If you're a good enough shot to hit him in the ankle, surely you're good enough to hit the chest. It's a bigger target, even."

"There were officers behind him. I couldn't count on the bullet staying inside him, and I didn't want to risk hitting them as well." Even if they were wearing bullet-resistant vests. After all, the bullet might have hit a place not protected by the vest.

"I see. That makes sense." He looked around. "Well, I've got to be getting back to work. Take care."

I could have left, and I was tempted, but a bit of a reaction to the rescue had set in. The adrenalin had all worn off, and I was tired.

I was also hungry, so I found the cafeteria and had some supper. It wasn't any worse than usual for hospital food, and at least I knew it would be nutritious.

After eating I went back to the Emergency Room. Two detectives were there, looking for me as it turned out. We found a little privacy, and I told them all about what happened, and my part in Malik's falling on his face with a shattered ankle. I wasn't in any trouble; the reports of the officers involved, including Grant, had taken care of that. They just needed to get all the paperwork filled out. Justified or not, a shot had been fired.

After that I was able to pay a visit to Erika. She was feeling better, and they had let her clean up after the exams. She was also pleased by some news from the officers who had taken her preliminary statement. Using a parking lot ticket found at the house they had found her car undamaged in long term parking at the airport.

With that established I went back and waited for word on Malik. I was curious about just how much damage I had actually done to his ankle.

Some hours later a tall, burly doctor in surgical scrubs came out and introduced himself as Virgil Sampson. Unlike Oldcamp, Sampson had heard the news reports on the rescue. "Well," reported Sampson, "He'll be able to walk without too much pain, but he'll have limited mobility at best. Maybe none at all. Too soon to tell for sure."

"So he'll have a limp?"

"Try walking without moving one of your ankles," he said. "About like that. Not as bad as if you'd shot him in the knee. Now that would cause a limp!"

"The idea was to stop him, Doctor, not to cripple him for life." Not that it bothered me that I had.

"Well, stop him you did. For good, from the looks of things."

"But other than that he's okay?"

"Oh, yes, he'll live all right. Oh, by the way, he was on PCP, in case you're interested."

I shook my head. No wonder he had been able to toss those three cops! "Thanks for the information, Doctor," I said.

He just waved as he headed back in the direction of the operating rooms. Maybe he had another patient waiting for him.

With that all taken care of it was time to leave. I wanted to go home, but I went by the Maja first. I had to make sure they all knew that Erika was safe, and thinking of them. I also had to give

Morgana a list of the clothing Erika needed from her apartment so she would have something to wear when she left the hospital. Then I headed for home and my bed.

CHAPTER 13

The news media had a field day with the capture of Harvey Malik, the discovery of a body, and the rescue of a beautiful young woman who had been the 'object of his affections.' At least that's what the next morning's paper called Erika, though of course they identified her as Susan Trumble. Their real problem was in saying what she did for a living. The paper called her a dancer, two of the TV stations called her an 'entertainer,' but only one radio station had the balls to call her a topless dancer and identify which club she worked at. Everyone else just gave her name and left it at that.

I wasn't mentioned at all, which suited me fine. The stories all declined to mention who had shot Malik, leaving the impression that it had been done by one of the SWAT team members who was being left unidentified for 'security reasons.' The stories also said that an 'alert citizen' had spotted Malik's hideout and told the police.

At other times this might have annoyed me, but right now getting my face plastered all over the place was about the last thing I wanted. That could make it more difficult for me to prove that Alexis Brogan and James Casey had conspired with Cari Roland to murder Ed Brogan.

Now, with Erika rescued and Malik in custody, I could concentrate on the Brogan case. I decided to start by finding out everything I could about Cari Roland, particularly who she was. There was no way I would believe her paperwork. I could not accept that two women could have babies in the same small town on the same day and give them the same name. Especially since there was only the one birth certificate.

The problem was that one of the main ways of identifying a person with a false name had already failed. The police had already run her prints through AFIS, the Automated Fingerprint Identification System, and come up blank. There was no record on her in the system.

This made little sense, because usually the reason someone will change their identity this way is because they have done something illegal. They will become someone else, someone the police have no reason to look for. If you do it right, it is possible to live out in the open for many years with nobody the wiser.

But commonly they will have done something along the line that will put their fingerprints in the system. Relatively few people suddenly commit a major crime with no criminal record before that. Most start with small crimes as children and teens, such as shoplifting, then work up to the felonies.

So I was essentially left with two possibilities. One was that she had changed her name for reasons unrelated to crime. For some reason known but to her, she had taken on this other identity. Not only that, but she had done it this way rather than change her name in the usual legal way, by going through the courts.

The other possibility was that she had committed a crime, the police somewhere were looking for her, and she had managed to change her identification before being taken in. Not only that, but she hadn't gotten into any earlier trouble that would cause the police to take her prints.

Frankly, of the two, I considered the second more likely. The next question was where this crime had been committed. It wasn't local, that much was certain. She had to have been from outside the area, possibly out of state.

There was one possible way of telling where she was from, even without prints or her real name. The problem was that it was Saturday, and I didn't know what Kellerman's work schedule was. I called the Homicide Division just in case he was available. Unfortunately, he wasn't. "Who worked the Brogan shooting with him?" I asked the secretary who answered the phone.

"Hang on just a moment," she said. Less than thirty seconds later she was back. "Lee Conrad was the other detective on that case," she said. "He's in if you'd like to speak to him."

"Yes, I would, please," I said, trying to hide my delight. Lee was another old friend from my cop days, but there was no way of telling if he would go along with my request. Or if he could, for that matter.

The phone only made it through one ring before it was picked up. "Homicide, Detective Conrad."

"Dan Muncie, Lee. I wonder if you could do something for me."

"Oh? What do you need?"

"Have you had the formal interrogation of Cari Roland yet?"

"Yes, we did, the morning after the shooting."

"Taped as always, I presume?"

"Of course. Audio and video."

"Were you in on it?"

"I was." Now he sounded wary.

"I've been hired to find out if it was a domestic violence incident, or if it was actually a murder. What I'd like to do is borrow the tape from that interrogation."

"What, the transcript isn't good enough for you?"

"No, it isn't. I'm not as interested in what she has to say as how she says it. I'd like to have an expert listen to it to see if we can figure out where she's from."

"Where she's from?" I had caught him by surprise. "I thought she was from Fleming, up in Laurie County."

"I don't think so. I found a birth certificate from there, but the baby was described as black."

"You don't say." Now I had his interest. "So she isn't who she says she is?"

"That's my guess. The problem is that under the conditions there is no easy way of telling where she's from."

"So what is it you want to do with the tape?"

"Take it to Sharon Lindon. She's an expert on dialects. Maybe she can give me a good starting point."

There was a moment of quiet. "Are you sure she'll even talk to you? Last I heard, you weren't one of her favorite people."

"That was three years ago, Lee. Hell, I was still a cop, then. And it wasn't as bad as you make it sound." Not quite, anyway. "Besides, she likes a challenge." Enough to make up for when we broke up, I hoped.

"It's your neck," said Lee, unconvinced.

He said nothing more for about half a minute. "Okay," he finally said, "I've got a clean copy of my own. I can't let you have the original, but I'll loan you mine for a couple of days. Think you can have it back by Monday?"

"Sure thing," I said. That was no problem at all. His idea of 'clean' and mine were not the same. I'd want to make my own copy anyway. "How about the Big Hole?" I asked. That was the name of a donut shop not far from police headquarters. He could go in there without anyone wondering.

"In twenty minutes?" he asked. "I've got some paperwork I need to finish, and then I've got some people to talk to."

"Twenty minutes will be fine." And from there to the Sound Experience, where Jordan Hardacre would make me a copy of the tape without a lot of the background noise.

Twenty-one minutes later I was sipping a cup of coffee and working on a maple-iced donut when Lee sat down beside me. He's an easy man to spot in one way. He is a natural blonde, with hair so light in color he's been accused of bleaching it. "Have you called her yet?" he asked.

"Nope." I said. "I'm going to make my own copy of the tape first. This one will be too noisy."

"It's not so bad," he said dismissively. He ordered a coffee to go. "So do you think you can prove Brogan was murdered?"

"I do."

"Why would she shoot her sugar daddy?"

"Because sugar daddy's wife wanted her to."

I got a "you've got to be kidding" look. "His wife was involved in it? Hey, most of the time it's the spouse that does the shooting. Why would she want her husband dead?"

I made him wait while I sipped a little more coffee. "Because she's having an affair with James Casey, executive vice-president of her late husband's company."

"You're sure of that?" he asked a little sharply.

I just nodded. He didn't say anything more to me, but I could see he was doing some thinking. He paid for his coffee and headed for the door. He left behind him a small unmarked manila envelope, the kind used to handle audio tapes. I casually picked it up and put it in my picket. It was a "pass" that wouldn't fool anyone watching for it, but the casual observer wouldn't notice.

I finished my coffee and donut, then headed for the Sound Experience. It was a "Sound Reproduction Equipment Market," meaning the owner, Jordan Hardacre, would sell you just about anything you wanted to buy for the purpose of reproducing music or other sounds. You could get stereos, speakers, recorders, and a variety of other equipment, but you could not get TVs, computers, or other electronics, unless they had to do with sound. The only requirement was that the equipment had to meet his exacting standards. This eliminated a lot of "cheap" items, but there were even expensive systems he refused to carry.

I went in and was met by one of his sales people, Larry Dix. Larry may not have known as much about sound as Jordan, but he knew plenty. Jordan was as picky about the people who worked for him as he was about the products he sold.

"Hi, Dan," Larry said. "Are you here to see Jordan?"

"I am."

"He's in back. You know the way."

I did. I headed for the back of the store, through the "Employee's Only" door, and went into Jordan's private workshop. It was a room most recording studios would envy, for mixing sounds if not to actually record them. Jordan was working at a console at the far end; his back to the door. "Hi, Dan," he said as I approached him.

"Hello, Jordan," I replied. I didn't bother asking how he knew it was me. He knew the sound of my steps.

"What've you got for me?" He stopped whatever it was he was doing and turned around. His tone was a bit belligerent, but that was normal for him. To say he 'didn't suffer fools gladly' was an understatement. I didn't meet his high standards when it came to my ability to recognize sounds and tones, but I passed as a person to do work for. I trusted his judgment and didn't try to tell him what to do.

"I've got a tape I need cleaned up," I told him. "I'm going to be having someone listening to it for accents, and I want to get the crap off of it."

He grunted and put out his hand. I handed him the tape and he rolled his chair over to a player. He started the tape and listened to about the first ten seconds. It was Steve Kellerman setting the scene, that he and Lee were interviewing Cari Roland in the shooting of Edward Brogan. Jordan stopped the tape and looked at me. "That's pretty crappy, all right."

Actually, for one of those tapes it was pretty good, but not by his standards. "Think you can clean it up?"

"Sure. Going to take a little while, though. You want to come back for it?"

"No," I said, "I'll wait." I had expected that, and brought some reading material.

"You want the original back?"

"Yes, untouched."

He just nodded and turned back to his work.

At first I tried to read, but I couldn't. I got caught up in listening to the interrogation. If you didn't know better you would say she was giving the police reasonable explanations of how she came to shoot her married lover when he tried to beat her up. I knew better, though, or at least was pretty sure I did. I just needed to prove it.

As Jordan went through it the background noises decreased, and the voices cleared up. By the time he finished you could close your eyes and it sounded like you were in the room with them as they spoke.

Finally he stopped. He looked at me. "Tape or CD?" he asked.

"Could I have one of each?"

"Sure." He loaded a tape into one unit and a blank CD into another, then pushed a few buttons. "That's the best I could do," he said. "Without working on it overnight, at least."

It sounded damn near perfect to me, but like I said, he's a perfectionist who can hear things the rest of us can't. "That's fine, Jordan. It's plenty clear for us ordinary people." I smiled at him with little effect. He knew I intended it as a compliment, and he knew he wasn't ordinary. Anything less than perfection left him dissatisfied.

He said nothing as we waited for the copying to be finished. It didn't take long with the high-speed machines he had. When he was finished he handed me the CD and two tapes. "I'll send you the bill," he said instead.

"Thanks anyway," I said as I started to turn. I didn't bother asking how much the bill would be. It wouldn't be cheap, but I would pass it on in my own billing.

"By the way, she's lying."

I turned and looked at him. "Excuse me?"

"She's lying. I can hear it in her voice." He wasn't looking at me, but had returned to whatever he was doing when I got there.

"Thanks again," I said as I left. There was no need to ask if he was serious. He wouldn't joke about anything like that. He also wouldn't have said anything if he wasn't sure.

One thing I had done while waiting, before trying to read, was to call Mayfield State University to see if, even though it was

Saturday, Sharon was teaching today. Happily, it turned out she did have a class that would be finishing up soon.

I made it in time, but not by much. I hadn't been standing at the door more than a minute when the students started to come out. Sharon wasn't far behind. She pulled up short when she saw me.

"Well," she said, "long time no see." She was not pleased to see me.

"Hello, Sharon. You're looking good." She was, too. Five foot nine and 140 well-shaped pounds, with honey blonde hair down to her shoulder blades, hazel eyes, and a smile to die for.

When she was smiling, that is. She wasn't right now. "You're looking about the same. What are you here for?"

"I need your help."

"My help? What can I possibly do for you?"

"I need to know where someone is from. You're the expert on American accents and dialect."

"And why should I do this for you?"

"Take your pick. You can either do it as a favor for an old friend, or you can do it for the money?"

The last got her attention. "How much money?" she asked suspiciously.

"Whatever we can agree is reasonable."

"Suppose I wanted fifty an hour?"

"You've got it."

"Are you serious?"

"Yes, I am."

"Follow me," she said after a moment, and then she walked off. She still looked good from the rear, too.

Before long we got to her office. She unlocked the door and went in. "Sit," she ordered. I sat down in the only chair other than hers that didn't have papers, books, and folders piled on it.

She clearly wasn't ready to trust me. "So what's this all about?" she asked.

"Did you hear about the man who was shot by his girlfriend earlier this week? Supposedly he had started to beat her up."

"I heard about it." She was politely neutral.

"I don't think it was domestic violence. I'm convinced it was murder. The woman who did the shooting isn't who she says she is, and the victim's wife was having an affair."

"Having an affair doesn't necessarily prove anything." From her tone I still had not been completely forgiven.

"Even when," I held up a finger, "the victim owned his own multi-million dollar company," another finger went up, "the victim's wife was having her affair with her husband's number two man, the executive vice-president," I put up a third finger, "and the bereaved widow appoints said executive vice-president to take over running the company on the death of her husband? It may not be proof, but it all sounds suspicious to me."

Sharon looked at me thoughtfully. "You're not joking about this? You need my help?"

"I could use your professional expertise," I said, crossing my heart.

"Tell me more," she said after a moment.

I took the next few minutes filling her in on the rest, from how I got involved to how I found out that Mrs. Brogan had a lover. I even told her that I had been "hired" by the insurance companies to prove it.

"So what happens if you can't prove it?" she asked after thinking over what I had said.

"They pay my bill and give the widow her money."

"So you get paid either way?"

"I do." I let a smile show. "Though I do expect to get some extra money if I prove her guilty of murder."

"How much extra?"

I shrugged. "Hard to tell, but if I can provide the evidence that gets the three of them convicted of murder, possibly as much as five percent of the value of the policies."

"And how much would that be?"

"The policies? Two and a half million."

She whistled, impressed by the number. "So how am I supposed to hear her speak?"

I pulled out the 'clean' tape Jordan had given me, and the CD. "You can start by listening to one of these. She's telling the police what she wants them to believe happened."

She hesitated a moment, then put out her hand. "The tape, please." I gave her the tape and put the CD away. She turned around and put the tape into a player behind her. In seconds I was listening to the interrogation again.

Five minutes later she stopped the tape. "Where's she supposed to be from?"

"Fleming. Laurie County."

"The hell she is." She rewound the tape.

"So you'll do it?"

"Sixty an hour?"

"Done. How soon can you give me an answer?"

"Tomorrow," she said over her shoulder.

I put one of my business cards on her desk and left. She had gotten out some headphones and was already listening to the tape that way. She didn't even notice when I left.

CHAPTER 14

While Sharon was presumably busy listening to the tape, I started doing more research into James Casey. All I knew so far was that he was Alexis Brogan's lover and what his bio on the company website had said about him.

It took little work to find some discrepancies. While the bio was rather vague and general, as expected from such information, he was reported to have worked with a brokerage company in New York. What I was able to find, though, indicated that he had never lived in the New York area. The closest he had ever been was central Pennsylvania, where he had lived for about two years.

Another problem was his education. It didn't take much longer to find out he had not graduated from where he said he had. In fact, he had not been anywhere near the campus when he should have been studying there.

Even more interesting, he had a criminal record. Possession of marijuana when he was 16, and shoplifting when he was 18; not serious, but still troubling.

One thing did check out. I was able to trace him all the way back to where he was born, and when, and that much matched. In that respect at least he was who he claimed to be.

By the time I finished, I had found enough to call his honesty into serious question. Education and experience claims both showed 'inaccuracies' that would be hard for him to reconcile. As far as I was concerned, he was a liar.

Being a liar, though, didn't make him a murderer. There are plenty of people who are less than truthful but who have never committed a violent crime of any kind, much less murder. The limited nature of his criminal record did not help matters any, either. Possession and shoplifting were hardly the standard immediate precursors to homicide.

Next I started checking out Alexis Brogan. Alexis was four months younger than her husband, and with Edward as a starting point it wasn't long before I had a handle on her.

There wasn't much to see. The information I could find about her matched what little I already knew. No criminal record, no missing periods, and nothing to indicate she had done anything much out of the ordinary for a woman of her age. If there was anything in the least surprising it was that she and Edward had been married for almost eleven years, yet had no children. I hadn't realized that they had been married so long.

By the time I finished checking everything out I was ready to call it a day. I had gotten plenty of information, but no real answers. Other than the obvious, I still had no reason for a woman who had apparently been happily married for ten years to start messing around with the vice-president of her husband's company.

Or maybe that "ten years" was part of the problem. Had she been bored? One thing I had found was that she had no outside employment. She had apparently been a dutiful "corporate wife" for a few years, until Edward had started a company of his own. Then she had shared in his success, or at least the material aspects of it.

The hell with it. I decided that I deserved the night off. Besides, it was Saturday night, and while people might talk to a police officer, few would willingly talk to someone like me when they could be out enjoying themselves.

I slept in the next morning. Not only was it Sunday morning, but I needed it. I had enjoyed my own Saturday night. Erika was not back at work, and in fact likely wouldn't be since it was now "known" that she was underage, but that had not kept Morie from thanking me for my efforts. The other dancers found pleasant ways to "thank" me as well.

In fact, if they had been any more "thankful" I think Sandy would have started getting jealous instead of amused.

When I finally woke up I sat up a little to confirm that it was as bright out as I thought. It was. "Timzit?" Sandy mumbled from next to me.

I checked the clock. "Almost noon." She pulled the covers back over her head. I got up.

Thirty minutes later I was just about finished with some soft boiled eggs when the phone rang. "Hello."

"Dan?"

"Good morning, Sharon."

"It's afternoon, Dan," she said, a chill in her voice.

"I just got up, and I'm finishing my breakfast. That makes it morning no matter what the clock says. When I finish cleaning up, then it will be afternoon."

After a few seconds she chuckled. It wasn't much, and she soon stopped, but it was enough. "Okay, do you want to know what I found out from that tape?"

"Of course."

"She's a Yankee. She's lived down here long enough to pick up a good bit of the accent, but it's not the one she grew up with."

"That's what I thought." While I wasn't the expert Sharon was, something about her accent hadn't sounded quite right to me.

"She's lost too much of her original accent for me to be more specific, or she's covering it up well, but I'd say she was from western Pennsylvania. Most likely the Pittsburgh area."

"Pittsburgh, huh? That's a big help, Sharon."

"You're not making fun of me, are you?"

"What? No, of course not! I'm serious, Sharon. That cuts way down on the areas I have to check if I'm going to find out who she is."

"So you truly have no idea where she is from?"

"I do now, but I didn't until you told me. All I knew was that she isn't who she says she is. You've confirmed that."

"Why would she do something like that?" asked Sharon. "Change her identity. You say she doesn't have a criminal record?"

"None that the police could find." A small warning bell sounded in the back of my head, but I couldn't take a good look just then. "It's possible she has a record as a juvenile, one that didn't make the FBI's database."

"Well, I hope what I told you helps."

"It will. Go ahead and write up a full report and send it in with your bill." I hesitated. "How much am I being billed for?"

"Six and a half hours." I heard some hesitancy in her voice, saying she wasn't sure how I'd react. "I did most of it last night, but I listened again this morning to make sure."

"Go ahead and put in a bill for seven hours, Sharon. This is a big help." Now I knew what police departments to call. I just wished I could be sure they would tell me what I needed to know.

"I'll do that," Sharon said, sounding relieved. "I'm glad I could help out." There was a short pause, and I had the feeling that she wasn't finished. "Call me if I can be of any more help," she added.

"I'll do that. Take care of yourself, Sharon." We finished our good-byes and hung up.

"Who was that?" asked Sandy behind me, her voice fuzzy from recent sleep.

"Sharon Lindon. She was letting me know where Cari Roland was from."

Sandy came around from behind me. As usual she was naked. She frowned as she asked, "Isn't she the old girlfriend who broke up with you after she caught you in bed with another woman?"

"She is."

"But she was still willing to help you?"

"Paying her sixty dollars an hour helped convince her."

"Wow. Being paid that much would convince a lot of people."

"Yep."

"Are you going to feed me or do I have to feed myself?"

So I fed her. She had a good appetite, and we spent the next half hour concentrating on food. Then we went back to bed for a while before she left.

I spent the rest of the day cleaning up and washing things, and thinking. That little alarm bell had finally come through. Several lines of inquiry had opened up, but I couldn't go after them until the next morning, so I got my home in order for the next week.

By the time I reached my office the next morning I was ready to get started. As soon as I got in I called Steve Kellerman.

"Yeah, Dan, what is it?"

"Two questions. First, when you ran Cari Roland's prints, did they go to the feds, or did you use the state records?"

"State records. Since she's a native, I saw no need to go to the FBI."

"Okay, now, did you ask the BATFE for a trace on the handgun she used?" The Bureau of Alcohol, Tobacco, Firearms and Explosives would have access to the records of the gun, at least to the point of sale. The store should then have records on who it was sold to. Sales after that were much less certain.

"No, we didn't. We were getting ready to when the D.A. decided he wasn't going to prosecute. After that, why bother?"

"I see. Would it be possible for you to do both?"

"Both what?" He wasn't being stupid; the question had just caught him by surprise.

"Run Roland's prints through the FBI database, and get the BATFE to trace the murder weapon."

"Well, the prints I suppose I could, but why should I try to trace the pistol? For that matter, why should I send her prints to the FBI?"

"For the prints, remember when I told you she wasn't who she said she was?"

"Yeah, I remember." I could hear the wariness in his voice.

"I borrowed Lee's copy of your interrogation and had a copy made, one with the noise cut way down. Then I gave it to Sharon Linden, so she could listen to it."

"You gave a copy of an interrogation tape to a civilian?" he asked, more than a little outraged. Of course, he was forgetting that I was a civilian, too. "What the hell did you do that for?"

"Like I said, so she could listen to it."

"Just what the fuck are you trying to do, Dan?" he asked, interrupting me. "Are you trying to impress her so you can get back together with her?" He had known Sharon back when we had still been dating.

"Not in the least, Steve," I said quickly. "She's an expert on accents and dialects, remember? I wanted to have her listen to Roland, to see if she could tell where Roland was from."

That calmed him down, and he even took a few seconds to think about the implications of what I had been saying. "So let me guess. Sharon says she's not from around here."

"Western Pennsylvania," I said. "More specifically, Southwestern Pennsylvania; around Pittsburgh."

"But we got a hit on Cari Roland, in Fleming," he said, but this time he sounded less sure of himself.

"Cari Marie Roland, yes. Take another look, Steve. That Cari Roland was black, and died less than a year later."

"Oh, shit!" he said bitterly. I said nothing for a few seconds. "That still doesn't make her a murderer, though," he added warily.

"No, it doesn't. I'm still working on that."

"So give me another reason to send her prints to the feds. And why should I bother the BATFE for the info on the gun?"

This part was weaker. "I ran a check on James Casey."

"The vice-president of Brogan's company?"

"Exactly. He appears to be who he says he is, or at least he seems to be using his own name. But he is not what he says he is in other ways. He has made a bunch of claims about his education and experience that look to be fake."

"So what the hell does that have to do with Roland?"

"He spent two years in western Pennsylvania."

I vaguely heard a breath being drawn, but he said nothing for about three seconds. "The Pittsburgh area, right?"

"You've got it."

"When Roland was still living there?"

"Hell if I know. But the records on Roland only go back a few years, and he was in the Pittsburgh area from seven to nine years ago. Right now, we don't know where she was during that time. Or for that matter if they might have been in the same area either before or after that. Even if they were in Pittsburgh at the same time, it's a big city. They might very well have never met."

"But you're betting they knew each other before this whole mess happened, aren't you?"

"I am. Let's just say I find this to be a bit too much of a coincidence."

"But why were you checking on Casey? Because the Brogan woman put him in charge of the company? He's the logical choice."

"Yes, he is, especially since he's also screwing her."

"He what?"

"James Casey is Alexis Brogan's lover."

"How certain are you of that?" Steve demanded.

"Ninety-five percent? Not confirmed, but I'd put money on it." That should tell him how certain I was. I didn't put money on anything unless I was convinced I would win.

"What makes you so sure?"

"Wednesday night I went by her house. There were the usual mourners there to give moral support to the new widow. I stuck around until everybody left. Everybody but one, that is, a man I didn't get a good look at, though I could see the widow smile at him after the others had left, and she didn't look in the least bit grieving."

"Do tell," murmured Steve.

"One of the cars left behind was leased to Brogan's company, and Casey is using it. The car, and owner, spent the night." Which reminded me, I still had to confirm that the car was leased to Brogan's company, and not Casey personally.

"In the widow's bed?"

"Don't know, but I only saw lights in one bedroom."

"How interesting."

"It gets better. I went back the next night, and he was still there. This time I did get a good look, and it was Casey. He spent the night again. This time I was parked where I could see two figures against the curtains in the upstairs bedroom."

"Interesting," Kellerman said thoughtfully. "So Alexis Brogan is screwing Casey, Casey may well have been in the Pittsburgh area when Cari Roland was there, and Roland shot and killed Ed Brogan. Very interesting indeed."

"I thought so."

"I'll send the prints in, but give me a reason to send the gun's serial number to the BATFE."

"Too many coincidences? Or maybe just covering the bases."

"Hmm, it's a bit weak, but I'll put it through. I can't justify a rush on it, though. No telling how long before they can come back with an answer."

"That's okay, Steve. Ed Brogan will still be dead."

"That he will. And better a solid case than a fast one."

I recognized the quote. It was one of the favorite sayings of the lieutenant in command of the homicide unit. He'd say it just before letting you know he expected it to be both solid and fast. "That's the idea." I said.

"So is there anything else you can tell me while I'm here?"

"Ed Brogan knew his wife was screwing around on him."

"How do you know that?"

"He told me. The night I found out about his affair with Roland he happened to come into the Maja, and sit near me. We got to talking, and he told me that he had gotten a mistress because his wife had a lover."

"Interesting coincidence, that."

"Yes, and proof that sometimes coincidences do happen."

"Did he know who the lover was?"

"He didn't say, though if I had to guess I'd say no."

"Why not?"

"He said he couldn't divorce her right now because of some business matters, but he was going to when he could, and she'd get nothing out of the settlement. My gut feeling is that if he had known who the lover was he would have said something about getting him, too. After all, I don't know about you, but if I owned a business I don't think I'd be willing to give a pass to an exec who'd been fucking my wife. Especially if I was going to be getting a divorce because she'd been unfaithful."

"Sounds reasonable."

"Iffy," I admitted, "but reasonable."

"Unless Brogan paid Casey to be with his wife. That's been known to happen."

"True, but the tone of his comment said he didn't know who the culprit was, or even care." Then I thought of something else. "Oh, one more thing. I presume you read the autopsy report. Was there any mention of injuries to Brogan's right hand?"

"No, there wasn't. I don't recall it mentioning his hands at all, really."

"Could you confirm that with the medical examiner? After all, if he's supposed to have popped Cari in the eye he'd have bruised knuckles. Like the ones Casey has."

"Like the ones- Casey has bruised knuckles? I'll check with the ME right away. Well, I'd love to talk some more, but I've got to be going. I'll let you know when we get something back."

"Okay, Steve. Bye."

I hung up the phone. It was time to do some legwork.

CHAPTER 15

I went out to the neighborhood where the Brogans had lived, well, where Alexis Brogan still lived, and looked around. I wasn't sure if this was the right kind of neighborhood for what I was looking for, but there was only one way to find out.

I used a fictitious "crime survey" as an excuse for my questions. I learned plenty about the neighborhood while I was talking to them, but the main thing I found out was that Casey had started coming by the Brogan house when Edward was not there starting about four months previously. I just got hints of it until I managed to find the neighborhood busybody. She was able to fill me in on lots of details.

She was a repressed bitch, but it worked out for me since she took it out on her neighbors. In this case it meant that she was aware of the misadventures of her neighbors to an astonishing degree, including the many visits of James Casey to Mrs. Brogan.

She lived on the other side of the street, three doors down, with a good view of their house. When I finished talking with her I had found out what I needed to know. There was no doubt that the relationship between Alexis Brogan and James Casey was no new thing. If he had started coming to their house that openly four months before it was a sure bet that the affair had been going on for some time before that. This fit what the women had told me at Ed Brogan's funeral.

Still, it wasn't this relationship that interested me. I was far more curious about that between Casey and Cari Roland, or whatever her real name turned out to be. I had no doubt there was a connection, and that it predated the one between Casey and Alexis. While coincidence was possible, I found it hard to believe that the two of them could have been living in the same part of western Pennsylvania without meeting, only to be "brought together" by the murder of Ed Brogan.

I went to lunch and considered my options. They were few enough at the moment, but one obvious choice was to start a more detailed investigation into Cari Roland and her actions since moving here. I wanted to find out how she had arranged to meet Ed Brogan.

After lunch I called Homicide, but, as expected, Steve was still out. I left no message, and headed out to the store where Cari worked. Harrison's had several stores in town, and she worked at the one on Baker Boulevard. Once I got there I asked for the store manager. I flashed my private detective ID, and impressed the hell out of one of the office staff, a young woman with an overbite and a budding moustache. "I'll get him for you," she said, overawed, as she scurried away.

It was only a couple of minutes before the manager arrived. He came in, a slightly pudgy man, a little short of breath from rushing back. "Hello, there, I'm Leonard Welty. What can I do for you, Detective?"

Detective? "I'm sorry," I said. "I think the young lady misunderstood me. I'm a private detective, Mr. Welty, not a police officer."

"Oh? What can I do for you?" Before I could say anything he added suspiciously, "May I see your identification, please?"

"Of course." I pulled it out again and showed the manager. "I'm sorry about the confusion."

"So what can I do to help you?" he repeated warily.

I put on an embarrassed expression. "This is about a rather personal matter. Could we speak in private, please?" I had decided to play it honestly, sort of.

"Of course," he said reluctantly. He hesitated a moment before turning and walking down the hall. I followed him to a cluttered office. It reminded me somewhat of Sharon's office, but less organized. He sat behind his desk and looked at me somewhat suspiciously. "Just what is it you think I can do for you?"

Time for my own display of reluctance. "I hate to bother you with this, but I've been hired by an insurance company to investigate a murder."

"A murder?" Clearly he hadn't made the connection.

"Yes, sir. The death of a Mr. Edward Brogan."

"Oh. But that wasn't a murder!" He looked nicely confused.

"Well, you see, that's the problem. There are a couple of insurance policies on Brogan that total up to over two million dollars. The insurance companies would save a lot of money if it turns out that it wasn't a shooting in self-defense."

"And you're supposed to prove it was really a murder?" He was decidedly suspicious of me now.

"Well, that's what they'd like, but it's a pretty clear cut case." Of murder, but I couldn't say that. "In the mean time, if I'm going to keep them happy I have to at least go through the motions, to prove I've earned what I bill them. What I'd like to do is find out what you can tell me about Cari Roland. How long has she been here, how well does she get along with the other people here, and so on. I'm going to have information like that in my report when I send it in."

"But you're not going to try to say she did something she didn't do?"

"Heavens, no!" I said with a shocked expression. I wasn't, either. I was going to nail her for what she had done, not frame her for anything. I shook my head. "Not at all, Mr. Welty. Heck,

I could lose my license for inventing stuff in a case involving a felony." That was true. "All I want is what I need to put together a good report."

I must have been looking sincere as hell, because Welty relaxed, and actually smiled at me. "That's okay, then. I just don't want to get her in any kind of trouble for something she didn't do."

"I don't either, Mr. Welty." Just for the stuff she did do. "I only want to find the truth."

"Well, where would you like to start?"

"Why not with the basics? I don't know that much about her, like where she was born and went to school. Would it be possible to get some of that information from you?"

"Of course," he said, warming to me. He picked up his phone and dialed an internal number. After a few seconds he said, "Agnes, would you bring in Cari Roland's personnel file, please? That's a dear. Thank you."

He hung up and smiled. "She'll be right in," he said.

Less than thirty seconds later the young woman with the overbite came in, bringing a file folder with her. She handed it to Welty, smiled hesitantly at me, and left, closing the door behind her. "Let's see what we have, shall we?" Welty said.

As expected, her application form gave her birthplace as Fleming. It also claimed that she had graduated from high school there, and had taken some college courses.

As for her work, to listen to Welty, everyone just loved her. I could well believe it of the men, but I had my doubts about the women there. She also had a good ability to make the sale, and knew what she was talking about when it came to appliances. She could not only talk features, but could explain technical terms as well, something not always easy to do.

I came across as pleased by all this, of course. In fact, I was so pleased at how well she was doing that I was able to schmooze Welty out of a copy of her employment application.

On the way out I stopped at the secretary's desk and gave Agnes one of my cards. I told her I had "forgotten" to give one to her boss. Then I made a bet with myself that I would hear from her before long.

Then I went back to where Cari lived to canvass the neighborhood. My tack there was different. While I was still investigating the murder, this time I was "bored," just going through the motions.

It's amazing, but some people will close up if you prod them, but if you simply show disbelief in what they say they will go out of their way to prove their statements. Or at least to tell you more, in hopes you will believe them.

Mark Talbot was like that. He lived in the house next to Cari's, and he had heard the shots being fired. "I told the cops I heard three shots," he said. Mark was an accountant with the city, in Public Works, and about thirty years old. He was out sick with a nasty cold. "Bang," he said, "then a pause, and bang, bang."

That certainly caught my attention. "It wasn't three in a row?" I asked skeptically. "Just bang-bang-bang?"

"No, sir," he said, shaking his head vigorously. Then he regretted the motion, as it aggravated his headache. After a few seconds he repeated. "No, sir, it wasn't like that at all. There was the first shot, a pause of at least fifteen seconds, then the second shot, then the third. There was maybe one second between the last two shots."

I put on my skeptical face. "That doesn't sound like a self defense shooting."

"I tried to tell the cops that, but they just didn't want to listen, I guess."

"So what reason would a woman like her have for killing her rich lover?" I asked, mixing scorn with skepticism.

"Maybe it's her other rich lover," he said with a touch of anger. I was getting to him.

"Her other rich lover?" Good lord, could it be that easy?

It was! "Yes, her other rich lover, the one with the Mercedes. One of the big ones, almost big enough for a chauffeur. One or the other was out there nearly every damned night. If it wasn't the BMW it was the Mercedes." He paused. "In fact, if anything the

Mercedes was there more often, since the Beemer wasn't there more than two nights a week."

"And I suppose you can describe him, as well as his car?"

"Sure. Male, mid thirties, average to just above average height. Average build, but looks like an office worker. Soft, you know, not muscular. Dark hair, with a bald spot starting at the back of his head. He had an arrogant look to him, too."

That was Casey, all right. "Have you seen him here since the shooting?"

Talbot shook his head. "Nope. He hasn't been around since." He grinned. "Maybe he's afraid to come back."

"Could be." Or maybe he was just lying low, trying to keep their relationship from public notice. Besides, he was busy with both the company and with Mrs. Brogan. He didn't have time to be with Cari. Not yet, anyway.

I handed him one of my cards. "Would you let me know if the second man comes back? Or if anything out of the ordinary happens, for that matter."

"Sure." He frowned at me. "So you can use what I told you?"

"I believe I can prove Mr. Brogan was murdered, if that's what you're asking. One thing. Would you be willing to testify in court about Miss Roland's other visitor?"

"Of course. If that will help prove murder, how could I not?"

"Thanks. Not everyone is willing to do that."

He shrugged it off. "What's right is right. If they did murder that man then they should be put in jail."

"I agree, Mr. Talbot," I said. "That's why I'm trying to do exactly that."

"But with real evidence?"

"As real as your testimony about the spacing of the shots."

He couldn't argue with that, so I took my leave.

It was starting to come together. It was all circumstantial right now, so circumstantial that if I were on the jury I'd have to vote not guilty. That was changing, though. I had already found out things they would have to explain away, and every time I found something new it would be harder for them.

But I still needed something more solid. While I could call the supposed facts of the case into question, I still couldn't prove that it actually was a murder.

One of the keys could well be finding out who the woman calling herself Cari Roland was. I phoned Lee Conrad, but he wasn't in. Ray Bancroft was, though, and he was willing to talk to me. "We haven't heard from the ATFE yet, about the gun, but we got a name to go with the prints, sort of."

"You have a name, sort of? What the hell's that supposed to mean?" Either you had a name or you didn't, right?

"It means that the Pittsburgh PD has a crime, some prints, and a good suspect, but they can't officially tie the suspect to the prints. She has none on record, and by the time they were ready to go after her prints she was gone."

"So that's why she was willing to let you have her prints," I said. "She thinks they aren't on record anywhere."

"They officially aren't," said Ray. "All we have is some prints from a crime in Pittsburgh along with the name of the prime suspect."

"We know more than that," I said. "We can now tie this murder to a woman calling herself Cari Roland. All we've got to do is get the Pittsburgh police to confirm that Cari is this other woman, what did you say her name was?"

"I didn't, but it's Lisa Brown."

"Okay, so all we've got to do is confirm that Cari is this Lisa Brown, and we can wrap up two cases at the same time. Or at the least solve one case and create a strong question in another one."

"Oh, really?" said Ray sarcastically. "So you think the D.A. will reopen the case just because we can show that Cari Roland isn't really Cari Roland? It's going to take more than that. He'll need some proof that it actually was a murder. The basics of the case still haven't changed from his point of view. He still sees it as Brogan beating on his girlfriend and she shoots him in self-defense."

I started to protest, then it hit me. 'Still sees?' "You've already approached him?" I asked. "You've already approached him and he turned you down?"

"I didn't, but he has been told of the development. He was interested, but he says that doesn't change the facts of the case. All he will do is call the Pittsburgh police and let them know we have someone here who might be their chief suspect in an old crime. If it does them any good."

"If it does them any good?" Then I realized what he meant. If the crime wasn't murder then the statute of limitations could have kicked in, and she'd be free even if they could prove she had done it. Or maybe not. It depended on the crime and the state laws of Pennsylvania. Not to mention exactly how long ago the other crime had been committed.

"We're still trying to find out what they wanted her for," said Ray, "and when the offense occurred."

"For the statute of limitations," I said, my assumption proven correct.

"Got it in one. But we don't think it's a capital crime. The only real question is how serious a felony."

"So what can you tell me about Miss Brown besides her name?"

"Not much right now. We're still waiting on a fax from the Pittsburgh PD with more info. One thing we do know is that if she has any other kind of record it's all when she was a juvenile."

True, or her prints would have been on record. Still, I had no doubt that she had a criminal past. She may not have been arrested for any of them, but the acts were there. Very few people choose murder as their first crime.

Which reminded me, could it be that James Casey had a hidden criminal past as well? That would have to wait, though. "Well, I hope the D.A. wasn't too upset you're still working the case."

"Well, he wasn't exactly pleased, but he wasn't upset, either. From what they said he was mainly pissed at being played for a sucker. On the other hand, he's not going to prosecute unless he's pretty damn sure of getting a conviction." Ray chuckled. "After all, being taken for a fool is bad enough, but how would it look to change his mind and then lose the case?"

"That would be bad," I agreed. "Keep me informed, will you?"

"Sure thing, Dan," said Ray. "Talk to you later. I've got some cases of my own to work."

"Okay, Bye," I said. I hung up and considered what I had just been told. One thing good was that Sharon had been proven right. Not that I was surprised. She had a damned good ear for that kind of thing. That was why I had gone to her.

I was ready to call it a day when my cell phone rang. "Hello."

"Mr. Muncie?" a timid voice asked.

"Yes, this is Dan Muncie," I said.

"Mr. Muncie, this is Agnes Granville, from Harrison's? Do you remember me?"

It took me a second, then I realized it was the quiet Agnes from the store where Cari had worked. "Yes, Agnes, what can I do for you?"

"Actually, it's more like what I can do for you," she said. "I just wanted to let you know that Cari isn't that well liked around here. She's good at what she does, all right, but she has a way of playing up to the male customers that others here don't like. Especially with the single male customers. I've seen her at work, and when it's a single man her voice gets all sultry, and the next thing you know her blouse is open another button or two down. Then she leans forward to make sure that they get a good view of the display." It was easy to hear the disapproval in her voice.

I resisted the temptation to ask what was on display, and instead said, "I understand what you mean, Miss Granville."

"They also don't like the way she talks down to you. Not openly, just that hint that she thought she was better than the rest of us. Frankly, I think most people here would be just as pleased if she never came back."

"I can understand that," I said sympathetically. I especially understood why someone like Agnes Granville would be pleased if she never came back.

"Well, that's all I needed to tell you, Mr. Muncie."

"Thank you, Miss Granville. Good-bye."

"Good-bye." She hung up abruptly enough I wondered if someone was coming that she didn't want to know she was talking to me.

Not that it mattered. I didn't believe her story any more than I believed Welty's. The truth was undoubtedly somewhere in the middle. Exactly where didn't matter.

But that was enough for one day. I was hungry, and it was getting late. Besides, when I went by my office to check for messages I found one from Roger Youngblood. He had offered to buy me a beer or three at the Maja. That sounded good to me.

CHAPTER 16

Sandy spent the night with me, so I sent her on home after breakfast and headed for the office. Having a better name for Cari Roland was a start, but only a start. When I got there I called Steve Kellerman. I was lucky and caught him still in.

"Yeah, Dan, what can I do for you?" he asked. From his tone it was clear he had a pretty good idea what.

"You can fill me in on what you found out from the Pittsburgh police," I said. "Anything useful?"

"Not much. It was a B and E about eight years ago; the homeowner was beaten when he came home in the middle of it. He wasn't too badly hurt, and the actors were only able to get away with a few things. The statute of limitations has kicked in, so officially they aren't interested in her any more."

But unofficially? That could be another matter. "So how did they come to suspect her?"

"She was the girlfriend of the kid they did nail for the case. They had his prints from the break-in, too, and he was on file.

They got him easily, but she had disappeared. Oh, one other thing. It's her all right."

"It is? I thought they couldn't confirm her identity?"

"They can't officially. Since they were never able to take her prints they can't put her prints on file attached to her name, but they were able to find other examples of her prints. She was the other person in the break-in. If they had been able to find her they had no doubt they'd get a conviction, but that isn't enough to legally attach her name to those prints."

"I see." So she did have a criminal history. "Anything else?"

"Yes. The homeowner said that it was the man who knocked him down, but the woman who kept kicking him."

"So she has a history of known violence, too. That's good to know." I'd be more careful around her if I ever got her alone.

"Yes, it is. We'll keep that in mind when we arrest her."

I grinned to myself. "So has the D.A. agreed to resume the investigation?"

"Yes," he said, "but as a low priority. We can do that only when we don't have anything better to do." His disgust was obvious and understandable.

"I see. By any chance is there anybody I can talk to in the Pittsburgh PD?"

"Yes and no. It likely wouldn't be a good idea to have you talk to the Pittsburgh department directly, but I'm told there's a retired detective who might be willing to talk to you." He gave me the number of Harry Miscowski, a former detective who had worked the break-in case. "I've got to run," Steve finished. "I've got that bar stabbing from last night to work on. Bye."

"Bye, Steve." It had not been a fatal stabbing, but it would still be handled by Homicide, likely as an attempted murder.

I looked at the number, and decided what the hell. It turned out that Harry was not only at home, he was willing to talk. "Mr. Miscowski," I started.

"Call me Harry," he interrupted. "I'm too old to be formal."

"All right, Harry. My name is Daniel Muncie. I'm a private detective, and I'm trying to put a woman named Lisa Brown in prison for murder."

"Lisa Brown? You found her?" From his voice I could picture him sitting up straight. I decidedly had his attention.

"I did. She's going under a different name, but yes, we have identified her."

"Identified her? So you don't have her in custody yet?"

"Not yet. That's what I'm trying to set up, though."

"And for murder, you said. Can't say I'm surprised. I had no doubt she'd kill someone eventually. She was a vicious little minx." He chuckled. "She still a pretty girl?"

"I'd say more like a beautiful woman, but yes, she's still quite pretty."

"Which is going to be one of your problems," said Harry. "Juries don't like to convict pretty women. They'll want solid evidence before they do it, and you're not going to get it through a confession. The bitch is tough. She'll look you in the eye and tell you to go to hell. Shit, she'll spit in your eye if you get too close."

"She does look like a tough nut to crack."

"Damn tough. Now, tell me more about the case."

"Okay, but one quick question. Would she be willing to use sex to get what she wants?"

"She'd fuck the devil himself if she thought it would get her what she wants."

Well, that was graphic as hell! "So then it wouldn't bother her to have two lovers at the same time?"

"Hell, she'd love it. In fact, it wouldn't surprise me if she had a couple more you haven't found out about yet. So tell me what happened with her. Who'd she kill?"

I found his suspicions about additional lovers interesting, but it was time to tell him the rest of the story. "I was hired by a woman, Alexis Brogan, to find out if her husband had a lover," I said. "It didn't take long to find out that he did indeed, a woman named Cari Roland. The wife, Alexis, then decided that I had told her all she needed to know, and that I didn't have to get evidence that would stand up in court."

"She just wanted to know if her husband was catting around on her? Nothing more?" His skepticism came through every word. "That's bullshit!"

"Agreed. Anyway, I confirmed that he has a lover on Thursday, and on the following Tuesday the lover, Cari Roland, kills him. She claims that he had hit her, and she has a black eye, but it just doesn't fit. The timing of the murder is too close to be coincidental."

"Damn straight!"

"Anyway, I also had heard that the wife, Alexis, also had a lover. I check it out, and sure enough, she does. Even more interesting is the identity of the lover."

"Why's that?" he asked. He sounded almost eager. It showed the power of gossip, even about people you don't know.

"The victim, Ed Brogan, owned a company down here, and Alexis Brogan's lover was his executive vice-president, James Casey. Now he's running the company, with the approval of the widow Brogan."

"Really." He understood the implications clearly.

"One more thing. On the nights when Brogan couldn't be with Roland because he was with his wife, James Casey was with Roland."

Harry said nothing for a moment. "So both men were fucking both women?"

Rather crudely put, but accurate. "Yes, they were. And the other way around as well."

"But who knew what? Oh, and which one is Lisa Brown?" With his first question he had hit on one of the key elements.

"Lisa is Cari Roland, Brogan's lover. As to who knew what, it's hard to say. Best guess, Roland slash Brown all but certainly knew that both men were with Alexis Brogan. Likewise, Casey undoubtedly knew that Brogan was with Cari when he wasn't with his wife. The crime here works better if they both know everything.

"As for the two Brogans, Ed knew his wife had a lover. My guess is that he didn't know who, but that's just a guess. I doubt very much that he knew Cari was also with Casey. That would have made him seriously suspicious, even without knowing that Casey was his wife's lover. I also believe that Alexis Brogan knew full well that Ed and Cari were lovers, and that Casey and Cari knew each other. In fact, if I'm correct, Casey and Cari knowing each other is vital to the crime. But I don't think she knows that Casey and Cari were also sleeping together." And may still have been for all I knew, if he had any nights away from Alexis.

"Vital to the crime? Sounds to me like you think this Brogan character was set up."

"I do think so. You see, for one thing we have evidence that James Casey lived in your area for a few years. It is quite possible that he and Brown knew each other before they moved here." A thought occurred to me. "In fact, it's possible that he's the reason she's in the area. He could have brought her here."

"Damn! This keeps getting more interesting!"

"Yes, it does. Now, two questions. First, would Lisa Brown be willing to become a man's lover as part of a larger scheme?"

"As long as she saw something in it for herself, damn straight she would. She's a mercenary little bitch. Hell, she'd do it just for the pretties he'd buy her during the relationship. In fact, I suspect she's done some whoring when short of cash."

"Second, once having taken this man as her lover, would she be willing to kill him?"

"My guess is yes. She didn't kill anybody here, not that we know of anyway, but she showed all the signs of working up to it. I suspect that if you could fill in the time between when she left here and now, you'd find a body or two. The only person she gives a damn about is herself. This Casey character had better be careful, or she'll get what she can from him and leave him holding the bag."

"Leave him dead or alive?"

"Whichever way puts more money in her pocket or saves her the most trouble. She won't kill him out of spite – she's too smart for that – but if killing him is the best way to get what she wants, or to keep herself out of jail, she'll do it."

"Sounds like you know a lot about Lisa Brown." It was a cautious question.

"I studied her while I was still in the department. I worked the break-in that caused her to leave town, and after that she became a bit of a project. I've got a ton of material about her, from her background to the crimes she committed that we didn't know about before. Well, we knew about most of them," he amended, "we just hadn't realized that she was involved."

"Would it be possible for you to send me some of that material? I need to know all I can about her."

"Hell, cover my printing and mailing costs and I'll send you copies of the whole thing!"

"Done!" I said immediately. "Just let me know how much."

"Or there's another way," he said. "A lot of it is in computer files. I could send you some disks with much of it, or e-mail you. You do have a computer, don't you?" His voice was light as he asked the question. He knew how important they had become.

"Could you e-mail a summary, then mail the rest? Disc or paper, I can handle either."

"Sure thing. I'll use disks, since it's easier and cheaper. I'll get started on it."

"Oh, and Harry, if you want, throw in some money for yourself. Call it a consulting fee."

I got a laugh for that. "A man after my own heart. Since you brought it up, I'll just do that."

"Thanks for your help, Harry."

"My pleasure. It's nice to be involved in a case again."

"I'll call you if I need anything else, then." A sudden thought occurred to me. "Oh, one thing. Would there be any reason for her to know anything about appliances? Household appliances, I mean. Stoves and refrigerators."

"You mean something other than the fact her father owns an appliance store? None that I could think of," he finished smugly.

"An appliance store? That explains a lot. She works in one down here and apparently does pretty well for herself. Thanks, and I'll call you if I need more help."

"You do that. Now find that bitch and put her sorry ass behind bars. Or better yet, on Death Row."

"Consider her gone. Bye, Harry."

"Bye, and thanks again." He hung up and I did the same. As I did I heard Mike come in. I was glad he was there; I had thought of another line of approach.

I gave Mike a couple of minutes to settle in, then went over to his office. "Mike," I asked, "do you know the CFO for Brogan Plastics by any chance? Or what company does their auditing?"

"Not offhand, but I can find out. Why?"

"Two reasons. First, I'd like to know the financial status of the company. Second, I'd like to warn them to keep an eye on things. I have reason to believe that there's been some hanky and more than a little panky going on there. Not of a financial nature that I know of yet, but I expect it to turn that way."

"Really? How soon?"

"That I don't know, but offhand I'd guess within the next six months." Neither Alexis Brogan nor James Casey struck me as the kind of people who would try to keep the company going. Most likely they would gut it and then sell whatever was left. Unless, of course, they could get a good offer for the company intact.

"So you still think Ed Brogan was murdered?"

"In cold blood, Mike. It was a setup."

"I'll see what I can find."

I thanked him and headed out. I had other things to do. For one, I had to confirm that the Mercedes Casey was driving was leased to the company rather than to him personally. That didn't take long. I had to go to their offices. From previous experience I knew they wouldn't give that information out over the phone, but once there my ID impressed them enough that my suspicion was confirmed. The Mercedes Casey drove was leased to Brogan Plastics.

There was still one thing that I hadn't been able to figure out. What had brought Ed Brogan and Cari Roland together? It was almost a certainty that Casey was involved somewhere in that. I simply couldn't believe that it was pure chance that she has ended up as Brogan's lover, and Casey was the logical person to arrange it. Not directly, though. He didn't perform the introduction, but he let Cari know the best place and way to meet Brogan. That was the only thing that made sense.

I hoped. I couldn't avoid the question of what if I was wrong? What if everything was as reported? What if Brogan had actually hit Cari? What if it was just coincidence that Casey and Alexis Brogan were lovers? So I looked the case over again, say from the point of view of a juror.

Which led me to conclude that I still had to find out just how Cari and Brogan met. Unfortunately, of the two who were best in a position to tell me one was dead and the other I couldn't trust to tell me the truth. Still, I called Homicide and left messages for Conrad and Kellerman asking one of them to call me when they had the chance. Maybe she had said something off the record which would give me a starting point.

I had barely hung up when the cell phone rang. In fact, I hadn't even had a chance to put it away. "Muncie."

"Dan Muncie?" It was a suspicious male voice.

"That's right." I wondered if I had annoyed someone.

"I hear you're investigating the murder of Ed Brogan." He didn't sound friendly.

"I am."

"Good. I've got some information you'll want to hear. Where can we meet?"

"Public or private?" If public it would likely be safe to meet with them. If private it might be a setup for a beating.

His response surprised me. "Public, private, who gives a shit? Do you want to meet or not?"

"I'd like to meet." I looked around. It was too early for the Maja, but I wasn't far from Tourtelli's, an Italian restaurant with a party room. It would be empty at this time of day. "Do you know where Tourtelli's is?"

"Of course. They have great Chicken Alfredo."

"Tell Maria you're there to meet me." Tourtelli's was actually owned by the Thermopolis family, and Maria was the greeter there. She was married to the eldest brother. I was one of the few people outside the family who knew her name was actually Naomi and she was Jewish.

"I'll be there in fifteen minutes or so."

"Who should I tell her is meeting me?"

He said nothing for a few seconds. Then he responded, "One of Alexis Brogan's former lovers." He hung up before I could ask him anything more.

CHAPTER 17

Barely five minutes later I was looking at Maria Thermopolis. I shook my head. "It's been too long," I said. "I didn't even know you were pregnant."

"So maybe you should eat here a little more often," she said with a smile. "I guarantee we have better food than where you usually eat."

"Undoubtedly," I agreed. "I'm not that good a cook."

She laughed. I looked her over, a dark-haired woman standing just over five foot six, slender except for a decided tummy bulge to confirm that there was a little Thermopolis on the way. She was pretty anyway, but the pregnancy agreed with her, giving her a glow that added to her beauty. "Are you here alone?" she asked, looking behind me. I usually went there with a date.

"For the moment. Could I borrow one of your party rooms? Someone wants to talk to me, and I'd like to keep it private if possible."

"Sure." She signaled one of the waiters, and a minute later I was sitting down in their party room. Two minutes later he came back with a Coke and a man.

"Your guest is here," said the waiter blandly as he handed me my drink.

"Thank you," I said to the waiter. Then I turned to my visitor. "Would you like anything?"

"No, thanks," he said. He pulled out a chair on the other side of the table and sat down.

"Thanks, Frank," I said. "We'll let you know if we need anything else." Frank nodded and left, closing the door behind him. I turned back to my visitor.

I didn't know him, but I knew his type. He was about 30, in a expensive suit, wingtips, and with his black hair perfectly done. He had a diamond on the ring finger of his right hand, and a gold necklace. I had no doubt that the slim attaché case he brought with him was real leather. He had that arrogant look that went with young businessmen who had made at least a small fortune early on, and considered themselves better than most of humanity. I was reasonably sure that he had driven here in a German car, either a Porche or a BMW. A mere Mercedes would be too pedestrian for him, unless it came with a chauffeur.

He looked back, a sour expression on his professionally tanned face. I got the impression he regretted making the call, but felt committed. I decided to prod him a little.

"So what have you got for me?"

The blunt question startled him a bit. "Excuse me?"

"You called me," I pointed out. "You called me and said you were one of Alexis Brogan's former lovers. That may be nice for you, but what the hell does it do for me? Why should I even care?"

My response confused him. "What? You don't care that she was cheating on her husband?"

I snorted. "Hell, I can prove that without your help. Give me a reason to care that she had an affair with you. What can you tell me about her that I don't already have?" The last thing

I wanted him to know was that he was the only lover other than Casey that I knew about.

Then he surprised me: he turned human on me. "So she's been fucking someone else lately, has she?" he asked, sounding disgusted. "I knew it."

"Knew what?"

"That she couldn't keep her legs together. And that she'd keep looking for someone to help kill her husband."

The last part was completely unexpected. I managed to avoid blurting out the question that came to mind. Instead I paused, and asked it more calmly, and with a skeptical tone. "She wanted help to kill her husband?"

"She did. Does that interest you?" he asked dryly.

"It does," I admitted. "But before we get too far, who are you, and how much can you prove?"

"Carlton Reynolds," he said. "I can prove I had an affair with Alexis Brogan. But you'll have to take my word for it that she talked about killing her husband."

"Okay, I'll accept that, for the moment, at least. Now, how did you find out I'm trying to prove Alexis murdered her husband?"

"I'm a sales representative for a company that makes machines used in molding plastics, and Brogan Plastics is a customer of mine. I've been selling to them for three years now, and I have some friends there. One of them mentioned it to me."

I saw no good reason to ask who the friend was. "So let's start with the basics. When and how did you first meet her?"

"I was invited to a party they threw for their customers, and I met her there. I presume you've seen her?"

"I have."

"Then you know she's a damn good looking woman. Close up she's sexy. She hits you with an almost physical effect. That was especially true that night, because she was wearing a dress with a plunging neckline and no back. I think the damned thing had been made just for her, because, if she sat up straight, it gave a good view of the sides of her breasts. Impressive, and erotic, but not all that unusual.

"If she wanted to, though, she could move in a certain way and make sure you got a look at her entire breast. I mean nipple and all. Everything would be exposed."

"And she made sure you got an eyeful."

He shook his head. "Boy, did she ever. Then it got worse."

"Worse?"

He nodded. "The dress only came down to just above her knees. At one point I was sitting in a chair against the wall. She came over to talk to me, and she put one foot on another chair. Then she lifted the dress enough to show me her pussy. The bitch was wearing the dress, a pair of shoes, and those stockings with the built-in garters. That was it. Other than her jewelry she wasn't wearing another damn thing. I mean, here she is at this fancy party for people at her husband's company, people from their clients, a few from their suppliers, and she's walking around with her bare pussy hanging out!"

He shook his head. "Then came the kicker. I'm sitting there doing my damnedest to not stare at her pussy when I see her right hand moving. I look up, and damned if she hasn't moved the strap over her right breast aside so I get a head-on look at her whole damn breast!"

"Wasn't she concerned that someone else might have seen her?"

"Nah, she was too careful for that. I was close enough to a corner that everybody else was seeing her from behind, or at least from enough behind that they couldn't see what she was doing. Do you want to know the craziest part of it all?"

"What was that?"

"She knew I'm from Atlanta and she was asking me about what things are like there. To listen to her, you'd never know she was showing me her tits and her cunt."

That was interesting, but I wondered if he had any real proof. "Nice story," I said, putting some skepticism in my voice. "How much of that can you prove?"

Without taking his eyes off me Carlton placed the case on the table and opened it. He glanced in and pulled out a small packet. He tossed it to me, letting it slide across the table. I stopped it and picked it up.

I could guess what was in it by the feel, and I was right. When I opened it I found it full of photos. Some were of her in a nice apartment, in various stages of dress and undress, including totally nude in suggestive poses. From the look of her I had the distinct impression she was intoxicated.

The rest of the photos, about twice as many, were of the two of them having sex. Based on the angle and such I guessed that they were taken by a fixed camera, triggered either by a timer of some kind or by a remote control.

I put the ones of them having sex down and picked up the first batch. "She looks drunk," I commented.

"Stewed to the gills," he agreed calmly. "I'm sure that she wouldn't have agreed to let me take the photos if she hadn't been. When she woke up the next morning she didn't even remember that I had taken them."

"And you didn't remind her, did you?"

"Of course not. She would have wanted them erased."

I put the first batch of photos down and picked up the others. "And these?"

He shrugged. "Let's call it a hobby. I don't normally share these, and I'm only doing it with you to prove I'm telling the truth. I did have an affair with her." He put his hand out. "May I have those back?"

I looked down at the two piles of photos. I sure as hell didn't want them.

Not all of them, that was. I when through the two batches and pulled out one of each. From the first batch I took one where she was using her dress as a plaything while dancing naked. From the other I picked out one where she was easily identifiable, but he wasn't. I put the rest back in the envelope and slid it back across the table.

Carlton glared at me, and opened his mouth to say something. Before he could I asked, "Want some advice?"

"What kind?" he asked suspiciously.

"Free, but professional."

He was still suspicious. "Okay, what is it?"

"Destroy those photos. Every photo you've taken of Alexis Brogan in your apartment. The chips, too, and get them off your computer. Burn the prints. Hell, destroy every photo you've got of her that doesn't have her husband in it as well."

"Okay," he said warily. I knew what it meant. He wasn't agreeing to do what I said, he was just saying he had heard me.

"Then get rid of the video recordings you've got with her. Don't just throw them away, and don't erase them. Burn them at the same time you burn the photos."

I had surprised him. "Videos?" he asked. "What videos?"

I looked at him like he was an idiot. Well, when it came to this he was. "The videos you made at the same time you were taking the photos of the two of you in your bedroom gymnastics. Don't bother trying to deny it, I know better. If you went to the trouble of installing a still camera, you damn well installed a video camera or two at the same time."

The bastard actually grinned at me. "Three."

"So burn the discs. All of them, along with the photos. And you never took them."

"Why should I do that?" The fool still didn't understand.

"Because if you don't the cops are damn well going to find out about them. Then they will be subpoenaed as evidence. Now, do I have to tell you what effect that will have, or do I need to explain it for you?"

It only took a second, and I could see it in his face when he realized what would happen. I suspected that he had only told a few of his 'guests' that he was making videos recording their activities. Once it became public knowledge that he had videos and photographs of Alexis Brogan, all the former 'girlfriends' who didn't already know would come after him, wanting to know if he had photographs and videos of them as well. Some would likely sue him, too. The legal problems could tie him up for years.

So I told him the rest. "Oh, and by the way, taking those photos and video recordings without their consent was illegal. Chances are you would end up facing criminal charges on top of whatever civil problems you have."

Though probably not in the case of Alexis Brogan when it came to prosecuting her. They might well have to give him immunity to get the Brogan videos and photos out of him. Otherwise there could be a conflict with the Fifth Amendment. Some of his other 'lovers' could, thought, and the immunity wouldn't cover them.

That wasn't my concern, though. I just wanted him to get rid of the photos and DVDs. They really wouldn't help the case, and would just add to the 'circus' factor.

"I'll do that," he said. "As soon as I get home this evening." Then he looked at me and frowned. "Hey, wait a minute. You take photos and videos of people without their permission all the time, don't you?"

"Not the same," I explained. "I'm permitted to do it when they are the subject of one of my cases."

"Sounds the same to me," he said sullenly.

"Not that it matters, but let's try this. Suppose I'm tailing a man to see if he is cheating on his wife. He goes into an apartment building. I get a room at a motel across the street, and set up to photograph the apartment he's in. Are you with me so far?" He nodded.

"Okay, so the subject goes into the apartment, and he and his girlfriend start getting it on. As I'm setting up my camera I look around, and in the apartment next to theirs I see another couple doing the same. Are you still with me?" He nodded again.

"Now, since it is my job, I can legally take photos and such of the first apartment, where the subject and his girlfriend are. But if I were to take photos of the second apartment I'd be as much in violation of the law as you were when you photographed your activities without telling your partners."

"I see."

"Or for that matter, if I were to take some photos of the girlfriend when the subject wasn't around I'd be breaking the law." Though there were a few times I hadn't let that stop me.

Carlton was thoughtful for a moment. "What would happen if they caught you doing that? Like photographing the other apartment, I mean."

"At the least I'd lose my license." If caught officially, and the district attorney decided to push it. "But all this has nothing to do with what you are here for, does it? Now, you told me you were 'one of' Alexis Brogan's former lovers. Tell me more. Starting with how she ended up in your bed."

He started to answer, then said, "Mind if I get something to drink? I'm a bit thirsty after all."

I checked my watch. "Hell, let's order some lunch. It's late enough." I went to the door and caught Maria's eye. "Will you be needing this room for a while?" I asked when she came over.

"No, it's not reserved until a birthday party mid-afternoon."

"Fine. We'll be out by then. Would you send Frank over? We're going to be eating lunch now."

Frank came in and we ordered. Then when Frank had left I had Carlton start on the story. A week after the party Alexis had called him up and asked if he had liked what he had seen. Then she had informed him that Edward was leaving on a business trip in a couple of days, and would he, Carlton, like to help keep her from being lonely. He would. "I hesitated for a moment," Carlton said, "but I couldn't get rid of that image of her standing there in front of me, her bare tit hanging out and showing her bare pussy. Then I realized that with a woman like that, if I said no she'd just go with someone else, and if she was handing it out anyway I might as well be the one to collect."

We kept talking as we ate. Carlton had some wine with his lunch, but I stuck to Coke. He described how long the affair had lasted, and how she had brought it to an end.

He described her as "one great fuck, willing to do damn near anything." Well, anything that didn't involve whips, chains, and ropes. And while he didn't have a chance to find out himself, he was pretty sure that she'd do a threesome as long as it was her and two men. She had also mentioned some previous lovers, but none by name.

As we were finishing our meals I got him to the key question. "There is still one thing you haven't mentioned yet. You said she wanted you to help her kill her husband."

He was silent for a moment, then nodded. "It took her a while to get to it," he said. "At the time I thought she was working up to it herself, now I'm not so sure. Now I think she was planning this for a long time and was looking for the right partner."

He paused before continuing. "She never came out and asked me to help her get rid of her husband. At first it was just complaining about what a bad husband he was. Then she got into how he mistreated her. Nothing bad enough to cause bruises, but mean. After doing that for a while she started in on how it was too bad he didn't just drop dead."

He shifted in his seat, as if finding a new position would make him feel more comfortable. "By now I was getting worried. I had this feeling that she was working up to murder, and I didn't want to have anything to do with that. Finally she broached the idea of having him killed, and I told her I wouldn't know where to find anyone to do the job. So she looked at me and asked, 'so you wouldn't slay the dragon for your lady fair?' I replied that the dragon in question was a friend of mine, and besides, I was a coward when it came to violence."

"What did she do?" I asked.

"Nothing then, but she only came over to my place twice after that. I think once she realized that I wasn't going to kill her husband for her she lost interest."

Sounded that way to me, too.

I spent another half hour going over what he had told me, until I was fairly sure I had gotten most everything out of him. Then he went back to work, and I went back to my office.

I had thought of a way that Brogan and Roland could have met.

CHAPTER 18

I called the Harrison's store where Cari worked and asked for Agnes Granville. She was in, and I identified myself. Then I laid it on thick and asked if she could check on something for me. Had Edward Brogan ever bought any appliances there?

Agnes pretended reluctance, but I could tell she was delighted to help me. She checked, and sure enough, three months before Ed Brogan had bought an upright freezer. Not only that, but Cari Roland was the salesperson who had sold it to him.

Clearly she had sold him something else as well.

One thing Agnes could not tell me was whether or not Alexis had been there for the sale, but I was willing to bet that she had not been. It is much easier to put the make on a man if his wife isn't with him.

At the least the wife wouldn't have to pretend she doesn't see what's going on.

So now I could be fairly certain how Brogan and Cari/Lisa had first met. Given that Cari would have information from Alexis on where Ed Brogan would be and when he would be there, it was entirely possible that if their first meeting wasn't enough, Cari would be able to "run into him" again and plant the hook. Since by then he knew his wife was cheating on him, he was primed for an affair of his own, especially when presented with a beautiful young woman who seemed 'ready, willing, and able.' Not to mention completely available.

I realized there was still something missing. I needed to talk to someone who knew Ed Brogan well, someone who was not a part of the conspiracy. Once it occurred to me the right person was obvious. All I needed was a name and a phone number.

So I called the personnel office of Brogan Plastics. I told the clerk who answered who I was, and that a minor problem had come up in regard to Brogan's insurance. I didn't lie to her; I gave her my real name and the real name of one of the insurance companies I was working for. I used the private insurer's name, though, not the one providing the company policy.

I was right about one thing: the clerk simply asked, "What can I do for you?"

"I need to check on some points of Mr. Brogan's schedule over the last week or so before his death. Would it be possible to speak with his executive secretary?"

"Oh, dear, I don't know," she said. "Mrs. Willingham has been on vacation since the shooting. She was broken up about it, you know. She had been with him for a long time."

Better and better. "Would it be possible to put me in touch with her? I just need to ask a few questions."

"Well, I can't give you her phone number, you understand, but I suppose I can give her your number if you'd like."

I'd like! "Yes, thank you," I said gratefully. "I would sincerely appreciate that." Which was totally true.

She took my number and promised to call Mrs. Willingham right away. I thanked her again and hung up. There was no way to know how long it would be before I was called back.

As it happened, I only had to wait about five minutes. The phone rang and I answered. "Muncie Investigations."

"Daniel Muncie? Marjory Willingham. I understand you want to ask me a few questions about Mr. Brogan." The voice was female, at least in her thirties, I guessed. She sounded articulate and educated. I considered that a good sign. She was also wary, which was entirely to be expected.

"Yes, I do, Mrs. Willingham. Would it be possible to meet with you? It might be easier to ask them in person. Besides, it would be less impersonal that way."

She said nothing for a moment. "Do you really work for that insurance company?" she finally asked.

"Not directly, no," I replied, "but I have been hired to investigate the death of Mr. Brogan."

"Investigate how?" she asked suspiciously.

I decided to take the chance. "To see if by any chance Mrs. Brogan might be involved in his murder."

There was a second's pause before she replied, "He was shot in a case of self-defense, Mr. Muncie. Don't you read the paper?" I heard the irony in her voice.

"Yes, ma'am, he was. I also saw where Jimmy Hoffa retired to Florida and Elvis is living on a ranch in Wyoming."

She chuckled. Her voice was more serious when she asked, "Do you believe he was murdered, Mr. Muncie?"

"I'm convinced of it. I just need a few more answers before I can prove it."

"You're not just saying that because that's what the insurance company wants you to prove?"

"No, I'm saying it because I'm convinced he was the victim of a conspiracy. The insurance companies hired me because they heard I was suspicious."

"Really?" There was a short pause, then she asked, "How soon can you get to 3774 Gardenia? It's out by the Delta Park Mall."

"Give me fifteen minutes."

"That would be fine. You have no objection if there is someone else with me, would you?"

"Invite the family if you want, Mrs. Willingham. They might get bored, but they are welcome to listen in."

"In fifteen minutes then, Mr. Muncie." She hung up before I could respond.

I went back to my car and headed for the Delta Park Mall. Once there I pulled over momentarily and checked the map for Gardenia. It didn't take long to find it, and it was the fourteen minute mark when I pulled up in front of 3774, a pleasant two story house, built in the nineteen sixties from the look of it. I parked and walked up to the door.

The woman who answered was about 45, with a pile of dark hair on her head. She was aging well, though she could have stood to lose a few pounds. "Yes?" she asked.

The one word was enough to tell me that this wasn't Mrs. Willingham. "I'm here to see Marjory Willingham," I said. "I'm Daniel Muncie." I had my ID card out, and I showed it to her.

She let me in, a bit reluctantly. "Marge," she called, "He's here." Then she turned to me. "Come with me."

Marjory Willingham was a couple of years younger than her companion, and a little better dressed. There were a few gray hairs in with all the brown, and she had a cheerful round face. She looked like the kind of woman who knew how to take charge when the need was there. I had the feeling that it would take a lot to get her flustered.

There was another woman with them, a black woman about the same age and build. "I remember you," she said. "You were the man at Ed Brogan's funeral who told Polly and Doris you thought Mr. Brogan was murdered."

"I was there," I admitted politely, "though I don't remember meeting you."

"That's because you didn't," she said. "After you talked to Polly and Doris they came over and told me. Then they pointed you out to me."

I remembered that the two women I had talked to there had gone and talked to a group of three other women, standing by a car. One of them had been black. "Yes, now I remember you.

With two other women, standing by a blue Chevy if I remember correctly."

She grinned at me. "That's right."

I looked at the first woman. "You still look suspicious. Tell you what. Call the police department, homicide division. Ask for any of the detectives, and ask them what they know about me. They'll tell you that I'm not here to harm anyone."

I wasn't surprised when she started reaching for the phone. "That won't be necessary, Angie," said Marjory. "I trust him." She looked at me. "Would you care to have a seat, Mr. Muncie? Or may I call you Daniel?"

"Dan, please." I sat down at the round table Marjory and the black woman were sitting at.

"Then you must call me Marge. This is Angie Turkin," she waved at the woman who had let me in, "and Sela Franklin," indicating the black woman. "I must admit that I was a little wary. If there was a conspiracy to murder Mr. Brogan they might be willing to kill others. I hope you're not offended."

"On the contrary, it was a sensible precaution," I said. "The fact that it is unnecessary makes it no less sensible."

Somewhat mollified, Angie asked, "Would you like some coffee?"

"Yes, thank you."

"Were you serious at the funeral?" asked Sela. She was wary in another way. "Do you really think Mr. Brogan was murdered?"

"In cold blood," I said seriously. "He was murdered by Cari Roland at the instigation of Alexis Brogan and James Casey."

Sela gasped. "Mr. Casey was directly involved?"

"Very much so. I can't prove it yet, but I'm convinced that he was working directly with Alexis Brogan to murder her husband."

"I see," said Marge. "What do you want to know?"

I hoped I wasn't reading too much into it, but I found it hopeful that she had asked what I "wanted" to know rather than "needed" to know. "For a start, how long had he been aware that his wife was cheating on him?"

"For years now," Marge said calmly. Sela looked at her, startled by the answer. "He knew she had her first affair about six years ago, and about two a year since then."

"Did he know that James Casey was her most recent lover?"

"Not at first," she said, "but then I heard the office gossip." Her eyes flicked at Sela, so I could guess the source.

"So why didn't he divorce her? And why didn't he get rid of Casey once he found out they were having an affair?" Well, so much for thinking Brogan had not known who the lover was.

"He was going to, just not yet. The company is in the middle of expanding, and changing executive vice-presidents would not have been a good move. As for his wife, she owns a large block of stock in her own right, and he wanted to get control of that stock before he divorced her."

"He had a plan on how to do that?"

"He did, but he was too busy with the expansion to implement it. He was going to do it as soon as he could. He was tired of her affairs, and having one with Casey was the last straw."

"So why didn't he divorce her sooner? The stock?"

Marge shrugged. "He loved her. He kept hoping that she was just, oh, sowing some wild oats, and that once she had gotten that out of her system she'd settle down."

"Until James Casey?"

"Until Jim Casey, right. That was just too much. After that he couldn't ignore that she wasn't going to change." She smiled sourly. "Unfortunately, she beat him to the punch. Can I ask how you got involved?"

"Believe it or not, I was hired by Mrs. Brogan to find out if Mr. Brogan was having an affair."

"You're kidding!" said Marge.

"You gotta be shittin' us!" said Sela, barely waiting for Marge to finish. Angie just raised an eyebrow, but then, she apparently didn't work at Brogan Plastics.

"I'm serious. She didn't hire me directly, but through a divorce lawyer I work with. I followed Brogan to a meeting with Cari Roland, and then to her apartment. That was the Thursday before he was shot."

"But what got you involved in proving that it was murder?" pressed Marge.

"I didn't like the timing. I find out he's cheating on Thursday, and on the following Tuesday he's shot to death? That was just too much to be a coincidence. So I started checking, and found some information that confirmed my suspicions."

"Such as?" asked Marge.

"I'll keep that to myself for the moment, but let's say I've found out enough to make a good case for a conspiracy. The problem is I still can't prove it in court, not solidly enough to be certain of getting convictions."

"So that's what you're trying to do now?" asked Marge.

"That's right. And you've already been a help."

"That's good. What else can I do to help?"

"You can tell me more about what Brogan knew about his wife's affairs. And whatever you know about Cari Roland."

"I didn't know her last name, but if you had asked me three weeks ago I would have told you that Cari was one of the best things to ever happen to Ed Brogan. She revitalized him, and brought zest back into his life."

"You sound like you thought it could be something permanent."

"I did. Obviously I was wrong."

"By any chance did he say where they met?"

"Yes. They needed a new freezer, and they were supposed to meet at the Harrison's Appliances on Baker Boulevard. Alexis didn't show up, and when he called her she said she had a headache so he was to go ahead and buy one without her."

Bingo! "And Cari was the one to help him with the purchase."

"That's right."

"Is that when the affair started?"

"No, it didn't start until they met again a week later. He went to lunch at LaRouche, and she was there."

"Did he eat there often?"

"At least twice a week."

"Who would he go there with?"

"He usually went there alone. To unwind, he said."

I thought about the timing of the purchase. "So this was after he had found out about Alexis and Casey?"

"That's right."

"How soon after that second meeting did his affair with Cari Roland actually start?"

"A couple of days later. I think it would have started that afternoon, but he had a meeting he couldn't get out of."

"She impressed him that much?"

"You've seen her, haven't you?" she asked dryly.

I grinned at her. "Did he buy her many gifts?"

"A few. Jewelry, mostly."

"Have you ever seen any sign from him which would indicate that he would try to beat up his girlfriend?"

"None," she said immediately. "He was a gentleman, and always treated us well. I know that some men can be nice in public and be dangerous in private, but I can't believe that he would do that. Besides, even his wife hasn't tried to claim he beat her."

Actually she had, in the interview with the police. There was only her word for it, though, so we could disregard that.

I looked at Sela. "Do you agree?"

"Absolutely," she replied with conviction. "Mr. Brogan wasn't the kind of man to sit in his office all day. He liked to get around and see what was going on. I never heard that he said anything nasty to any of the women working there."

We were talking violence rather than sexual harassment, but I understood her point. I spent about two hours talking to the women. By the end even Angie had accepted me, and offered me a piece of chocolate cake. I wasn't sure how much the information was going to help me convict the killers, but I did have a better feel for what kind of man Ed Brogan had been.

As we had spoken I got a feeling that Marge was not staying away from work simply because she was too upset over Brogan's death. For one thing she was too calm as we spoke. I had no doubt she was grieving, but she was never even close to breaking down in tears. If anything, she was angry.

Finally I was ready to take the chance. "Marge, would you be willing to help me with the investigation?"

"If I can," she said. "What can I do to help?"

"Go back to work. You said they have asked you to come back, didn't you?" That had come out as we had been talking.

"They have. I'm just not sure I want to be around Jim Casey."

"Yet clearly you have knowledge they want. It could be useful to know what. It may simply be business matters, but even that could be useful."

"So how do I explain going back?"

"You haven't given them a flat 'no way in hell,' have you?"

"No."

"Tell them you're willing to go back in memory of Ed Brogan, to help his company. Invent something they will buy."

She was thoughtful for a moment. "Do you think it will help?"

"In all honesty, I don't know. You could give me a lead, you might just be helping keep the company going. Are you willing to take the chance?"

Marge looked at me quietly for a moment, then grinned. "I'll do it. But only because you said it might not help."

"What?" asked Sela, confused. "You're helping because it might not help?"

"Yes, Sela. He's being honest with me. He's not trying to snow me by telling me that it is needed to help prove murder."

"Oh. I see." I wasn't sure she did, though. Not that it mattered. It was Marge I was trying to convince.

"I'll go in tomorrow," Marge said. "No sense warning them."

I smiled at her, even though I had no idea what they could be "warned" about. "I would appreciate that," I told her. "Even if that doesn't work out, you've been a big help with the information you've given me today."

"I'm glad. Call me again if there is anything else I can do."

"I will. And you can call me with anything you may find out, or any questions you may have. You, too, Sela."

"I'll do that," said Sela.

"Well, I'd like to thank you for your help so far. I'll let you get ready for tomorrow. Thanks again." I stood to leave.

"You're welcome," said Marge. She also stood, and went with me to the door. As I was ready to leave, she asked, "Are you sure that you can prove they murdered Mr. Brogan?"

"Absolutely sure? No. But I think there's a damn good chance."

"Then make it a sure thing," she said. "There is one more thing I wonder about. Why would Alexis hire a private detective to tell her what she already knew about?"

"Simple," I replied. "By having my report she had the 'proof' she needed that her husband was cheating on her. Without that, all the police would have saying that Cari Roland and Ed Brogan had been having an affair was Cari Roland's word. So to prove that they had been seeing each other for a while they needed outside corroboration. That was my job."

"I see. Once they had that they could go ahead and murder him. Is that what you meant by the timing make you suspicious?"

"Yes, it is. I find them together on Thursday and he's killed the next Tuesday?" I shook my head. "No. That's just too much of a coincidence. So I did some checking and that's when I found out that Alexis Brogan and Jim Casey were having an affair."

"Thank you, Dan. Good-bye." She shook my hand, and turned to go back into the house. I think I wasn't supposed to see the tear in her eye.

I checked my watch, and decided it was late enough to call it a day. I'd review what I had that evening to see for sure what I had and what holes needed filling.

CHAPTER 19

When I went in the next morning I was ready to start filling in the remaining blanks. The first thing was to go back over James Casey's history. With Marge Willingham's information I was better able to check out sites I hadn't known about before, and fill in the missing details. There were even more differences between what I found and his "official" biography on the Brogan Plastics website.

I finished that about eleven, and went to LaRouche, taking along a photo I had shot of Cari and one of Brogan I had gotten from Marge. I wanted to see what they could tell me about the meeting there.

They all remembered Brogan because he was a regular customer. Several also remembered Cari. The two who remembered her the best were the hostess and the waiter who served them.

I spoke to the hostess first. She was a sweet young thing, interested at being interviewed in a murder case. She remembered that day, though. And the beautiful woman who had joined Ed Brogan for lunch.

"I knew Mr. Brogan well," she said. "Other than when he was out of town, he would come in at least once a week, and twice wasn't uncommon."

"What about Miss Roland? What do you remember about her?"

"She was beautiful, but I wouldn't trust her. She's the kind who only cares about herself. She was completely on the make." She shook her head. "A woman like that may be beautiful, but she has no morals worth speaking of."

"What about when she came here? What can you say about that?"

"Well, for one thing, she knew Mr. Brogan was there. When she came in she looked for him."

"You're sure of that?"

"Of course. Before long you can tell the difference between people casually looking around while waiting for their table and those looking for someone in particular. She was looking for him."

"How long after he arrived did she come in?"

"Maybe two minutes. She looked around, saw him, and said hey, there's a friend. May I join him? She tried to make it sound like she hadn't been looking, and hadn't known he was there, but she knew all right."

"So you took her over?"

"Sure. Why not? The worst he could have done was say he'd rather eat alone."

"But you didn't expect him to, did you?"

She grinned at me, and pointed at the photo of Cari. "Name me three men who wouldn't want to have lunch with her."

"Good point. So he invited her to join him?"

"He did. She made it worth his while."

"How's that?"

"Her skirt went down to mid thigh. Her neckline didn't go down quite that far, but it was trying."

"I see. So she was on display."

"Very much so. And she has plenty to display." The last came almost reluctantly.

"Yes, she does. So she ate lunch with him. Did she also leave with him?"

"She did. What happened after that I don't know."

"He went back to the office," I said. "Alone. He had a meeting he had to go to."

"That wasn't from lack of effort on her part."

I grinned. "Mind if I talk to the waiter now?"

"Sure thing. I should be getting back to work anyway." She returned to her station. I looked around. I knew about LaRouche, but hadn't actually been in before. It was too fancy for my taste, and even more for my wallet. I could afford it if I wanted, but I wasn't interested in paying fifty dollars for a steak dinner I could get someplace else for fifteen.

Before long the waiter came over. He remembered Cari very well, too. "She was seriously putting the make on Brogan," he said. "She was using every trick in the book. The low voice, direct looks, little touches, everything."

"Was it effective?"

"Hell, it was giving me a hard-on and I wasn't even the one she was trying to impress. The only way it couldn't be having an effect on Brogan was if he was queer. And he wasn't queer. He was enjoying himself."

"So he knew what she was doing?"

"Of course. He wasn't blind. Or deaf."

"She was that obvious?"

"People three tables away could see it. The women especially. She ignored them all, though. She was concentrating on Brogan."

"What did they have to eat?"

"She had a seafood sampler. He had a steak with the works."

"Is that what he always had?"

"No. You could never tell what he'd have. He could choose damn near anything on the menu."

"Did he tip well?"

"Very. Twenty percent or more, depending on his mood. He was pleasant to serve, too."

"Is that unusual?"

He shrugged. "It varies."

I didn't push the issue. "So you are convinced she was serious about doing something with Brogan?"

He shook his head. "Man, if getting his attention would have meant going naked I have no doubt she'd have done it. She wanted to get him into bed and didn't care who knew it."

"Get naked right there in the restaurant?" That certainly fit in with what Miscowski had told me about her.

"She was damn near doing it as it was. Hell, there were times that I could see her nipples, and I know damn well that Brogan could. She was making sure of that." He snorted. "One good thing. I got a hundred dollar tip from him that day."

"That would make it memorable," I commented.

"Damn straight. And that's on top of seeing that woman. I'd remember her all by herself." He hesitated, then asked, "Was she the one who shot him?"

"That was her."

"Damn! And she seemed so interested in him. What in the world led her to shoot him?"

"It was murder. She meant to kill him right from the start."

It took a few seconds for what I said to sink in. "What? She meant to kill him?"

"That's right. When she came here to meet with him she already knew she was going to be killing him."

He was shocked. "You're shittin' me!"

"Nope. That's why I'm investigating. I am convinced that he was murdered."

"Damn! And they met here?"

"No, they had already met. But this was where she set the hook. This was where she made sure he knew she was available."

"She was available all right." He glanced up. "Hey, I've got to go take care of my tables. I hope I helped."

"You certainly did. Thanks a lot."

He stood and shook my hand. The lunch crowd was coming in and he was needed. I left the restaurant and headed out to my own lunch someplace cheaper.

After lunch I went by the office and got a surprise. Steve Kellerman had left a message that I should call him. Almost as surprising, Maggie had not only written the message down right, but had put it in the proper slot.

I took the message slip to my office and called Kellerman. I got lucky. He was in and willing to talk to me. "Hi, Dan," he said when he came on the line. "I thought I'd let you know that the feds have been heard from."

"Which ones?" I asked. Lord knows there are enough agencies to choose from, but I knew which one I wanted.

"Someone at the Bureau of Alcohol, Tobacco, Firearms, and Explosives just screwed up badly. They accidentally got us the information requested in time to actually do us some good, I think." He chuckled. "Heads will roll for that mistake."

"Oh, really? What did they have to say?"

"They traced the gun to a shop in western Pennsylvania. It was sold to a Robert Casey, of Blawnox, Pennsylvania, just over six years ago. Never having heard of this thriving metropolis, I looked it up. Care to guess where it is?"

"Well, unless I am sadly mistaken, I would guess that it is somewhere near Pittsburgh." *Robert* Casey?

"Got it in one. Blawnox is one of a collection of small towns that make up the northern suburbs of the city, along with some places with fascinating names like Aspinwall, Sharpsburg, and Montrose Hill. And while we're still checking, it looks like Robert Casey is James Casey's brother. But older or younger we're not sure."

I couldn't stop smiling. Now I could link James Casey directly to the murder. Or rather we could, since I had no doubt that the police were working their end as well.

Why didn't they get the gun some other way? Since she had no criminal record Cari could have acquired a gun easily. She could have bought one from a gun store and passed the Brady background check, or in a private purchase. Or for that matter, she probably wouldn't have had any trouble getting one from the underground market where the other criminals get theirs.

So why would they get a gun from Casey's brother? It didn't make any sense that I could see. Well, there were always questions in everything but the simplest cases which could only be answered after the arrest, and then only if the person doing the crime was willing to talk.

The important thing was that now we had a link between Casey and Lisa Brown. "Has anybody been in touch with the brother?" I asked Steve.

"Not yet," Steve said. "We're trying to decide how to do it. Should we call direct, or should we get the Blawnox department to do it for us? That kind of thing."

I had an idea. "How about an unofficial contact? Let me call Harry Miscowski. Maybe he can talk to this brother."

"That's an idea," said Steve. "Let me pass it by the Loot."

"Okay. Call when you get an answer." I knew it would not take long. Lieutenant Kevin O'Malley was not the kind of person to dither about decisions.

We hung up and I got onto my computer. Mentioning Miscowski reminded me that he was to have sent me some information. I checked, and sure enough there were three e-mails from a name I didn't recognize, but the subject on all three was "Lisa Brown." I opened them, and started reading the information.

I was impressed. What I got was a good summary of what he had found out about her. It was every bit as bad as he had said. While she had managed to avoid arrest, it looked like Mr. and Mrs. Brown's daughter Lisa had been a very bad girl. Shoplifting was the least of her crimes, though apparently she had gone against type in one regard. There was no evidence that she had ever been a drug user.

Well, not the hard drugs, anyway. I expected that she had at least used pot. In fact, I'd have been astonished if she hadn't.

Still, one thing missing was any evidence that she had ever actually killed anyone. This was hardly surprising, though. It only covered her time in Pittsburgh. Whatever had happened after she left was not included.

I started looking over the materials again, this time going for impressions more than for facts. At first I didn't see anything I hadn't already noticed. Then I realized that one thing was missing. I tried not to read too much into its not being there, but there was still something missing that I expected to see.

Guns.

There was no mention of firearms at all in the descriptions of her crimes. It wasn't much, and there were several viable reasons, but it still bothered me.

I was so wrapped up in reading what Miscowski had sent me that I was startled when the phone rang. I picked it up. "Muncie." I didn't bother to say more since the caller ID said it was from the police department.

"Hi, Dan, sorry it took so long, but we were out on a call."

"Homicide?"

"Nah, a suicide. A jumper. Fifteen floors and landed on a gravel walk."

"Ouch!"

"No shit. I wanted to let you know you can call that Miscowski character. We'll keep it unofficial for the moment, but word is it can turn official real quick if it needs to."

"Got it. I'll see if he can get anything. I need the brother's address, though."

"We've only got his old one, but if Miscowski can't find him he's not much of a detective."

Assuming he was still in the area, at least. "Okay, Steve. I'll let you know what he finds out." Besides, I had a question of my own.

"Do that. See ya." He hung up before I could say any more.

I hung up and got Miscowski's phone number. Less than a minute later he answered his phone. "Miscowski."

"Harry, Dan Muncie. Thanks for that information. I can see a lot of work went into getting all that together."

"Sure did. Gave me something to do, though."

"I've got a question for you. What does Lisa think of guns?"

"She hates them. Word is she knows how to use them, but she refuses to carry one herself. In fact, she doesn't even like it when others have guns. She's rather fond of knives, though. Personally, I'd rather have a gun. Knives scare me."

"By the way, did I tell you how she killed that man down here?" I couldn't remember one way or the other.

"No, you didn't, but I presumed he was either stabbed or beaten to death. She's pretty good at just beating people, too."

"He was shot. No other wounds."

"You're kidding me!" His surprise was clear.

"Nope. Shot in the heart three times."

"Bullshit," he said firmly. "She's not a shooter. That's too impersonal for her. She likes her violence up close and personal."

"That's what it sounded like from what you sent me. Now, how'd you like to get a little more directly involved?"

"In what way?"

"Remember I told you that one of the people connected to the murder was a man by the name of James Casey?"

"Sure. He's the one fucking the wife."

"That's right. Well, we found out that he has a brother, Robert. Six years ago Robert bought a handgun. That gun was the one used to commit the murder."

"No shit?"

"No shit. Anyway, at the time of the purchase Robert Casey was living in Blawnox. Do you know it?"

"Sure thing."

"We were wondering if you'd care to have a talk with Robert Casey, if he's still in the area."

"Who is we?"

I grinned. "We is me and the Mansfield Police Department. They are willing to keep it unofficial for the moment, but if he gives you a hard time he can get official visitors. Either way, we want to know how James got that gun from his brother, as well as when."

"Got it. What's his address?" He sounded eager.

"It's an old one," I cautioned. "It's from six years ago, when he bought the gun."

"Don't worry about that," he said dismissively. "I'll find him. If he's not in the area I'll let you know."

"Okay. Call me when you have something." I gave him my cell phone number.

"I'll do that. And thanks. I'm looking forward to this." He sounded quite happy. For his sake, and mine, I hoped Robert Casey was still in the area.

"You're welcome. Talk to you later." I hung up. Then I checked the time. I wanted more information before I went any further, but for now I needed to clear my mind. I spent the rest of the afternoon at 'Gunny's,' the shooting range where I get most of my target practice. I fired off a few hundred rounds at a variety of targets, fixed and otherwise, before I felt relaxed. Then I went home, fixed myself some supper and watched an old movie.

CHAPTER 20

The next morning, I was still eating breakfast when my cell phone rang. It was Harry Miscowski. "Have I got news for you," he said. From his voice I guessed he had a big smile on his face.

"Have you now? So give me the good news."

"I didn't have any trouble at all finding Robert Casey," he said, his voice becoming more formal. I suspected it was his "testimony mode." That didn't stop him from sounding pleased. "He moved a couple of years ago, but he's still in the area. I called him, and after confirming he's James Casey's brother I asked if he'd be willing to speak to me. He was."

"Really. That's interesting."

"Yeah, I thought so too. So I went out to his place. We talked for a couple of hours, and I think you'll like what he had to say. For a start, he never bought a gun. Of any kind, at any time."

"So how come the BATFE boys think he did?"

"Bob doesn't know, but he has an idea. And he's pissed about it, too. I told him when he supposedly bought this gun, and he said his brother had been visiting then. He thinks Jim may have, ah, 'borrowed' his driver's license one day and used that to get the gun. He said Jim Casey had a felony conviction and can't legally own a gun."

"While Robert has a clean record and can own a gun. So they look alike?"

"Robert says they are fraternal twins, but look a lot alike. Especially in those lousy driver's license photos."

"So it was James who bought the gun and has presumably had it ever since. That is fascinating."

I was also amazed at his stupidity. This would link him even more closely to both the murder and to Lisa Brown. It would be interesting to hear how he might try to explain his gun ending up as the murder weapon. For the plan to work properly there should be no connection between him and Brown.

But that brought up a question. "Might Robert be willing to testify in court that he didn't buy the gun?"

"He would. They had a serious falling out later on, and he would just as soon forget he even has a brother, much less a twin." Harry chuckled. "I told him it could have been worse. They could have been identical twins."

I couldn't avoid a little chuckle of my own. "How did he react to that?"

"He agreed. He said fraternal was bad enough." Harry found the answer amusing. "Either way, that's why Bob is willing to testify. He's been had just too many times, and brother or not, he's ready to tell what happened, and the hell with what it does to Jim."

"What about the rest of the family? Isn't he concerned they might not like him doing that?"

"No problem. They all got burned, too. They'd all cut him out of their lives before then. I've got family dirt like you wouldn't believe. Bob's wife was there, and she joined in a little. She said that Bob's loyalty to his brother damn near broke up their marriage. I think 'ratfink bastard' was one of her milder terms for Jim." He laughed. "After that she started getting nasty. I think she's a real lady most of the time, but you couldn't tell that from her language last night."

"So James Casey can't look for any help from the home front?"

"If he was drowning I think they'd toss him some concrete blocks. To go with the concrete galoshes, you know." Harry was having a good time.

"So what kinds of things did he do to piss off the family?"

"Well, for a start, his dad caught him screwing a hooker on the kitchen table one time."

"What?"

"Yep. Damn near got him kicked out of the house. The only thing that saved him was that he was seventeen and still had a semester of high school to finish."

I shook my head. That was interesting, but not anything I needed to know. I got us back on the subject. "So James has effectively cut himself off from the family, huh?" I wasn't surprised by the news.

"Completely. Not only that, he hasn't made any efforts to mend fences, either. As far as Bob knows there is a complete split."

That fit with my reading of James Casey. He was a user, and once he had used you he discarded you. Even family wasn't excluded from that. In fact, they were usually the first 'victims.'

A question came to me. "His background claims he went to college. Did he?"

"Yes, and got good grades, too. Bob says he may be a jerk, but he's a smart jerk."

"Did his parents pay for college?"

"No, they didn't. By then he had burned them again, and they kicked him out."

"So how did he afford college?"

"Bob isn't sure, but he said that whatever it was, it was probably illegal. You know, providing the frat boys with their pot and coke. A young man could make some good spending money that way."

He could also get himself quite dead if he screwed up. Clearly Casey hadn't. "Bob doesn't know for sure?"

"He said he didn't want to know. I think he was afraid that if he knew that would make him a target, too. Can't say I blame him. We may not have the drug problems of Miami or New York, but we certainly do have them." He paused, and before I could ask another question he added, "Then again, he also said that Jim was seen around town with an older woman. Could be he was filling another kind of need."

I thought of him and Alexis Brogan. "Could be." Not that there was all that much of an age difference between him and Alexis. It had more to do with the way I was unsure who was using whom.

Then again, they could be using each other, each with their own private agenda.

"Nice work if you can get it, I suppose," said Harry. He didn't sound convinced.

"I wouldn't know," I said. "I've always preferred to earn my money in ways that were less, ah, intimate."

Harry chuckled again. "Yeah, me, too." I knew that subject was closed. "I guess that's the price we have to pay for being moral."

"Yes, it is," I replied. "So did Bob have anything else to say for himself?"

"Sure, but I'll just send you copies of the tapes. That'll be easier than trying to remember everything."

"Sounds good." Even if I would have to listen to a lot of nonsense along the way. I could imagine how the conversation went.

As if reading my mind, Harry added, "I'll do some editing, though. Cut out the unimportant stuff and the duplicated stories. No need for you to listen to all that shit."

"Thanks, Harry," I said gratefully.

"Don't be too thankful," he said. "I'll be charging you for my time. Just like I'm charging you for talking to Bob."

"Money well spent, I'm sure," I said. By now I had finished breakfast, and was ready to get dressed. "Anything else you have to report?" Just to make sure he hadn't forgotten anything.

"Actually, there was one more bit of news. Are you sitting?"

What the hell? "I am." From his voice he had intentionally saved the best for last.

"Then I thought you might be interested to know that one time just before the final split, Jim came by with some little bitch, good looking but from the look of her she had no more morals than Jim had. Bob said she looked to be about nineteen or so, and he wondered what the hell she was doing with Bob, who was 25 at the time. Care to guess who she was?"

I started to ask if she was a black hooker when it hit me what he was saying. "You're shittin' me! Lisa Brown?"

"None other," he said, sounding almost proud. "He remembers her quite well. They came to his house late at night, and he tried to chase them away before they woke up his wife. He remembers her so well because just before they left Lisa lifted up this sweater she was wearing and flashed her tits at him. Then she said 'what, these aren't good enough for you?' Then Jim said he knew when he wasn't wanted, and they left."

"He's sure it was her?" This was fantastic news! If it was true, that was.

"Abso-damn-lutely. The bitch has a small mole just to the right of her left nipple. Bob remembers it well, because he told me this when his wife wasn't with us, and he still remembers them as the most perfect tits he has ever seen in person."

"How do you know about the mole?" I asked, intrigued.

Harry chuckled, but this time it had a slightly nasty sound to it. "I've got photos," he said. "Back when I was first checking her out. I found some stuff of hers, including a business card from a photographer. It turned out he had taken a full set of photos of her. They started out more or less normal glamour shots, but by the end she was nude. Some of them were legitimate art stuff, the kind you see in the photography magazines, but others were the kind of art you're more likely to see in one of those magazines they keep in the plastic covers. He told me he was delighted to have a model as beautiful and relaxed as her, and was even thinking about jumping her bones, when suddenly she asked if it made any difference if she was only sixteen!" Harry burst out laughing.

"I can imagine how that went over."

"Damn straight. He said he couldn't get her dressed fast enough, and out of his studio. At first he was just going to burn the lot, but she was so beautiful he couldn't bring himself to do it. He just hid them away, and brought them out to look at once in a while."

"So he let you look?"

"Hell, no! I gave him a hard time and he gave me the whole collection! Negatives, prints, and everything. Even a videotape he made of her while she was posing. Well, I think he may have kept a couple of prints, but I scared him out of all the negatives."

"By pointing out she was underage when he took the photos?"

"Of course. What else? And can I help it if I forgot to mention that she was seventeen by the time the photos were actually taken?"

"Just seventeen or almost eighteen?"

"About half way in between. Close enough to eighteen that if she had intended the photos to be published it would have been legal."

That was a good point. Strictly speaking, while a model has to be 18 for nude photos of her to be published, the date that is important is the publishing date, not when they are taken. She can be 17 during the photo shoot, just as long as they are not seen in public until after her next birthday. Taking photos when they are younger than 17 is dangerous, because of the kiddy porn laws, but nobody will worry about some taken in the second half of 17.

"So she was eighteen by the time you got the photos?"

"Closer to nineteen by then. Not that knowing that would have done him any good. He had chased her out before he got a release signed, and by the time I got to him she was on the run."

Not to mention that any release she might have signed at the session wouldn't have been legal anyway, not without a parent's signature as well. "So what did you do with them?"

"I've still got them. Would you like to see some?"

"Sure. Why not?"

"I'm glad to hear that. I sent some up with the other stuff. A copy of the tape, too."

"Thanks." Though I wasn't sure it was a good thing.

"Should be there in another day or so. Well, I'll be letting you get on to work, then. Have a nice day!" I could have sworn I heard him laughing as he hung up.

I finished cleaning up and getting dressed, and then went on to the office. When I got there I called Homicide, and asked if Steve Kellerman was in. He wasn't, so I left a message.

Fortunately, for my sanity, it wasn't long before he called back. "Hi, Dan," he said. He sounded tired.

"Hi, Steve. I heard from Harry Miscowski in Pittsburgh this morning. He has interesting news."

"Oh, wonderful," said Steve flatly.

His reaction brought me up short. "What's wrong, Steve?" I could think of only one thing. "Is the D.A. giving you a hard time?"

"Yeah. The silly shit has told us to lay off the case. He's made his decision, and doesn't want to have to change it unless the case is handed to him on a platter. So unless you've got proof that can stand up in court, forget it. He doesn't want to know."

I knew the D.A. was bad, but I didn't realize it had gotten that bad. Screw him. "How about you? Would you like to know?"

"Oh, sure, what the hell. What did Miscowski have to say?"

"For a start, Robert Casey never bought a gun. He thinks James borrowed his driver's license and bought one in his name."

"Is that so?" Steve asked, perked up by the news.

"Yes, that is so. He has also burned his bridges with his family. They don't want to know him."

"Interesting."

"It gets better. Robert Casey identified Lisa Brown as being with his brother."

"So they knew each other then?"

I smiled. He was alert now. "Yup. No doubt about it," I said. "Casey and Brown knew each other in Pittsburgh."

"That does change things. Well, for us, anyway. I don't think the D.A. will care. We'll need something harder than that to convince him to reopen the case."

I was half expecting that. "I'll get it, Steve. I'll talk to you later." We finished the conversation, and I hung up.

Like it or not, it looked like I was going to have to prove that something was going on. But what would be the best way to handle it?

What had been a square had turned into a triangle. My question was which was the weak corner? While I couldn't ignore Lisa/Cari, I had the feeling that she was going to be the tough one. I'd cover her, but I doubted she would break.

Alexis was another matter. She didn't have the kind of criminal record that Lisa and James did, which made her the weak link. While I didn't doubt she had been getting advice from Casey on how to behave with the police, she wouldn't have the experience to act on that advice. They had treated her somewhat gently earlier, but once she was being seriously questioned the pressure would be on, and tougher to handle.

Then again, she came across as one tough broad, and a lady like that didn't break easily.

The real question mark was James Casey. On the one hand, he had experience with the police, which could make him hard to break. I doubted they could brow-beat him, and he would know to get a lawyer.

Yet that could work against him, as well. He struck me as the kind of person who had no loyalty to his co-conspirators. While he would protect himself and them as best he could, ultimately he would do whatever it took to minimize his own responsibility. If putting someone else on Death Row would cut his sentence in half, he would do it.

While he might not be vulnerable, I decided that Casey deserved some of my attention. For a start, I wanted to put some pressure on him.

I had come in late, so there was a good chance that Mike was in his office.

I went over, and he was. "Hi, Mike. Got a moment?"

He looked up from some balance sheets he was working on. "Sure thing. What do you need?"

"Did you ever find out who the CFO is for Brogan Plastics?"

"Sure thing. Bradley Chambers. I've met him, but that's about all. Lee Stasson says he's good and pretty honest."

I didn't bother to find out what he meant by "pretty honest." I simply took it as a compliment. Lee Stasson I'd never met, but Mike had told me he was an officer in the local accounting association. He knew every accountant in town who wasn't simply an 'office drone,' and quite a few of them. "Do me a favor, will you? I'd like to have a quick meeting with Mr. Chambers. It won't take long, and I promise to not ask him for any information he can't freely give me."

Mike cocked an eyebrow at me. "I've already passed your comments on to him."

"How did he react?"

Mike said nothing for a moment. "Let's just say he wasn't as surprised as I expected him to be."

"No kidding? Sounds like he already had some suspicions of his own. That could be useful."

"Do you still want to meet him?"

"Yes, please. I think he deserves to have a better idea what is going on."

Mike nodded. "In that case I'll call him. When would be good for you?"

"Whenever he's available. I'm flexible."

"Hang on." He picked up his phone and made a call. I barely listened as he got hold of Chambers, then asked him about a meeting. It took a moment, but before long they had something worked out. It surprised Mike, but he wrote something down. Then he finished the conversation and hung up.

"Well, he says you can come by his house tonight. Would eight be acceptable?"

"I'll be there," I promised.

He gave me the address. I thanked him and headed back for my office. There were more preparations I needed to make.

CHAPTER 21

One of the problems I had was that the rules were different now. The laws were rather free on what I could do during a divorce case, for example. I didn't need to get anybody's approval before planting bugs or cameras, except for the client, and that only because he or she was going to have to pay for it.

But now I was involved in a criminal case, and so I had to follow the same basic rules as the police did. Unfortunately, I was even more limited, since I couldn't go to a judge to get either a search warrant or permission for electronic surveillance. That meant I couldn't bug their homes or put taps on their phones.

Well, I could, but whatever I found out couldn't be used in court, and likely couldn't be used directly to find out things that could be used in court.

But since the District Attorney wouldn't let the police work on the case until there was much more solid evidence, it was up to me to provide that evidence.

So which would be the easier target, the amateurish but tough Alexis or the experienced but self-serving James Casey?

There were advantages to both, so I decided to go after both. In fact, I'd be starting some direct action when I met with Bradley Chambers. If I could disconcert Casey in other ways he would become more vulnerable to later direct attempts to gather the proof I needed.

Alexis Brogan would be harder to annoy, I suspected. But that reminded me I needed to make a call. I phoned Roger Youngblood, and didn't have to wait long before he was on the line. In the meantime I had an interesting conversation with his secretary, one that left me wondering if the rest of her lived up to her voice. Even though I hadn't known Roger all that long I was pretty sure she did.

"Daniel, my boy," said Roger when he came on the line. "How are things going?"

"Quite well in some ways, not so well in others," I told him. "On the good side, I have strong evidence that Alexis Brogan has been having affairs for at least six years."

"Do tell!"

"Yes, indeed. According to Ed Brogan's private secretary he became aware of her affairs six years ago. I also met with a former lover of hers. Without actually asking directly she sounded him out to see if she could get him to murder her husband."

"Did she really? How terribly interesting."

"I also heard more from Harry Miscowski."

"Harry who?" Roger ask blankly.

I realized it was Thursday, and I hadn't spoken with Roger since Monday night. "Harry Miscowski. Remember I told you that Cari Roland is really Lisa Brown, from Pittsburgh?"

"I do."

"Well, Harry Miscowski was a detective on the Pittsburgh force, and he investigated the break-in they wanted her for. He's retired now, and has made something of a hobby of building up a full file on our Miss Brown. It makes for interesting reading."

"It must."

"Anyway, we heard from the BATFE that the gun used to murder Ed Brogan was bought in the Pittsburgh area six years ago, supposedly by Casey's brother, Robert. Harry talked to Robert Casey, though, and he denies ever buying a gun."

"Do you believe that?"

"If Harry believes it, so do I. Not only that, but Robert is willing to testify to that effect in court."

"How interesting. Robert must be quite upset with his brother." Roger sounded pleased.

"It gets better. One night James came by with a young woman. Harry showed Robert a photo, and he identified the woman as Lisa Brown." I didn't bother to keep the satisfaction out of my voice.

"Really, now!" That decidedly pleased him. "So they knew each other in Pittsburgh? How convenient. Tell me more."

I spent the next ten minutes going over what I knew in more detail. By the time I finished Roger was convinced that we would be able to put all three on Death Row. Personally, at that point I would have just settled for some prison time. I still had no real plan on how to find the evidence we needed. Still, it was nice to know Roger had confidence in me.

Finally Roger was satisfied that he was up to date. "Thank you very much for the call," he said. "I trust I will be getting more good news from you soon."

"I expect so," I said with more confidence than I felt. I hesitated, then asked, "One thing, Roger. Your secretary has a very pleasant voice. Is the rest of her as good?"

He chuckled. "Do you think I would have a secretary who isn't pleasant to look at? But come visit me some time and find out for yourself."

"I may do that."

"Please do. Until later, Dan." He hung up before I could respond, so I hung up and got back to trying to figure the best approach to try on Casey.

But not for long. Barely two minutes later Maggie came in with a package. "The mailman just dropped this off," she announced. She dropped it on my desk and headed back out front.

It was from Harry Miscowski, and was big enough to hold a video tape. It did, along with three disks, an envelope with some photos, and a note from Harry, wishing me luck.

I settled down to going over the material, starting with the photos. There were eight of them. Two were standard 'glamour' shots, two were nudes, but in good taste, and two were blatantly sexual. The last two were interesting, in that they were glamour shots, except that in one the dress top was down, revealing her breasts, and the other was the same with the addition of providing a clear view up her skirt. I could see what Harry had been talking about. Most photographers would be delighted to get a model like her.

I also could see the mole he had mentioned.

I set the tape aside. Right now it would be a distraction. Instead I started with the disks. There was a tremendous amount of material on them. I didn't have the time I needed to read it all, but I'm pretty good at scanning.

Clearly Lisa Brown had led a busy life. Not only had she been involved in more criminal activities than I had known about, but she had also had an abortion at the age of 15.

I was on the third disc when I noticed it was about time for lunch. The rest could wait until after I had eaten something, so I stopped. Out of habit I checked my e-mail, and in with the junk I found one from Harry Miscowski. I opened it, and found that he had done some more checking on James Casey. It filled in some detail on his background, but didn't tell me anything I didn't already know. Still, I sent him a return e-mail thanking him for checking on Casey without being asked.

But speaking of Casey, there was something nagging at me about him, and after lunch it came to me. If Casey was directly involved in shooting Brogan, which he had to be to pop Cari in the eye, how did he get there?

He certainly didn't walk to Cari's house from his, so where had he parked? Had anybody asked him about an alibi? And for that matter, had they checked to see if Brogan's hand showed any sign of being used to poke someone in the eye? While I had told Steve about Casey's knuckles, had they ever confirmed it?

I called Homicide, and left a message for Steve. Then for a little while I got back to looking over the materials Harry had sent me. It was maybe thirty minutes later when Steve called back.

"What can I do for you?" he asked.

"First thing, did the medical examiner find any injuries to Brogan's hands?"

"Nope. Both hands were perfectly normal."

While far from proof, that seemed to indicate he hadn't hit Cari in the face. Not that I expected anything else, since I knew Casey had a sore right hand. "That's what I expected. Second, was James Casey asked where he was on the night Brogan was shot?"

"No, he wasn't. There wasn't any good reason to ask, and by the time we had a reason the case was closed." Steve wasn't happy about that.

"Okay, third, I'd like to know who was on patrol in the area around Cari Roland's house that night."

"I don't know for sure who was on patrol, but the first officer on the scene was Billy Ray Seaton. He called in the confirmation."

So Seaton either had that area, or he had been patrolling a nearby area and would know who did. "Thanks, Steve. I'll let you know when I have some more information."

I hung up and considered how to get in touch with Seaton. I knew Billy Ray. Not well, but enough to know he was a good cop. He liked patrolling, and as far as I knew had no ambition beyond eventually making sergeant in the patrol division. That's hardly unusual. Lots of cops actually prefer working the street, being out with the people they were hired to protect.

I didn't have his number, but I knew which substation he was assigned to. I called and got the "A" shift patrol sergeant. Pat Hanratty was an older version of Billy Ray, making sergeant for a few years just to get the larger pension when he retired. "What can I do for you?" he asked. I had ridden with him a few times as a rookie.

"I need to talk to Billy Ray Seaton, Pat. Could you ask him to call me?"

"Heck, I can do better than that," said Pat. "He's here filling out some paperwork. Hang on a sec and I'll get him."

It wasn't more than half a minute before Billy Ray came on the line. "Hello? Dan?"

"Hi, Billy Ray. How's things going?"

"Oh, 'bout as usual. What can I do for you?"

"I understand you called in the confirmation on the Brogan killing," I said. I had to stop myself from calling it a murder.

"I did. I got the call that there had been a shooting, so I went there and checked it out. The woman let me in and showed me where the body was. I took a look, and I didn't need to check his pulse to know he was dead. He was laying there on his back with his eyes wide open and a surprised look on his face."

"That's not what I need to know, Billy Ray. Were you the primary car in that area?" The way the Mansfield police did it was that the city was divided up into patrol areas, and each area was given a three digit number, with the first digit indicating which substation was responsible for that area.

The primary car for a given area had that number with a trailing zero. Any additional cars, up to three in some of the "busier" areas, would replace the zero with a one, two, or three. So the primary car in area "123" of the, for example, would be "car twelve thirty," while the secondary car would be "twelve thirty-one," and so on.

"No, I wasn't. I was working three twenty-five. Jack Kittimer had three twenty-two, but he was ten ninety-nine after working a traffic accident."

"10-99" was officially the "coffee break" call, but what it usually meant was a bathroom visit. "How close is 325 to 322?"

"The line is about half a block or so from the house," said Billy Ray.

I'd never worked that substation, so I didn't know where the lines were. "Are you going to be there for a while?" I asked.

"Sure. What's going on?"

"I think it was a murder, Billy Ray. I'd like to ask you some questions about your patrols that night."

"Hell, that has to be more interesting than this damned paperwork," he said. "Sure, come on by."

So I did. I went to the substation, and they let me back to the sergeant's office. More to the point, there was a large map on the wall, with the various areas marked on it. Now I could see that the house was in 322, but the line for 325 was the next street to the east. 317 was only two streets to the north, while the others were further away. I quickly explained to Pat and Billy Ray what I needed. Billy Ray couldn't help me. He hadn't seen a Mercedes anywhere that night.

By now some of the officers assigned to the "B" shift were coming in. They started at either two or two thirty in the afternoon. Jack Kittimer came in, but he didn't remember seeing a Mercedes either. A couple of others wandered through, but they either hadn't seen anything or had worked another area.

I had just about given up hope when Brian Liston came in. Brian was one of those unflappable people who never seemed to get excited. Or if he was, he was good at hiding it. "What's going on?" he asked. He was sucking on the straw stuck in the top of a cup of soda from a fast food chain, and looked only mildly curious.

"I'm doing some checking on the night Ed Brogan was killed. That was a week ago Tuesday."

Before I could say any more Brian said, "I remember the night. Quiet except for that shooting. What is it you're checking on?" I couldn't tell if he was curious or just being polite.

"I'm trying to find out if anyone saw a Mercedes parked in the area around the shooting that night. It was most likely parked on the street."

"Dark green?" he asked casually. He slurped his drink again.

His question brought me up short. "That's right," I said cautiously.

"Yeah, I remember it," he said. "I ran the plates, since that's not a Mercedes kind of neighborhood. It was owned by some lease firm."

"Where was it?" I asked.

"Here." He pointed to a street three blocks north of where Roland's house was. "In the middle of the block."

"Do you remember what time it was?"

"Nineteen thirty the first time. He was still there at twenty fifty-five. After that I can't say. I didn't go through that street again that shift. Haven't seen it since, though."

So he had seen the car at 7:30 and 8:55, while the shooting occurred at ten minutes past nine. I realized I was grinning.

"So what's so important about that car?" asked Brian.

"I believe the shooting was a murder, Brian, with malice aforethought. I'm convinced that not only was he killed by his mistress with the help and agreement of his wife and the executive vice-president of the company he owned, but that she was brought in for the very purpose of setting up the murder."

Brian looked at me steadily for a moment. "So what's with the Mercedes?"

"The company's vice-president drives a leased dark green Mercedes. This indicates that he was in the area at the time of the shooting."

Brian finished off the drink and tossed the cup into a trash can. "Not surprised," he said. "Women hardly ever shoot after being belted just one time." He turned and headed for the door into the assembly room. As he reached the door he turned back. "By the way, the car had a video camera installed. I think we're holding onto the tapes for thirty days now before we reuse them."

As he headed for the assembly room I considered the news. Assuming they did hold onto the tape for 30 days, and that the murder had only happened nine days before, that tape should still be available!

Pat had been out of the office briefing the sergeant who had the "B" shift duty. He came back in, and I asked him, "Have you got the car tapes from last week? Brian says he saw a Mercedes only three blocks from the Roland house, and his car had a camera. Maybe he got it on tape."

"Let me see," said Pat. He sat down at a computer and pulled up some logs. Then he went into a vault in an adjoining room. It was "fireproofed" to protect the contents, but the lock just needed a key. After a moment he came out with a tape. He put it in a VCR in his office and turned on the TV there. "I can't let you look at the tape, you understand," he said. "Not without a formal request. But every so often we check picture and sound quality."

He first ran the tape ahead to about the four hour mark. Then he stopped it, and hit play. I could make out the time mark. As he used the fast forward I watched the time recorded on the tape. The player had two fast forward speeds, and when it got close to the seven thirty mark I had him use the slower speed. As it was I still almost let the tape get past the part I was interested in. Then there it was, a dark green car parked on the street. The bad news was that Brian had approached it from the front, and an old pickup blocked the view of the license plate. Brian may have been able to see the plate, but the camera could not.

Then we advanced to eight fifty. I watched carefully, and bingo, there it was. This time he came down the street the other way, and not only passed closer to the car, but there was no other vehicle blocking the view. While the image quality was not all that great, we were easily able to make out the plate number. I got my notebook and confirmed, but there was no doubt that this was the Mercedes James Casey drove. "I would say the picture quality was just fine, Pat," I commented. I didn't bother hiding my satisfaction.

"Looks that way to me, too," he said. Then he rewound the tape and put it away.

When he came back in I was looking at the map. "What is it?" he asked.

"I was just wondering how he left the house, and when. That area has alleys behind the houses, doesn't it?"

"Yes, it does. That's where the utilities run."

"And that's most likely the route he used. Out the back door, down the alley to the street, then back to his car and home."

"With nobody the wiser, except that Brian remembered seeing the car and his unit had a camera. So what do you do now?"

"I request a copy of the tape. I'll take care of that tomorrow morning. I have some other things to do." I had a couple of neighbors to talk to.

CHAPTER 22

I went back to Cari Roland's neighborhood, and started talking to other residents along her block. They confirmed that on the night Brogan was shot something had set off all the dogs in back yards on one section of the alley, from Roland's house to the street. Well, not all the dogs, but enough. Most weren't too sure of the time, but those who were placed it after Ed Brogan was killed. This supported the possibility that Casey had snuck out the back way.

That used up the rest of the afternoon, so I had some supper at a restaurant near my office. I made myself relax and enjoy it. Then over coffee and dessert at the Sweet Tooth I considered what I wanted to tell Chambers when I met with him. I also went by the office and put a few things in a briefcase I took with me.

Then it was time. I was actually a couple of minutes early, but I waited until exactly eight to knock on his door. It was a nice house in one of the "high rent" parts of town. It was also nicely conservative, a delight considering how ostentatious some of them were.

The door was opened by an older man, dressed in a dark green polo shirt and khaki slacks. The days of his slender youth were long gone, but he likely played something more strenuous than golf to keep in shape. He looked at me with at least as much curiosity as I had for him.

"Mr. Muncie?" he asked.

"That's right, Mr. Chambers." I recognized him from his photo on the company website.

"Come on in," he said. Without another word he closed the door behind me then led me to a room on the right side of the entry hall. It was an office and library. I glanced around, and noticed that this was not a "show" library filled with "Great Books" sets, with volume after volume standing in uniform rows like good little soldiers. Instead it had a variety of books that someone had actually read.

Instead of sitting behind the desk, Chambers went to a back corner where there was a little "conversation nook" with three overstuffed chairs. I took that as a good sign. He sat down in one chair and indicated I was welcome to one of the others. I took the first I reached, and found it quite comfortable.

"So," said Chambers as soon as I was seated, "Mike says you want to talk to me. What about?" He was curious, but he was also wary. I could convince him, but only by being honest with him.

"Saving Brogan Plastics for a start, Mr. Chambers." He said nothing, but one eyebrow went up. "If you can do it, that is."

"Why should you want to save the company, Mr. Muncie?" he asked skeptically.

"For the most part I don't give a damn," I replied. "It's just that when some people who have annoyed me want to do something that is likely unethical then I consider it my duty to see to it that they fail."

"And who is trying to do something unethical in connection with Brogan Plastics?"

"James Casey and Alexis Brogan."

He said nothing, but the eyebrow went up again. When I didn't say more after a few seconds he said, "You are speaking of the majority owner and the new president of the company, Mr. Muncie. Why would they de-stabilize the company? Mrs. Brogan especially. That would ruin the source of her wealth."

"Good question," I said. "You'd know that better than I would. I'm just a cop who works for himself instead of for the city. As the old saying goes, I know just enough about accounting to be dangerous. That's why I get Mike to look at accounts and ledgers for me."

"Wise move," he murmured. Then with more volume he said, "In that case, perhaps you would care to explain just what in the hell you are talking about."

"Murder, Mr. Chambers. Cold blooded murder."

"Murder? Who was murdered, Mr. Muncie? And by whom?"

"Edward Brogan was murdered, Mr. Chambers. I am convinced that he was murdered by either a woman known as Cari Roland, or by James Casey himself. Either way it was done in collusion with Alexis Brogan."

He said nothing for a moment. "I've heard rumors that someone was looking to prove Ed was murdered," he finally said. "I presume that someone is you."

"For the moment. Once I can come up with some solid evidence the police will finish the investigation."

"Do you truly believe that you can prove they murdered Ed?"

"I'm off to a good start. I suppose you've heard that Casey and Alexis Brogan have been having an affair?"

"I've heard such rumors," he said noncommittally.

"It's true. Casey spent the first two nights at least after the murder with Alexis."

That jolted him. "He spent the first night after the murder with Alexis? I was at the house that night!"

"Casey was there too, wasn't he?"

"Of course!"

"So at the end of the night everybody left but him."

"Do you have proof of this?" he asked suspiciously.

"Other than my word, no. I was there, watching the house, and when everyone left Casey stayed. Not too long after that all the lights were turned off, ending with the ones upstairs, and Casey was still there." Chambers was doing a slow burn.

"But I did get these the second night, after Ed Brogan's parents and a reverend and his wife left." I handed him the photos from the briefcase. The ones of Alexis smiling at Casey were especially effective.

"Okay," he said, his voice hardened, "what else have you got?"

"One. Cari Roland's real name is Lisa Brown, and she's from Pittsburgh, Pennsylvania. She left there to avoid criminal prosecution. Two, Casey is also from there. He had legal troubles of his own."

"I didn't know about that," interrupted Chambers.

"He had good reason to keep it secret, didn't he? If you'd like I can send you the documentation on what I've found." That was one thing I had forgotten to bring with me.

"I'd like."

"Three. The gun used to shoot Ed Brogan was bought in one of the Pittsburgh suburbs, supposedly by Robert Casey, James Casey's twin brother."

"Brother? He claims he's an orphan!"

"The family has disowned him for some of the things he did to them. But Robert Casey denies buying the gun. He suspects James took his driver's license to make the purchase. But regardless of which Casey bought it, what was it doing in Cari Roland's possession?

"Four, Casey and Brown knew each other in Pittsburgh. Their relationship goes back years, although they would have you believe they never knew each other. Yet it also is more recent. Casey has spent nights with Brown recently, at the same time Ed Brogan was having his affair with her."

I could see that Chambers was getting mad. This wasn't the time to let off, though. "Five, Casey's Mercedes was parked in the neighborhood the night Brogan was shot, only three blocks away."

"You can confirm that?"

"I saw it on a police video just today. A patrol car went past it twice that evening, and the second time you can see the license plate. It was his car, no doubt."

"I see. Tell me more."

So I filled him in on what I knew and what I suspected. I didn't give him every detail, but it still took twenty minutes before he was satisfied.

"So what do you want me to do about it?" he asked. "I'm not a detective, and I doubt I can find anything to prove his guilt. Or *their* guilt, I should say." He believed my evidence, but he still wasn't sure why I had come to him.

"It's simple, really. I can't see either James Casey or Alexis Brogan being interested in the long term health and success of Brogan Plastics. My gut feeling is that they are in it for the short term profits. The only real question is whether they will try to sell it for what they can get for it, or gut it and then sell whatever is left. Either way they want the money now, not in ten or twenty years."

"That is quite possible," agreed Chambers.

"So watch for the signs and do what you can to make things difficult for them. I'm not asking that you do anything illegal, or even in violation of your professional ethics, but simply to make life hard for them if they try to do any of these things."

Chambers sat back, thinking. "Sounds doable, up to a point."

"That's what I figured."

"But why should I do this for you?"

"You're not doing it for me," I replied. "Like I said, other than this desire to keep them from doing what they want, it will do me little good, if any. You would be doing it for yourself and the other employees of Brogan Plastics. I don't know if Brogan

Plastics can be saved or not, Mr. Chambers. I'm just trying to keep some murderers from getting rich from their crime. The rest is to your advantage, not mine."

I'm not sure if he believed me or not. "The best way to stop them would be for them to be convicted of murder, would it not?"

"It would."

"What is keeping the District Attorney from filing on the case? Or at least letting the police investigate further?"

"He committed himself to accepting a domestic violence defense way too soon. It will look bad when he backs off and admits it was really a murder. He would look stupid if he reversed himself, put them on trial, and then they walked. He wants to know he has a good shot at a conviction before he reopens the case officially."

"What else do you need to prove to encourage the D.A. to act?"

"Oh, better proof that Alexis Brogan and Casey were having an affair, proof that the affair between Cari Roland and Ed Brogan was set up ahead of time, preferably proof that Alexis Brogan knew about Roland before the affair even started, things like that."

"I see. I may be able to help there. I was treasurer for Frank Jeffries' last two campaigns." Jeffries was the state senator from the district that included most of Mansfield, and a good man. "I am not without political pull in my own right. Perhaps Samuel Ackright can be persuaded to lower his standards somewhat."

"Perhaps, but in the mean time I want to put a good case together. This is personal with me."

"Then I will do nothing for the time being in that respect."

"Thank you."

"One other question, if I may. Who is your client in this matter? Are you doing it on your own?"

"If you are thinking of offering to be my client, don't worry," I said. "Not only might it set up potential conflict of interest problems, but I already have clients. There are two insurance policies worth a total of two point five million to be paid to Mrs. Brogan. The companies are reluctant to pay that much money to someone involved in a conspiracy to murder her husband."

"I see. You are correct, of course, especially about a conflict of interest."

"I am? In what way?"

Chambers smiled grimly. "As you may well know, Brogan Plastics is not a publicly-traded company. The stock is held by some of the founders of the company, and certain officers. Sixty percent of it was held by the Brogans, with him holding forty percent and her the other twenty. Now she holds the entire sixty percent all by herself. If she were to be convicted of murder I expect the probate court would rule that the stock should go to whoever is the beneficiary in case they died together."

"And who would that be?" I asked, though from the look on his face I could guess.

"The employees, Mr. Muncie. The Brogans had no children, and his parents are already well off, so it goes to the employees of the company. Mostly to the officers of the company, but it would be spread around. At the least it would allow us to outvote even the two of them acting in concert." He thought for a moment. "Especially since I expect on conviction James Casey's shares would revert to the company."

Leaving Alexis with her original twenty percent minority instead of a sixty percent majority. I liked it! "Good luck, Mr. Chambers," I said.

"On the contrary," he replied, "it is I who should be wishing you good luck."

"I think my work here is done, then." I stood up. "I'll let you know if anything comes up." I got one of my cards and handed it to him. "In the meantime, if you hear anything that might help me I'd appreciate a call."

"I guarantee it," he said. He stood as well, and walked me to the door. Our handshake and good-byes were somewhat perfunctory since we both had other things on our minds.

On impulse I drove back to the Brogan house. I parked near the house, and looked at it. One thing that caught my attention was that it had a tall privacy fence around the back yard. Remarkably tall considering that the neighbors on both sides had single story houses. In fact, the closest two story houses were three away on one side and four on the other. Behind the house was a small wooded hill.

Now I was curious. I got out my low-light camera and moved the car to the end of the block. Then I went for a walk on that hill. I was able to get to the Brogan house before long, and saw that the privacy fence was lower in the back than on the sides. This was good news, since it made what I was about to do barely legal.

I also saw the reason for the fence. The Brogan house came complete with a swimming pool. It was being used at the moment, by Casey and the decidedly merry widow. They were having such a good time, in fact, that they had neglected to put on bathing suits.

I got a few good shots of them frolicking in the water, helped by the well-lit yard, then they got out and settled into some serious kissing and groping. While getting shots of them actually screwing would have been good for the case, the shots I did get were clear enough that it didn't matter when they ran inside to finish their business on something more comfortable than a lounge chair or the grass. In fact I was pleased they had. Watching that would have upset my digestion.

As for the fence, the reason for that became clear when I got a good look at Alexis in the nude. Like Erika, she also had an all-over tan. Unlike Erika's, I was pretty sure that Alexis got hers at the side of the pool. The fence was to keep the neighbors from seeing her as she tanned.

But enough of that. I put the camera in its case and headed back to the car. If there were any questions about the nature of their relationship this settled them. It was only nine days since her husband had been shot, and here she was playing grabass with

Casey while skinny-dipping in the pool. There was no way they could convince a jury that they had fallen for each other that fast.

I drove on home. At one point I had considered going to the Maja, but taking those photos had soured me on that idea. Instead I made myself watch the video Harry had sent me.

It had been made by the photographer, and showed him doing the shoot with Lisa Brown. I suspected he did it for self-protection when photographing women alone. This way he would be covered if one tried to claim he took liberties he actually hadn't. Or if they tried to claim rape after being a willing participant.

Not that it mattered. The point was that he had made the tape, and I watched it. If I'd been in a different mood it could have been erotic. She came in, and they set up for the glamour shots. He took them, and then she started doing another kind of posing. The neckline went down, the skirts went up, and before long she was naked.

When she started asking him about age, his reaction to realizing she was underage was comical. For one thing he used the word "shit" a lot, and expressed concerns about going to jail. I almost felt sorry for him.

When the tape ended I set it aside. I'd watch it again some other time. But I was through with the case for the night. Instead I read until I was tired enough to sleep. Fortunately it wasn't too late, for I had a lot to do the next day.

Despite my bad mood, I was pleased when Sandy came in later and crawled into bed with me. I don't think I was good company, but it would nice not to wake up alone.

CHAPTER 23

By the next morning I was in a better frame of mind, and ready to do with Sandy what I hadn't been in the mood for the night before. Not that it mattered at the time, since she had been too tired then anyway.

Still, I was in much better spirits by the time I fixed us some breakfast. We might have had a repeat performance, but Sandy was due at the gym and I had work to do.

When I got to the office one of the first things I did was e-mail Harry Miscowski, thanking him, and letting him know that the check was in the mail. It wasn't, actually, so the second thing I did was write out the check and mail it.

After that I put together copies of the documentation I had promised Bradley Chambers and got that in the mail, too. Then I looked over the case.

The trouble was that the evidence was purely circumstantial. I could prove that James Casey had been in the neighborhood of Cari Roland's house, but not that he was in it. I could prove that Cari Roland was really Lisa Brown, a woman with a criminal record, but not that the list of crimes included murder, especially this murder. I could prove that Alexis Brogan was having an affair with James Casey, and had been since before her husband's death, but not that she was involved in his death. I could prove that James Casey and Lisa Brown had known each other in Pittsburgh, and that he had visited her here before Brogan's murder, but not that they had conspired to commit murder.

All in all, it was strong enough to convince most people that they had probably committed murder, but it wasn't strong enough to put in front of a jury. There were still too many holes where a defense attorney could cast doubt, enough doubt to get an acquittal. I had to close those holes.

Still, I had the feeling that I was missing something. I was looking over the papers when I noticed the copy of Cari's employment application. I picked it up and re-read it, but there was nothing I hadn't seen before. Then I flipped up the sheet to the second page.

And I smiled. I should have looked at that second page sooner. That was where they asked for references. She had given three of them. One was someone I didn't know, hardly surprising since his address was Fort Wayne, Indiana. The other two were local, James Casey and Alexis Brogan.

This made hash of any claim Alexis might make of never hearing of 'Cari Roland' until I told her of her husband's affair. It was careless of Cari, yet I wondered if she had any choice in the matter. Given that she was a recent arrival in Mansfield, she would not know many people. Given the kind of person she was, I didn't think she would leave many people behind willing to give her a good reference.

I checked the time. It was still a bit early for most retail stores, but maybe the office staff at Harrison's came in before opening. I called, and asked for Alice Granville. I was lucky. She had just arrived.

"Hello?" she said after a minute.

"Alice, it's Daniel Muncie," I said, sounding as warm and friendly as I could. "I wonder if you could answer a question that has come up?"

"Sure," she said, "if I can. What do you need to know?"

"I was just looking over Cari Roland's employment application, and I was wondering if anybody had checked on her references."

"Yes, I did."

It took a second for what she said to click. "You called them personally, Alice?" That was good news.

"Well, the two local ones I did. Mr. Welty only talked to the one from out of town. That's because he was able to tell about how she was at selling appliances. The two local people were more like character references."

"Were they favorable to her?" I kept my voice casual, as if I had no idea what they would say.

"Very much so. If you give me a moment I'll get my notes of the conversations."

An opportunity like this couldn't be missed. "Better yet, why don't you fax them to me, Alice? I've got to be going in a minute, and this way I can study them properly."

"Okay," she replied casually. She didn't see anything wrong with my request.

"By any chance are Mr. Welty's notes on there, too?" I asked. "From his conversation with Mr. Florentino, I mean."

"Yes, they are."

"That's good. It will save you the trouble of getting that out, too." Not to mention that this could keep Welty from finding out about my call. If he did, I wouldn't put it past him to tell Cari I was double-checking her references.

She giggled. "That wouldn't have been any trouble at all, Mr. Muncie. Where should I send this?"

I gave her my fax number, and thanked her for her help. Then pleading a meeting I "had" to go to, I finished the conversation. She understood completely.

Barely two minutes later the fax machine started up. It was from Harrison's, and had the notes from the calls to Cari Roland's references. All three people, James Casey, Alexis Brogan, and Anthony Florentino, were complimentary. Amusingly, Alexis claimed to have known Cari for three years. I found that hard to believe.

Still, I decided to give Mr. Florentino a call. When I called his work number I was told he was no longer employed there. The bitch who told me was rather nasty about it. I avoided the temptation to say anything nasty back, and simply hung up on her.

Next I called his home number. He was there. "Hello?" he said when he answered. He sounded like he didn't much care.

"Mr. Anthony Florentino?"

"You got him."

"Mr. Florentino, I'm calling in regard to a reference you gave Cari Roland-"

"Who?" The question caught me by surprise. It was just odd enough that for a moment I didn't know what to say. It shouldn't have startled me like that, but it did. In the meantime he recovered. Or at least tried to. "Oh, yeah, Cari. Yeah, I know who you mean. What about her?"

It was a nice try, but it was too late. He honestly hadn't recognized the name for a moment, something that was hard to believe if she had been working for him for over six months, as he had claimed when he spoke to Welty.

I put on my "official" voice. "Mr. Florentino, we are investigating some criminal activity here in Mansfield, and your name came up. We see that you gave Miss Roland a good reference when you were called, and now it appears that this may not have been entirely honest." I heard a faint "oh, shit," so I continued, "Were you being honest, Mr. Florentino?"

"Of course I was," he said, but not convincingly. "I wouldn't lie about anything like that," he finished.

I said nothing for a few seconds, then continued, "Mr. Florentino, are you aware that there are laws against giving false information in a criminal investigation?" Which was true enough, but they didn't apply to someone lying to me. They only applied to official investigations. Besides, I didn't know if they could be applied to someone living in another state, unless he came here to tell his lies.

"There are even federal laws on the matter," I continued. Which as far as I knew only applied to lying to federal officers and agents, like the FBI or Secret Service.

"Now, Mr. Florentino, do you still insist that you were being entirely truthful when you gave that reference?"

He said nothing for a few seconds, then said "No." I could hear the defeat in his voice. "No, I wasn't."

I could feel a little sorry for him, but I didn't let it show yet. "So you lied when you gave that reference?"

"Not entirely," he said defensively. "She was damned good at selling appliances when she worked for me. Once she was my top salesperson three months running."

"That's nice," I said in a tone of voice that implied it was immaterial. "So let's start from the top. Do you know a Miss Cari Roland?"

He sighed. "Yes, but not under that name. When she worked here she called herself Janet Montgomery. I expect that isn't her real name, either."

"Why is that?"

"Because she wanted me to give her a reference as Cari Roland, and I knew she hadn't had it changed legally, in front of a judge and all. In that case, it wouldn't surprise me if Janet Montgomery was as fake as Cari Roland."

"So why did you?"

Another sigh. "Because she had something on me. She had been stealing from the store, and I found out about it. I threatened to report it, and she turned on the charm. She came up to me asking if I had to do that, and her blouse was open, showing me her tits. Next thing I know I'm banging her on my office desk, and she was the sweetest piece of pussy I'd had in a long time. We finish, and she tells me there's plenty more where that came from, but not if she's in jail. I try to resist, but before long I'm helping her cover up the thefts in exchange for three nights a week at her place. The bitch was damn near insatiable."

"So what happened?"

"So after a couple of months she says she's leaving. She's got a better offer somewhere else, and it's good-bye, Tony. Not only that, but I've got to give her a good reference under the name of Cari Roland, or I'm in serious trouble. She'll tell the company that I was the one doing the stealing, and tell my wife about the affair. So when I was called for a reference I did as she wanted. It wasn't hard in one respect. As I said she was damned good at sales. I just left out how she could steal from you while she was at it. And that her name was something else here."

"I notice you don't work there any more."

"Yeah," he said with a sigh. "Some auditors came through, and they discovered that money was missing. I managed to convince them that I hadn't taken it, which I hadn't, but they fired me for not turning Janet in. Then my home life blew up. She had given me a couple of photos of us screwing to show me that she could prove we'd been having an affair. She'd taken them without my knowing. Like an idiot I kept them, and a couple of days after I was fired my frigid bitch wife found them. She screamed at me, cleaned out our bank accounts, went home to mama with the kids, and filed for divorce. I suspect she's going to take me to the cleaners." He was still too numb to get upset.

"You kept the photos?"

"Yeah," he said dreamily, "I did. They are great photos of her, and sexy as hell. I just look at them and I can get hard remembering. Actually, Janet gave me five of them, and the bitch only found two. She's given them to her lawyer, but I've still got the other three."

From his voice it wouldn't have surprised me if he was looking at them as we spoke. "Has the store filed charges against her?"

"Hell, I don't know. I don't give a shit, either."

"Do you know if she had any boyfriends?"

"Most likely. While I did my best, I don't think I was enough to satisfy her completely. Don't ask me who they were, though, because I have no idea."

"What about this better offer? Did she say much about it?"

"Only that it was going to make her rich. A real killing, she said." He said it casually, not realizing what he had just told me. "She even laughed as she said it."

"A real killing." A phrase with a double meaning in this case. "Was that all she said? She didn't mention anyone else?"

"No, no other names. Just remember she would be Cari Roland in the future. By the way, what's she suspected of?" He didn't care; it was just idle curiosity. "Has she been stealing again?"

"Murder."

He said nothing for a moment. "Murder?" I had finally gotten through to him. "She's wanted for murder?"

"Not yet," I said, "but she will be as soon as I can prove it. You can help if you are willing."

"How can I do that?" he asked warily.

"Would you be willing to tell the police here what you just told me?"

"Sure, I'll tell-. Wait a minute. I thought you were a cop!"

"Yeah, sorry about that. Actually I'm a private detective, Daniel Muncie. This case, though, is real. She's not a suspect because they set it up to look like a self-defense shooting, but I have no doubt that it was murder. Her comment to you that she was going to 'make a killing' backs that up. She came down here knowing she was going to be involved in a murder."

"Shit!" The word had an entirely different tone now. It had awe, and a little fright.

"So will you tell the police here what you told me?"

"Sure I will. Theft is one thing, but murder is another matter entirely!"

"So you'd be willing to testify, too?"

"I would. What the hell, the damage here is already done."

With that settled I got some specific information from him, like the dates when she had told him she was leaving, when she actually left, and so on. Then I gave him the information on how to get hold of me, and hung up. That was my first real solid break, tying Lisa to the murder before it was a murder.

Then I had another thought. I didn't know how much a salesman at a store like Harrison's made, but it seemed to me it wouldn't be enough to afford a house like the one Cari was living in. I got back online, and checked on the ownership of the house. As expected, it was a rental. I got the information on the owner, and this time I decided to talk to him in person.

Benny Grimes was some kind of "middle management" person at a steel processing plant on the south side of town. He met me in the lobby of the building where he worked. A slightly chubby man in his mid-thirties, he said that the house was one of two he owned as an investment.

"When did she rent the house from you?" I asked after a few minutes.

"She didn't. I never saw her until I saw the story on the news. Good looking girl."

"You rented the house to a tenant you never saw?"

"Yes. Her cousin rented it. She said her cousin was moving here after a relationship went bad, and needed a place to stay."

My ears perked up. "She said? The renter was a woman?"

"Yes. She gave her name as Angie Roland. Under the conditions I asked for three months rent, the first and two in advance, plus a larger deposit than I would ordinarily ask for."

"How did she react?"

"She didn't bat an eyelash. She just came back the next day and paid me the whole thing."

"How did she pay?"

"With a money order."

"I see. How was Miss Roland as a tenant?"

"No trouble at all. The rent has been paid on time and in full, and as near as I can tell she took care of the house."

I got out a photo of Alexis Brogan. "By any chance do you recognize this woman?"

He took the photo, looked, then handed it back. "Yes. That's Angie Roland."

I didn't bother asking him if he was sure. "When did she rent the house?"

"She signed the lease on the 18th of May. I was pleased, because the current tenants were leaving at the end of the month, and this way the house didn't sit empty."

And "Janet Montgomery" had told Tony Florentino on the 16th that she would be leaving. "So she agreed to take the house on the 17th of May?"

"That's right."

I asked a few more questions, then thanked him and left. I didn't bother asking if he would be willing to testify, As a local resident he wouldn't have much choice, though I was fairly certain he would anyway.

I had some lunch, early for a change, and then headed back to the office. There were some things I needed to think through.

CHAPTER 24

One thing I wondered about was why Alexis Brogan had rented the house for Cari. That seemed a dangerous thing to do. It would have been bad enough for Casey to do it, but this was exactly what I had been looking for: a confirmed connection between the two women.

But why had Alexis risked it? One possibility came to mind, but I needed to check it out. I called Brogan Plastics, and asked to speak with Marjory Willingham. I was put through without even having to use the "cover story" I had come up with.

When she answered I said, "Mrs. Willingham, this is Dan at Sunshine Travel. We've had a problem with some of our records here concerning past travel, and I was wondering if you could confirm that Mr. Brogan was traveling in the middle of last May?" If he had been that would have given Casey the chance to visit his old friend "Janet Montgomery."

"Yes, he was, Dan. Do you need the exact dates?" From her voice I had no doubt she knew who I was.

"If you don't mind."

"Just a moment." I waited barely five seconds when she was back. "Mr. Brogan left on Monday the tenth of May and didn't return until the evening of Friday the twenty-first. They spent the first week in Indianapolis, the second in Chicago."

They?

"Did Mr. James Casey accompany Mr. Brogan?" If so, that would confirm my suspicions. Especially since their first week was spent in Indiana.

"Yes, he did."

What the hell. "By any chance did they travel separately at one point?" I asked. "Our records are a little confused on that."

There was a short pause. "Yes, they did," said Marge. "Mr. Brogan flew to Chicago on Friday night. Mr. Casey flew in on Monday morning. He stayed in Indianapolis over the weekend to visit with some friends." She was clearly wondering where this was headed.

"Thank you very much, Mrs. Willingham. You have been a tremendous help. Please, feel free to call me if there is anything I can do to help, or if there are any questions I can answer for you." Then to emphasize the point I added, "You do have my number, don't you?"

"Yes, I do, Mr. Muncie," she said, confirming she knew who I was. "As a matter of fact, I will likely be calling you later on a matter of some personal travel."

"I'd be happy to help. Good-bye, Mrs. Willingham."

"Good-bye, Dan." She hung up, and I did the same.

I was right! I could see what happened clearly, now. On the tenth the two men flew up to Indianapolis. They conducted their business during the week, then Brogan went up to Chicago while Casey stayed behind. But instead of visiting with friends in Indianapolis as claimed, Casey went up to Fort Wayne, where he met with Lisa. While there was no way of knowing how much they had talked before that weekend, clearly by the end of it she had agreed to come down to help with the murder. From the looks of things, part of the "cost" of that agreement would be that she have a place to live when she got down here.

Apparently Lisa insisted on the house, since she didn't quit her other job until the 19th, the day after the lease was signed and paid for. Since Casey couldn't take care of it, he had gotten Alexis to do it.

Even more interesting was the name Alexis had used. That told me that the name "Cari Roland" had not been chosen by Lisa. There was no way of knowing right now if Alexis or Casey had found it, but clearly Lisa had not, not if Alexis had used the same last name. It had been chosen ahead of time, before Lisa had even fully agreed to take the job.

That helped confirm this whole thing was preplanned.

Yet as expected everything had an amateurish flavor to it. Alexis should never have had anything to do with getting Lisa Brown here. Lisa should have rented her own place. Having someone do it for her may have been good for Lisa's ego, but now it merely served to link Alexis to Lisa/Cari.

All of which was good and useful, but still failed to do what I needed done most. I still had nothing to solidly put James Casey in Cari Roland's house on the evening Ed Brogan was murdered, and I had nothing to solidly tie Alexis directly to the shooting.

Still, there was one thing I needed to confirm. I had a number of contacts, but there were limits. Just to be doing something, I went over to Roger Youngblood's office, in a twelve story building on the north side of town. Once there I confirmed that his secretary was a pretty blond. "May I help you?" she asked, smiling at me. A nameplate on the desk identified her as "Miss Stephanie Delaney."

I wondered if I had her approval or if she was just this friendly with everyone. "I'm Dan Muncie," I said. "I'd like to speak with Mr. Youngblood if I may."

"So you're Dan Muncie," she said with a bigger smile. "Roger mentioned you. He's on the phone right now, but I'll let him know you're here as soon as he hangs up." She waved me over in the direction of a small waiting area to the right. "Feel free to sit, and have some coffee if you wish." There was a coffee maker on a stand in one corner.

I did, and when I sat I realized that I had a sideways view of Stephanie. Somehow I wasn't surprised to see that the frilly white blouse she was wearing was over a short maroon skirt, with no stockings. Equally unsurprising were the long, shapely legs revealed by that short skirt. They went well with the good figure and full breasts I had seen from the other side of the desk. After a moment she stood to file some papers, and I got a better look at the whole package. At one point she bent over at the hips to put something in a lower drawer, pulling the skirt tightly over her well-shaped buns. I could make out no panty lines.

After a moment she sat back down. Without looking at me, she asked, "Do you like what you see?"

"Very much," I said. Clearly she expected to be looked at, so why deny it?

She favored me with a quick smile, and was apparently about to say something else when the phone rang. I didn't intentionally listen in, but I could hear enough to tell she was passing some instructions on to another detective on a worker's comp fraud case. I knew Steve Bell. These cases were his specialty, so we were not competitors. I just did them occasionally.

When the call ended she made some notations, and did other work that was none of my business. It was almost a minute before she glanced at me again. "You're not going to ask, are you?"

"Ask what?"

She chuckled. "You're a man and you're a detective. Surely you noticed the lack of panty lines under my skirt."

"Of course."

"So you're wondering what I'm wearing under my skirt, aren't you?" The way she smiled at me she knew damned well the thought had crossed my mind.

"I did wonder about it a bit," I admitted, "but mainly I've been thinking you've got great legs."

The smile got even bigger. "I do, don't I?"

"Perfect legs," I continued. "Sculptors dream of such legs."

"Bullshit," she said, but there was no doubt she appreciated the compliment.

I shrugged. "If I were a sculptor I would dream about legs like that."

She stood up. "Then let me help those dreams." She pulled the skirt up to the tops of her thighs, all of six or eight inches. In addition to the view of all of her legs, I could see she shaved more than her legs. She twisted around so that I could see the sides as well as the front. She had a good ass, too. "You like?"

"I like." Damn straight I liked!

She "dropped" her skirt and sat back down. Without another word she picked up the phone and punched a button. "Roger, Dan Muncie is here to see you." She listened for a moment, then said "Okay." She hung up and said, "You can go in now." She smiled at me boldly as I stood and went in.

Roger was behind a large desk with papers all over the place. "Welcome, Dan. Close the door, why don't you?"

I closed the door behind me. "Hi, Roger. Nice place you've got here." The office was nicely decorated, and he had a good view of downtown from the windows.

"Yes, it is. So what's your opinion of my Miss Delaney?"

"A very attractive young woman."

"So did she show you her bush?"

Given what I already knew about Roger Youngblood, I was only a little surprised by the question. "What bush?"

"She's shaved again?"

"I don't know about again, but yes, she's shaved."

"Bikini or triangle?"

"It looked like a clean sweep to me."

"Ah. Ask her out to supper. She's sure to accept. If she invites you to supper at her place, accept, but take a change of clothing with you. You likely won't be going home tonight."

"So why don't you ask her out yourself?"

He looked horrified at the thought. "I never fuck the help, Dan. I did once, and it caused endless problems. Now, what can I do for you?"

"I'm not sure. I need someone with contacts so I can check some phone records. I have reason to believe that Alexis Brogan made at least one phone call to Lisa Brown in Fort Wayne, Indiana, just before Brown moved here and took the name Cari Roland."

"Really. Tell me about it."

So I did. It took fifteen minutes to fill him in on the latest discoveries. When I finished he asked, "So you want to confirm the phone calls between Alexis and Lisa Brown?"

"If at all possible. For that matter, between her and James Casey, too."

"As evidence?"

"No. Once I get the police involved they can get the records officially for evidence. I just want to know if the calls were made. That will help confirm what I suspect."

"I see. Give me the dates and people again." He made notes this time. One complication was that I didn't have anybody's phone numbers, but Roger was unconcerned about that. "They could have other cell phone numbers they don't hand out to just anyone," he said. "It wouldn't surprise me."

Nor me, once I thought about it. Then I had a thought. "Could you have them check on the night of the murder, too?"

"Of course." He picked up his phone and dialed a number from memory. I could tell when the phone was answered. "Larry, my boy, I have a project for you."

After that I more or less tuned out what he was saying. It was a professional courtesy. "Larry" was his source, not mine. Instead I looked out the window, at a good view of the city. My windows just looked out over a city street.

After a few minutes Larry had the names, including both "Cari Roland" and "Janet Montgomery" for Lisa. Roger hung up, and said, "He's not cheap, but he is well worth the price. I suspect he has his own contacts in the other phone companies, but I know better than to ask."

"So he can do it?"

"If anyone can. It will take a while, though. At least half an hour. Why don't you see if Stephanie would like to join you for a cup of coffee or something. I can do without her for a little while. In fact, tell her I insist that the two of you enjoy an adult libation and stay away for at least an hour."

I grinned at him. "I'll do that." I could certainly think of worse people to spend an hour with.

So I went back out to where Stephanie was doing some typing. She looked up at me almost expectantly. "Roger says I'm supposed to take you out for a drink," I told her.

"He did, did he? Well, let's do that, then. There's a nice bar just around the corner. You can buy me a drink or two there."

She stood up and grabbed her purse. "Are you right-handed or left-handed?" she asked.

"Right."

"That's good." I had no idea what she was talking about, but once we had gone through the door she walked on my left side and took my hand. Now I understood. She was leaving my gun hand free.

As we entered the elevator I said, "Roger says I should ask you out to supper."

"He's right," she replied without taking her eye off the floor number display.

"Would you care to join me for supper?" I asked.

Now she looked at me. "I've got a better idea. Why don't you let me fix supper."

"I accept," I replied. "When and where?"

We got that settled on the way down, and then walked to the bar she had mentioned. It was a sports bar at night, but during the day all but one TV was tuned to the news and business channels. We found a quiet corner away from all of that. She ordered a daiquiri, and I had a scotch and water. After that we talked. I wasn't surprised to find out that she had been a dancer for a while, but she had disliked having to do table dances for any man that wanted one.

"But I'm a damned good secretary, Dan," she insisted. "I'm not just an ornament, or some plaything he keeps on out of pity. I earn what he pays me."

"I don't doubt it," I replied. Roger might want a good looking secretary, but I could tell he would want one that could do the job as well.

Once we noticed that an hour had passed we finished our drinks and headed back to the office. When we went in I could hear Roger finishing a conversation, so I stopped in the reception area. I didn't know who he was speaking with until he said, "Thanks, Larry." Then he hung up.

I started to head for the door when Stephanie stopped me. She kissed me on the lips, then whispered "Don't be late." Before I could reply she had turned and was sitting down at her desk.

I knocked on the door and went on into the office. "Excellent timing," Roger said. "Did you have a pleasant visit?"

"I did. And I'll be having supper with her tonight."

"Splendid. Now, I have heard from my contact, and he has some interesting news. Very interesting. Do you have a few minutes to spare?" He was smiling grimly.

"I have all the time you need."

"Now, the faxes will take a few minutes, but to make a long story short, he found frequent calls between all of the people involved, especially cell phone calls. Most of them were between Alexis Brogan and James Casey. In fact, there weren't any calls to Janet Montgomery until April 27th. That one was made by Casey, and lasted over half an hour." He was reading from notes he had made.

"Other calls were made to her almost daily over the next two weeks, all by Casey. Or at least all from Casey's phone. Then there was a gap when Casey started that trip you mentioned. The next call we can identify was made on the 13th. Then again nothing until the night of Sunday the 16th. That night there was a long call on Casey's phone from Fort Wayne to Alexis Brogan. Monday was quiet, then on the evening of the 18th Alexis made two calls. One was to Janet Montgomery in Fort Wayne, the other was to James Casey in Chicago."

"And on the 19th Janet Montgomery gave notice," I said. This helped confirm the connection.

"There is more," said Roger. "I believe this is what you need. Do you remember what time Edward Brogan was shot?"

"About ten minutes past nine." I didn't bother asking why. Clearly he was going to tell me.

"At nine twelve there was a call made to Alexis Brogan. It was made on James Casey's phone. I just got word that they were able to roughly place where the call was made from. It was within about 50 feet of the house where Ed Brogan was shot."

There was the detail I needed. I was almost dumbstruck at the stupidity of his action. Here he has just killed Ed Brogan, and he calls Alexis to let her know her husband is dead?

"He's sure of that?"

"Certain. The exact position can be refined a bit when done for the police."

I checked the time. It was after three thirty by now. "They are sending faxes?"

"Yes. They will be here in an hour or so."

Which would make it too late to take to Homicide today. "I'll come back tomorrow to get them," I said. "I'll organize my evidence this afternoon, and get ready to go to Homicide tomorrow. Thanks, Roger. This is a tremendous help."

"So I gather. But aren't you forgetting something? Today is Friday. I won't be here tomorrow."

I had forgotten. "Shit," I said bitterly.

"Never mind, it is no obstacle. Stephanie is having you over for supper, isn't she?" From his smile I wondered if he was using "for supper" as a pun.

"Yes, she is."

"Then I will send them home with her."

"Thanks," I said. I was about to stand when a thought occurred to me. "Just for the record, how much is this going to cost me?"

"Depends," he said almost lazily, with a faint smile. "If we can block payment on the policies I'll take it out of your payment for the case. But don't worry, you'll still get plenty. If we get a murder conviction, I'll pay for it out of my share."

"And if something goes wrong and they have to pay up?"

Roger shrugged, dismissing the possibility. "Then I'll cover it. Otherwise you'd hardly get anything. Besides, I agreed to make the call."

I stood and shook his hand before leaving. On the way out Stephanie winked at me and said, "Don't forget."

"I won't," I promised.

I didn't, either. I went back to my office first, though, and began to organize the evidence for presentation to Homicide the next day. When I was finished with that I went home. I still had an hour before I was due at Stephanie's place. I checked my mail, changed, and feeling a little silly, I packed a small bag with a change of clothes. Finally it was time to go over to have supper with Stephanie.

She lived in a modest house, smaller, actually, than the one Cari rented. Stephanie greeted me at the door wearing a short sundress with a halter top. Well, the skirt was actually a bit longer than the skirt she had been wearing at work, but on the other hand the halter top meant there was nothing on above the waist but the halter itself. I doubted seriously she had bothered to put on any panties.

"Hi," she said. "I was beginning to wonder if you were going to show up." If she had been worried it didn't show in her face. She was smiling as usual.

"I'm only two minutes late," I protested.

"Heck, most men I invite over for supper are early," she said. "Come on in."

I followed her into the house. It was pleasantly neat, and clearly feminine. "There's an envelope on the dining room table for you," she said. "It's the faxes he told you about."

"Thanks."

"Do you like pork chops?"

"Yes, I do."

"Good. Dinner will be ready in about fifteen minutes. In the meantime, I won't be offended if you open the envelope."

"Thanks," I repeated. So I did. It didn't take long to confirm that these records did what I hoped they would. They confirmed an existing relationship between Casey and Cari prior to not only the shooting, but before Cari had come to town, as well.

Another sheet discussed the phone call on the night of the murder. While the circle was not centered exactly on Cari's house, it was certainly close enough.

I only gave it all a cursory look, for supper was soon ready. She had fixed pork chops with rice, cream gravy, and corn on the cob. It was delicious.

The company was good, too. We continued the conversation started at the bar, and I helped her clean up the table. When we finished clearing away the dishes she came over to me and put her arms around my neck. "You don't think I asked you over just for supper, do you?" she asked huskily. Then she kissed me thoroughly.

When the kiss was over I reached behind her and pulled on the tie of the halter top. It turned out that the tie was the only thing holding the dress on. She took my hand, stepped out of the dress now crumpled on the floor, and led me back to her bedroom.

Roger was right. I didn't get back home that night.

CHAPTER 25

As I was finishing breakfast the next morning my cell phone rang. It was Marge Willingham. "I'm sorry to disturb you so early in the morning," she apologized, "but I didn't want to call from the office and I wasn't able to call last night."

"That's all right, Marge," I said. I was far more "disturbed" by Stephanie. She was sitting across from me wearing nothing but a sheer robe. She gave me a rather jaundiced look at the name, but didn't stop smiling.

"Well, may I ask why you asked for that information yesterday? That was months ago!"

"Yes, but I have evidence that it was during that trip that Mr. Casey recruited Cari Roland to kill Mr. Brogan."

"No!"

"Yes, Marge. I expect that he and Mrs. Brogan will be arrested soon. And Marge, what you told me was a key piece of information."

"It was?" She sounded grateful.

"Yes, it was. Thank you for returning to work."

"Well, thank you for making me do it. It turns out they needed me here."

"And they'll need you even more before long, Marge."

"Yes, I suppose if Mr. Casey is gone, they will indeed."

"That's the spirit, Marge. Now, would you mind keeping what I said to yourself for a few days? The police will have to confirm what I tell them, so it's not like Mrs. Brogan and Mr. Casey will be arrested this afternoon."

"That's fine, Dan," she said firmly. "Just knowing they will be is good enough. Have a good day. Good-bye."

She hung up and I smiled at Stephanie. "Don't worry," I said. "She's a married lady."

Stephanie had never stopped smiling. "I'm not worried." She stood up and came around the table. She leaned over, putting her hands on the back of my chair. "Now, you weren't planning on going to your office just yet, were you?" she asked softly just before kissing me.

I had been, but decided it could wait. What the hell, it was Saturday morning.

But it couldn't wait forever. An hour and a half later I went into the office, and put the final touches on my evidence. Then I called Homicide, and asked if any of the people who had worked on the Brogan case were around. Steve Kellerman was in, and he took the call.

"Steve, it's Dan. I've got some information for you. I think you can reopen the Brogan case now."

"Oh, really?" he asked doubtfully. "What have you got?"

"How about proof that Alexis Brogan rented Cari's house for her while Cari was still working in Fort Wayne, Indiana, under the name Janet Montgomery? How about proof that James Casey was in frequent contact with that same Janet Montgomery in the month before she came down here?"

"Interesting, but hardly conclusive." Still, he was interested in what I had to say.

"How about solid proof that James Casey was in Cari Roland's neighborhood on the night of the murder. How about a phone call from Casey to Alexis Brogan made from Cari's house less than two minutes after the shooting?"

I got more reaction this time. "You're kidding! He called her from the house?"

"Want to see the evidence?"

"Of course. But what's this about solid proof Casey was in the neighborhood? What kind of proof?"

"A police video. Casey parked his car three blocks to the north. Officer Brian Liston was patrolling that area in a car equipped with a camera. He's got Casey's car on tape fifteen minutes before the murder."

"No shit!"

"Check it out yourself."

"I will, right after you get your ass down here and show us what you've got. I'm going to call the Loot about this. He'll probably want to sit in."

"That's fine, Steve," I said. "I'd be happy to have him there." I would, too. Kevin O'Malley could be a hard-nosed bastard at times, but he took pride in being a cop. I had heard he wasn't happy at the way Casey had been given a pass.

"Get on down here, Dan." He hung up before I could say any more. He was in a hurry, and as I hung up I smiled. I'd have bet money he was already dialing Kevin's number.

I collected the materials and headed out. Fifteen minutes later Steve was leading me back into Homicide. He took me into one of the small conference rooms. Kevin O'Malley was there, as well as Ned Harris, one of the Homicide sergeants.

Despite his Irish name, O'Malley was a tall, muscular black man. His father had been one of the first black officers on the Mansfield Police force, and had retired as a sergeant. Kevin was the second black to make lieutenant, and he was good at what he did. The men in his division didn't like him all that much, but they thoroughly respected him, and knew he would support them fully in their efforts to put the bad guys in prison. Right now, since it was Saturday, he was in a police polo shirt and blue jeans.

Kevin shook my hand. "What have you got for us, Muncie?"

"Plenty," I said, and sat down. I spread out my evidence and started talking.

It was an hour and a half before we finished. I had them convinced well before that, but they wanted to satisfy themselves that they could convince District Attorney Ackright.

We had just watched the video from Liston's car. Kevin had sent for it as soon as I told him about it. Now he sat back and looked at the TV screen, frozen on Casey's car where you could see the plate number. Abruptly he leaned forward and picked up the remote. Then he stopped the tape and turned off the TV. "Screw Ackright. Steve, get someone and start interviewing the neighbors around Roland's house. Ned, get some other people started on these other items, especially the phone calls. I want them on the official record before the end of the day. Hold off on the other cases for a couple of hours, unless someone is working a hot lead. Any questions?"

There were none. "Okay, get started." We all stood. "Thanks, Dan," Kevin said. "I hated having to stop the investigation."

"It pissed me off, too," I said.

"Do you want to be in on this?"

"Hell, Kevin, it's your case now. Though I wouldn't mind being able to sit in on a couple of the interrogations." I had done my bit. The cops needed to make the official case, and there was little I could do there.

Kevin smiled. "You've got it. Now if you'll excuse me, I've got some work to do."

"I can see myself out," I replied. So I did. It was Saturday, and I'd had a busy week.

I still hadn't heard anything back by Monday morning. This didn't especially surprise me, though. I expected that it would take them all through the weekend to confirm my data and to develop some evidence of their own. This gave me a chance to catch up on stuff around the office, and look over some other possible jobs. None of them especially appealed to me, but at least they would keep me busy.

I had just come back from lunch when the phone rang. It was Steve Kellerman. "Are you smiling?" he asked.

"Should I be?" I asked. He certainly sounded happy.

"Damn straight you should be. We confirmed most of your information, and found out a few things on our own. The Loot just came back from a meeting with the D.A. Ackright said we're to nail Casey, Brogan, and Roland to the wall."

Now I was smiling. "That's great! So he's finally convinced?"

"Enough to reopen the investigation. But he isn't willing to issue an arrest warrant yet, not until we have a lot more solid information. It looks like we're going to get it, though."

"That's good. By the way, Steve, by any chance do you have the autopsy report handy?"

"No, but I can get it."

"Good. Check something, will you? Calculate how far away the shooter was, and then check the angles of the wounds. My guess is that you'll find one wound slightly downward, matching a shooter James Casey's height. The other two will both be slightly upward. Those are the two fired by Cari as she stood over the body."

He said nothing for a moment. "Yeah, that witness did report a pause between the first shot and the next two. You could be right. I'll check that out."

"Good." The possibility had occurred to me over the weekend. The routine checks after the shooting had confirmed gunpowder residue on Cari's hand. That meant that she had fired a gun, though there was no way of telling how many times.

"I'll let you know what we find out. Bye."

"Bye, Steve. And thanks for the call."

I hung up and smiled for a moment.

But only a moment. I felt like a mechanic on a race car. I do all this work to get the car set up and working, then someone else gets to drive it in the race. It was silly, since that was exactly what I had been working for, but that's the way I felt.

I turned my attention to a new case, a store that was the victim of systematic shoplifting. It wasn't interesting, but it did pay well. It was just as well, because I didn't hear another word until Wednesday night when Steve called me. "You were right," he said. "One shot was slightly downward, the other two slightly upward, and the downward shot was right on the money for a person Casey's height. And since the gunpowder tests on Cari Roland came back positive, that fits, too."

"That's good to know."

"So O'Malley said you should be downtown tomorrow if you want to see any of the interrogations. We'll be arresting all of them at first light."

"So you've got enough?"

"More than enough. Word is that Ackright is going for murder one with special circumstances for all three."

That meant that he was going for the death penalty. I could live with that.

Bright and early the next morning I was down at headquarters when the three were brought in. I found that a change had happened in my attitude. It wasn't my case any more. In the extra days I had gotten over much of my involvement in the case. Now I was just an interested spectator.

Still, I was interested. The interviews were being videotaped, and the video was being fed to a small office where I could watch. I switched channels back and forth, and listened in while they started by questioning the two women.

To my surprise, it was Lisa who cracked first. She was shocked at the amount of information they had about her, including that the Fort Wayne PD wanted to talk to her about some missing money. Every diversionary trick she tried to pull they were able to counter. She had gotten away with so much for so long without getting caught that she just was not mentally prepared for something like this. While she didn't tell everything, she told enough to get all three of them hung.

Alexis Brogan, on the other hand, refused to say anything. She wouldn't even admit to being Alexis Brogan. Finally they stuck her in a holding cell.

With Casey it was more like he was holding court than being interrogated. He resisted at first, but once he realized they had him nailed he opened up. He wanted them to know what a smart man he had been, putting the crime together. Actually, all they saw was what a conceited asshole he had been. And still was, for that matter. Truly smart criminals don't brag to the cops.

Still, it gave me an idea. I stepped out of the office where I was observing the questioning, and spotted Lee Conrad. I made my suggestion, and he smiled. He went to get Alexis Brogan.

Alexis Brogan glared at me as she came in, but she said nothing as she stood next to me watching the television. Lee stood right behind her. The timing couldn't have been much better.

"So when did she bring up the idea of killing her husband?" Steve Kellerman asked Casey.

Casey said, "Not long before Ed took up with Lisa." Alexis gasped. "We were in bed one night and she commented how much better things would be if we didn't have to worry about Ed." It was his contention that they had brought Lisa down to have an affair with Ed Brogan to put Alexis in a better bargaining position in the divorce she already knew was coming. He didn't know Lisa had already confessed that it was murder all along.

"Then what happened?"

"I brushed it off at first, but she persisted. I know I should have reported it or something, but then I began to see that there were advantages for me. If I could take over then I could sell the company, or do something to make me a bunch of money. Potentially lots of money. Maybe millions, as much as ten million dollars." He smiled wistfully.

"What did you think Alexis Brogan would have to say about that? Wouldn't she have some say in what happened?"

"Not if I had been able to set things up the way I wanted. I didn't need her. She'd served her purpose."

"So you intended to dump Alexis Brogan from the beginning?" Kellerman asked. "Just toss her out of your life and leave her with nothing?"

"Of course. Why should I stay with her when I had Lisa waiting for me? This way I had the money and the woman I wanted."

"And it didn't bother you that you were leaving Mrs. Brogan with nothing more than cash on hand and whatever other investments she might have?"

"Not in the slightest. Hell, I could have left her penniless and it wouldn't have bothered me. She's pretty enough, but the bitch could be possessive as hell. After a while she seemed to think she owned me, and I had no intention of being owned. Then she started giving me orders on how the company was to be run. Why should I pay any attention to her? I was the businessman, not her. She didn't know what the fuck she was doing." He showed anger now.

"But with the death of her husband she owned the company. Didn't that give her any rights on deciding where the company should go?"

"When she would have ruined it? Not hardly! So I led her on and let her think I was doing what she wanted while I kept things running until I could work out the sale."

"The bastard!" said Alexis. "He's a lying son of a bitch! Killing Ed was his idea, not mine!" If looks could have killed Casey there would have been a bloody mess on the floor. For that matter I had no doubt that she would have attacked him personally if they'd been in the same room.

"So do you want to make a statement to that effect?" Lee asked immediately. "Right now all we know officially is that it was your idea. Hell, according to him the whole affair was your idea. He says you seduced him."

That seemed to piss her off even more than what she had just heard. "That shithead!" she said. "He seduced me! I'd been faithful to Edward before that!" I managed to avoid smiling, even though we knew she was lying about being faithful.

"Then tell us the truth," said Lee instantly. Not that he expected to get it. He knew all he would get was her version of the story. In addition to Carlton Reynolds, the police had so far been able to identify three other former lovers. Carlton and one other were also willing to testify that she had brought up killing her husband. Still, there would be useful information in whatever she told us.

She was just mad enough to be stupid. "Let's go," she said. She glared at Casey's image on the TV, a look he was blissfully unaware of, and then she left with Lee.

I watched Casey for a few minutes more, but he wasn't saying anything I didn't already know about, so I left. In fact, I left the building and went on home. It truly wasn't my case any more. It belonged to the police, and they could finish it up with my blessing. I had done my part.

One thing I knew that Alexis Brogan either didn't know, forgot, or was too angry to remember, was that legally all three were equally guilty of all the crimes that mattered. Even though she had been nowhere near the actual shooting, she was just as guilty of murder and conspiracy to commit murder as Lisa Brown and James Casey.

But that wasn't my concern any more. I set the whole thing aside and went back to trying to find out who was stealing plus size ladies clothing.

The trials of the conspirators were fun. The three of them were each tried separately, and each tried to blame the others. Lisa tried to get off by pointing out that Casey had actually fired the first shot, but she couldn't deny firing the other two, and she had clearly been deeply involved. Casey claimed that Lisa had fired all the shots, but couldn't deny that at the least he had given Lisa her black eye, and had supplied the gun. Alexis did her best to prove she had been taken in by the others, but it was clear that she had been involved in the plot from the start.

All three were convicted, but only Lisa Brown and James Casey were given the death penalty. Alexis Brogan got a sentence of life without parole, but from the time the jury was out it apparently was a close thing. Apparently the fact that she hadn't actually fired a shot made the difference, but not enough to give her a sentence that would let her get out of prison eventually.

While my bill had been paid immediately, when Alexis was convicted I got two checks totaling five percent of the face value of the two policies. That was a nice piece of change, even after taxes. Another 'bonus' I got was the occasional company of Stephanie. It was never a relationship, but we did spend some more pleasant evenings together, especially since I continued to work with her boss.

The injury to Harvey Malik's leg never did heal completely. It healed enough that he was able to walk on it by the time of his trial, but he had a bit of a limp for the rest of his life.

But after the day I shot him, the trial was the only time I was to see him again. I didn't even have to worry (much) about the shooting. Every cop in sight of it swore that Malik would have killed someone if I hadn't acted, and that I had taken the only shot possible. An attempt by Malik's lawyer to file criminal charges against me was flatly rejected, and his civil suit was quashed as soon as the judge got a look at the report of the shooting team.

I didn't pay much attention to that, either. It was only the conclusion I cared about and that supported me.

Not that it would have done Malik much good if he had won a civil case against me. With all the charges against him he would have spent the rest of his life in prison even if he hadn't been put on Death Row for the murder of Wilamina Farrell. His lawyer tried for an insanity defense, but the prosecutors were able to show too much 'logic' in his actions. There was no doubt he was a loon, but not in the legal sense.

Erika, or maybe I should say Susan, surprised me. She actually finished getting a high school GED, and then started going to college. I heard later that she went back to dancing, but in due time she had another career to go to when she was too old to show her tits and do table dances.

I was delighted that she had the chance.

ABOUT THE AUTHOR

Jerry grew up traveling as an Air Force brat (yes, that is what he calls himself). Started writing late in life and even tried a few different genre's, but the series we are publishing here needed writing and wouldn't let him rest. Married to the same woman for 34 years, he hopes that becoming a famous author doesn't give him the same problems it has for other authors (none of ours). They have one daughter. Due to these stories demanding to be told Jerry presents *The Dan Muncie Mystery Series*.

www.ingramcontent.com/pod-product-compliance
Lightning Source LLC
Chambersburg PA
CBHW070340260626
47160CB00003B/1098